CLIMBING THE MOUNTAIN

A HOCKEY ROMANCE
THE SEATTLE SKYHAWKS

BOOK 1

BY

SAM PARKER

This Book Contains

Trigger warnings/ mentions of,

-VERBAL ABUSE,

-BURNING/BRANDING

-ATTEMPTED SEXUAL ASSAULT

-PHYSICAL ASSAULT

-LOSS OF A PARENT DUE TO CANCER

-CHILD FIGHTING CANCER

-UNEXPECTED PREGNANCY

-EXPLICIT SEXUAL CONTENT

Copyright

You know what this page is for, don't steal my shit. If you wanna use something just ask. Don't be a dick.

Copyright © Sam Parker 2024

Cover design by Lovelee design

This novel is entirely a work of fiction. The names, characters and incidents portrayed in it are the work of the author's imagination. Any resemblance to actual persons, living or dead, events or localities is entirely coincidental.

Climbing The Mountain

Self Published by Sam Parker 2024

Dedication

For the ones who want a big thick hockey player that is a gentleman but will also edge you until you beg.

"FORGIVENESS IS BULLSHIT. NOT EVERYONE DESERVES TO BE FORGIVEN. THE THING ABOUT FORGIVENESS IS, YOU DON'T <u>HAVE</u> TO FORGIVE SOMEONE FOR WHAT THEY DID TO YOU. YOU CAN CHOOSE TO NEVER FORGIVE SOMEONE AND BE PERFECTLY FINE WITH IT."

-TABITHA

CHAPTER 1

Tabitha

People are screaming, cheering, and stomping their feet as the hockey players chase the puck across the ice. It's the Seattle Skyhawks vs some team I can't remember, something with a duck or a goose? Or maybe it's a moose? Oh well. I don't even watch hockey that much, but my roommate Riley and best friend Perry had pleaded for me to go on this triple-quadruple date. According to them, spending my nights either working or with my head buried in my text book wasn't the way to live. Perry had promised to do my extensions free of charge and Riley had offered to let me use her car for two weeks since she got rides from her guy. How could I say no to that? A night out with my friends and watching some grown men fight each other for a little rubber puck while I got free drinks? Count me in!

As soon as we all got to the arena, I'm mildly happy to find out my tinder date had bailed. Meh, I wasn't going to complain. Last guy I had matched with was disgusting. He kissed like an octopus and smelled like cheetos. The first time he had picked me up and I got in his car I actually gagged. The floor was littered with half filled pop bottles with cigarettes and dip spit into them and a couple of them were open without lids. As if that hadn't been bad enough, His heater didn't work and he had his window rolled down so he could smoke, letting me freeze my ass off as he drove us to the Olive Garden. I requested an Uber halfway through the date after he brought up being 'an alpha male'. I just grimaced and told him, "*Yeah, no. I'm gonna leave.*" And just left him at the table gawking. He was so gross I spent 2 hours scrubbing my skin after the date. Yea never again.

Don't ask me how, but we all ended up with random seats. Riley and her boyfriend ended up six rows back while Perry and her date were in the row behind me. But I think I got the luck of the draw since I ended up right next to the penalty box. Score one for Tabitha James. Only downside is the air around me reeks with the smell of popcorn, stale beer, and some type of sweaty-meat mixed with the un-deodorized patrons around me. The energy crackles with excitement. And I kinda love it. The energy, not the stench.

Seriously, people need to learn how to shower. I think, brushing a loose strand of my newly dyed caramel copper hair behind my ear.

The extensions added an ombre effect giving it major Bloom from *Winx club* vibes and I loved it.

I learned very quickly that the group of fellow season ticket holders next to me are the extreme type of fans, their heads painted in the opposing team's colors, red and white, decked out entirely in that team's fan gear. How do I know this fact that they are season ticket holders you may ask? The sign one of them held up for the first twenty minutes of the game read 'Season holders. Never miss a game.' That sign is now torn and under their feet since it had been covered in beer due to them going ballistic when the team came out onto the ice. Honestly it was comedic, their screaming like fangirls at a Taylor Swift concert. I mean kudos to being that dedicated. At this point we're halfway through the game, Perry and her guy are gone. No clue where.

Three players ram their bodies up against the plexiglass in front of me, as a fight breaks out over the puck. The refs rush up to pull the players off each other. One of the Skyhawks players comes out of nowhere and slams his large body against the other players, the moment he does, he rips his gloves off and his helmet. This causes the group next to me to go crazy as they begin to chant *"Fight! Fight!"* Fuck yeah! I may know next to nothing about hockey-other than what I've seen on *Shorsey-* but I do love a good hockey fight. I'm cheering along with everyone else because who doesn't love a good fight? The Skyhawks player, number fourteen, is on top of the opposing teams number seven. He yanks sevens jersey collar and slams his fist into sevens face, drawing blood from his mouth. *Fuck that's hot.* The guy next to me yells something in drunk-ish and throws his hands up which sends his jumbo cup of beer splashing into my lap. I'm on my feet letting out a disgusted "FUCK!" As the cold foam soaks into the fabric of my pants and shirt. He just laughs and slurs out what I think is an apology before boo'ing the refs for breaking up the fight. Both players are sent to the penalty boxes, the Skyhawk player is yelling at seven who is bleeding from the nose and mouth.

"Asshole." I hiss, shaking my hands. *Fan-fucking-tastic.* As a bartender this isn't abnormal for me to get splashed with beer but I mean come on! It's my day off. I just wanna drink and enjoy my night, not get drenched in cheap, stale beer. My drunk buddy seems to have heard what I said because he turns his full body to me and tilts his head, "Wha dis you juss say?" he slurs, squinting at me. He looks to be in his early thirties with a sad excuse for facial on his chin. It's like he glued hair trimmings on his jawline and called it five o'clock shadow. The paint on his face is peeling from his greasy, sweaty forehead and the toque on his head is stained with paint and dirt. He is pretty drunk so I go with a less bitchy tone.

"Just watch what you're doing. You threw beer all over me. I'm trying to enjoy the game just like you." I say calmly, trying to keep my irritation out of my tone.

He staggers a bit as he tries to loom over me. Dealing with drunk men and women was something I am so used to at this point that I know how to handle myself when they get too aggressive. Normally being stern and telling them to just carry on and go away works. Normally. He crowds me and wraps his arm around my shoulder tucking me into his sweaty, disgusting body. My stomach rolls and I feel vomit lurch up my throat. *Ew ew ew!!! He's damp! Why is he damp?*

"I thinks you sh-shuld be nicer ta me, baby." He leeres down at me, the smell of his breath and body odor causes me to almost gag, it is so bad I wonder if throwing up on him would make him smell better. I snarl, shoving him off me before I grab the second, full cup of beer from the cupholder in his seat and throw it at him. When I shoved him he'd lost his balance and with his drunkenness he fell onto the ground so the beer goes right into his face and up his nose.

"*Don't. Fucking. Touch. Me. Asshole.*" I bark as he coughs, screeching about his nose burning. I see two security guards walking down the steps and motioning toward us when they see the commotion.

"You two! No fighting." one of them shouts. There is no way I am going to hockey arena jail because of this asshole. I hold my hands up, "I'm leaving." I announce, turning to grab my bag. When I look up, I'm met with a pair of emerald green eyes. The Skyhawks player in the penalty box is looking right at me. He is drenched in sweat and his dark hair is plastered to the hunter green headband tied around his forehead. He raises one of his eyebrows, mouthing, *'You good?'* as if he could do anything.

Holy shit, even with the thick stubbled beard, I could cut myself on this mans jaw. Our stare off doesn't last any longer than a few seconds because the drunk group next to me start yelling slurred insults at him while security was trying to handle the one I'd gotten in a fight with. I say trying because Drunk man now staggers onto his feet and glares at me, his thick neck beet red.

"Dumb bitch!" he roars. He tosses the empty cup as he goes to shove me. The moment his greasy hands touch me, I kick my knee up and get him in the groin, then smack my palm up into his nose hearing it make a satisfying pop. His eyes bug out and he falls back into the chair holding his crotch with one hand and nose with the other while the group pushes forward to yell at the penalty box, completely ignoring their bleeding idiot friend.

"*Ok, screw this.*" I growl, putting one foot on my chair, I step up and over into the next row. I glance back and see the player in the penalty box, his eyes locked right on me, ignoring the idiots hurling insults and hitting the glass, acting like they aren't even there. The crowd around me grows louder as the timer for the penalty box counts down. He breaks eye contact first. He pulls his helmet on and turns his attention forward. The second the door to the box opens, he shoots out, flying down the ice to get the puck. Security is next to the man who tried to actually fight them now. His friends finally realize what's going on and try to help. I wouldn't really consider it helping since two more security guards come over and take away two of the group. The one I had punched being one of them.

As I make my way up the stairs, I sniff one of my extensions to check if it reeks of beer and to my dismay it fucking has a beer scent to it. Fucking asshole. Extensions are expensive and a bitch to wash. These were brand new! This is what I get for letting my friends talk me into shit.

Riley meets me halfway, giving me an apologetic smile as she looks up and down at my now ruined clothes.

"This wasn't as fun as you promised." I glower, giving her a stink eye. Riley gives me a side hug avoiding the wetness on my shirt, "Sorry chickadee. Are you okay?"

I shrug and dry my hands, "You owe me." I tell her as we leave the arena. Riley chuckles and I notice now that the black knit sweater she is wearing is mine and I had been looking for it all day. Her chestnut brown ponytail swishes as she walks, "Is that my sweater?" I ask. She smiles widely at me, "I love you." she blurts out, caught red handed like a kid with their hand in the cookie jar.

"Yea yea, I love you too. I want it back tomorrow." I roll my eyes.

Perry had gone off with her guy about twenty minutes ago, most likely banging him in one of the bathrooms or in his car in the parking lot. Otherwise she would have jumped right in in that fight. When it comes to Perry she'd dick a guy down anywhere, anytime. One time she took her cousin's date from her at prom and fucked him in a parking garage. The cousin had given her the go ahead but hadn't thought she would actually go for it. The rule of Perry is: never tell her to go for it because she will. And she did. Several times. She told me so. In detail. She would also fight a grown man if needed. I've seen it and have the video as a memento.

Riley kisses her boyfriend goodbye and we head home after we find Perry waiting by the car, her hair is ruffled and clothes wrinkled but she's happy.

As soon as we get to the house, the shower calls my name. The sound of the Netflix show Perry and Riley turn on is the extra bit of noise I need. The sound helps me not focus on my adrenaline crash or the memories trying to surface.

"Hey let me know if you need help with the extensions." Perry calls up to me mid shower.

"Will do!" I shout back, hearing her go back down the creaky steps.

Rileys house is a small light blue two story bungalow, the front door opens into the spacious living room, if you look to the right there is the staircase that leads upstairs where my room and a small bathroom is. The house is set up so if you went through the living room, there is a bedroom to the left that's Riley's room and across from her room is her bathroom. Further down the short hallway is the cozy kitchen. In the left corner is the door to the laundry room where there also was the back door.

I love this house. It's the first place that made me feel safe and at home. Riley received the full deed to the house after her stepfather died a few years ago. since it fully paid off the bills weren't too bad.

"Hey Tabs?" Perry calls knocking on the bathroom door. I pull my robe around my body and tie it as she opens the door.

Perry is beautiful, modelesque. She is five-nine with bronzed skin and to die for curves. Her black silky hair was now up in a messy bun. She is the one who had actually done the ombre dark russet brown to copper color on my hair at the salon she worked at and the extensions as well. She'd become a very talented hairstylist over the past few years.

"Hey, do you need me to pick you up tomorrow after work?" she leans on the door frame as she munches on some raisinettes.

"No, Dex is driving Riley to work in the morning so I'm gonna borrow the car. I have a double shift again." I explain, wiping the makeup off my face.

"Sorry the date fell through." Perry pouts, a small smile on her face.

"Don't be, I would have probably ended up even more soaked in beer than I was." Perry has been trying to help me out in the 'getting laid' department for months now. The whole tinder thing was so not working out at all. As soon as she told me she had made me an account I knew it would be a failure. While I appreciate and love her, I really don't need help getting a one-night stand. As soon as I could I was deleting the app.

Perry gives me a look. "I know you, you throw yourself into work and school and ignore everything else. Let someone take care of you and your needs once in a while."

"I am very capable of taking care of my 'needs'. Thank you very much" the laughter in my voice not convincing her.

"Ok, I am all for self love but you work so hard and deserve to get your back blown out by a sexy ass man who can give you the best orgasms of your life!" she calls as I toss my clothes in the hamper and go into my room. The laughter erupts from my mouth because sometimes Perry was just the most extra person in the world. She follows me into my small bedroom. I plug my phone in on the nightstand and opened the textbook on my bed.

"I don't want my back blown out by anyone. The orgasms would be nice, but I'm not you Pear. I can't really get into one night stands or random hookups with a bunch of guys." I admit. Perry acts offended as she throws me a pair of pj's out of my dresser before jumping onto the bed next to me.

"Did you just kindly call me a hoe?" she asks, cocking her head to the side.

"You're sex positive and more adventurous, so yes. Yes you are a huge Hoe." I deadpan. She makes a growl sound and grabs a pillow to hit me with it, "Ok, fuck you," she laughs, "I will give it a break on setting you up with dates." she says, holding her hands up when I held up my own pillow to hit her back.

"I love you, have fun studying." she kisses me on the cheek before hopping off my bed and skipping down the hall.

Perry and Riley shared a room whenever she stayed over. Perry had an apartment in the city but was always over when she wasn't busy or working. She didn't like being alone, never had. I understood that.

Once she left, I pull on the large shirt and crawled into bed, reading my chapter for school before going to sleep.

CHAPTER 2

Boone

The team piled into the locker room, Joch bumping his fist against the locker letting out a loud 'whoop!' as he pulls his helmet off.

"That is what I'm talking about baby!" he cheers, getting his gear off. Joch, pronounced Josh but spelled with a c because his parents were cruel like that, is a few inches taller than me with slightly shaggy blonde hair that was a sweaty mess at the moment. His blonde beard was a mess, the chin hairs sticking in every direction as the sides stuck out.

"That last goal Oliver, chefs kiss!" he said, kissing his fingertips and blowing me a kiss. I shoot him a smirk and pull my jersey off before getting to work on removing the padding. Joch is the captain and always energetic, keeping the team morale up. We just finished the twenty third game of the season and things are looking good. We've won eighteen games so far. My last season was off to a pretty good start.

"Hey, where was Kaminskey today?" I ask, packing the pads in my bag.

From the row behind him, Tig our forward spoke up, "Oh man, his wife called before the practice. Their house got hit, the place was trashed." he explained. That had me wincing. Damn, Kaminskey and his wife had just got the house and moved their two kids in at the start of this year. They barely got settled and now this? "Damn, how many does that make in the last six months? Eight?" Joch whistled, pulling his pants off. "Les is gonna wanna move now. She already sent me five houses from Zillow." Tig sighed. Over the past seven months, there had been a string of burglaries in the surrounding area and now they had gotten into a few athletes' houses. It was unnerving that two had happened in the development. It was gated and supposed to be safe. The worst part was these thieves somehow got past all the security cameras. None of them caught anything. I finished getting undressed, grabbed the towel and shampoo then head to the showers.

"Hey, Oli, you coming to the bar tomorrow with us? Some of us are heading to TAPHOWZE." Joch calls from the shower stall across from me. The last thing I wanted is to go out, but I needed to do something, otherwise I would just sit at home going stir crazy about the appointment tomorrow.

"Sure. what time?" I call back, wincing as my sore muscles loosen. Fuck this sport really does a number on you after so many years.

"Two, we're gonna watch the game against the Bruins.." Joch replies, drying his hair with his towel. I shut off the water and wrap the towel around my waist.

"Meet you guys there. I have some stuff I gotta do in the morning." Getting poked by needles wasn't how I wanted to spend my morning but I had no choice.

$$\times \quad \times \quad \times \quad \times \quad \times$$

I sit in my truck the next afternoon and look over the documents I'd gotten emailed from the hospital. All the instructions and the doses of medicine and what kind that I would have to take. I took a deep breath, exhaling before closing the emails. I absolutely hate this but I had to do it. Shaking the bad memories away before they started, I drive to Taphowze and park the truck in the side lot. I barely slept last night after the game. Then leaving the hospital this morning sucked. The bar is a local place in downtown Seattle that Joch and the others had been going to occasionally this past few months. Joch and the others had already arrived and were waiting for me at a table in the back. A few of them had beers already and Joch held one out for me but I shook my head no.

"No drinking for me today man." Joch was the only one who knew about what was going on with me so he doesn't push. I looked around the bar, it was pretty crowded for a Thursday. A table of rowdy frat boys were to the left by the entrance, their table was covered with a big tray of wings and beer bottles. Kaminskey and Tig joined us after a few minutes.

"Kaminskey, hey. Heard about the break in, is everyone ok?" I ask giving him a bro hug. Kaminskey is a right defenseman, similar build to me only a few inches shorter. He has a full lumberjack beard and is covered in tattoos from head to toe.

"Carol is really shaken up, she's still all messed up from the hormones from the pregnancy and she had Lucy with her so she was trying to not panic to keep her calm. It was not a good call to get." he winces, running a hand through his brown hair. Carol, his wife, had given birth four months ago and the baby was currently in the NICU due to being born two months early. Not only was she dealing with a toddler but also a very sick newborn.

"How is the little superman?" Joch asked, taking a swig of his beer.

"He's doing really well, gaining weight and will be home soon." Kaminskey sighs, he is smiling but I can see the tiredness in his eyes and how exhausted he is. Whenever he wasn't at work or home taking care of Lucy he was at that hospital with Carol.

"Let us know if you need anything man, I am a great babysitter." Joch smiles, holding his arms out. Kaminskey shakes his head, "After you dyed the dog purple last time I don't think Carol will take the offer, but I'll ask." he tips his beer toward Joch.

I unzip my coat and look around, my eyes catch the sight of the female bartender behind the bar. Her high ponytail of copper hair bounces as she zooms up and down the bar, grabbing drinks and taking orders. She looks up, doing a quick scan of the bar and when I see her mismatched eyes, I do a double take. I know her from somewhere but I can't remember where.

Patting Joch on the back I say, "I'll be right back man." before heading to the bar not looking away from her as if she would vanish if I do. She is bent forward grabbing two beers from the cooler, she looks up and her eyes meet with mine. A look of surprise comes over her face and she blinks at me, almost startled.

"Hey." she says, her voice cracking a little.

CHAPTER 3

Tabitha

I jerk up into a sitting position and suck in a breath, swallowing the scream as I wake up from the nightmare. My hair is matted to my forehead as sweat coats my chest and back making my shirt stick to my skin. *'He isn't here. He's not here. It was just a dream.'* I repeat, calming my breathing down. My throat burns as I take deep, shaky breaths. I sit forward, bending my knees so my elbows rest on them as I take in more deep breaths to help push the memories away. That fucking house. The smell of burnt skin. All of it gets pushed away into the dark recess of my mind.

A quick glance at the clock on the side table shows the time as five forty-five am. Great. Right before the alarm sounds too. I need to get more melatonin next time I am at the store. It had been so long since I had a nightmare that I had thought they had finally gone away for good. Or at least were only a once in a blue moon thing.

Getting out of bed, I quietly change into running shorts and a large black hoodie. The sky is a dark indigo color as I start my run, pepper spray and taser strapped to my left arm. I keep up with running every morning. The cold temperatures make it more challenging which I don't mind. Call me a sadist, but the burn from the cold air and pushing myself to run faster reminded me just how alive I was. And I loved it.

By the time I get home, the sky is a light blue with the sun cresting over the trees. Riley is awake and making food. She stands at the oven bopping around to music playing from her phone. Her hair is in a messy, puffy bun and she has on an oversized gray t-shirt. She winces as she burns her thumb on the skillet and sucks on it before looking over and sees me.

"Hey. Morning. You hungry?" she asks. Perry must still be asleep. I pull the hoodie off and nod. "Yeah I'm gonna grab a shower first." I say, thumping up the steps, not even bothering to be quiet. Perry could sleep through a building falling over.

After I had showered I got dressed for work. The snug white tanktop has the bars name across the chest stretching across my tits, 'Taphowze', and 'Bar bitch' is on the apron. Pulling on worn, light ripped jeans and tie my hair up into a ponytail, clipping it with a claw clip, I take a look in the mirror at my reflection. The black eyeliner makes the mismatched colors in my eyes pop and the foundation hides how tired I am. Judging from the smell, Riley had made eggs, bacon and toast for breakfast so I make a bacon and egg sandwich, taking a bite out of it before yelling a "Bye" to Riley as I leave the house. It's the middle of November and it's freezing for once. The weather has lately been balmy and warm. I shiver as I zip up my plum colored jacket before I climb into Riley's scratched up black corolla and crank the heat, letting it warm up a bit before backing out of the driveway. Work was about a forty-five minute drive out of the small town of Oak burrow falls into the city. It wasn't so bad.

When I get to the bar I idle in the car for a minute, letting myself mentally prepare for the shift, pushing back the memories of the nightmares from last night.

"Ok. I got this." I exhale, before killing the engine and head toward the entrance. Taphowze got its name years ago when the owner was drunk and filled out the paperwork wrong. He was too much of a cheapskate to change it and just left it. Riley had worked at the og location in highschool and had gotten me a job after I had moved in with her seven years ago. Riley eventually got a better job and quit. Georgia, one of the other waitresses, stands outside the back entrance smoking a cigarette as I walk up. Georgia is twenty-three, two years younger than I am, and has white, bleach blonde hair with black streaks in it. Her scene hair is pulled in a ponytail out of her face revealing a tattoo of a crescent moon on her hairline by her left eye. She nods at me as I walk past. She is dressed in ripped black shorts with a black puffy coat over her white shirt.

"Ready for the day, Sunshine?" she asks, slapping my ass when I pass by, making her laugh. Georgia pops a stick of gum in her mouth and follows me inside the kitchen. Georgia is always in a good mood, nothing really gets her down. She's also super private about her outside of work life. Which I respect.

"Georgia, were you smoking again?" Mick, the owner, calls from the grill. Mick is the size of a tank. Dark, tawny, bronze skin with olive colored eyes, standing at six foot two, almost two hundred-forty pounds of muscle. He had taken the ownership of Taphowze from his skeezy brother Mike, and moved the location to a semi better part of town. Not the most boujee part of town, but better than before. We didn't need to worry more than usual about walking to our cars in this location. Especially when Mick would watch us leave at night or have one of the bar backs walk us to our cars.

"What if I was? You gonna spank me, old man? Punish me for being a bad girl?" Georgia shot back, taking her coat off and hanging it up on the coat hook by the short hallway next to the office.

Mick wags the spatula at her, "If it made you stop that bad habit, I would definitely take you over my knee. Are you trying to give yourself cancer?" he scolds like a father would. Mick and Georgia have this odd relationship where they flirted but it was more like arguing in a cute way. They had almost a fifteen year age gap, with Mick being thirty-seven, but the sexual tension these two have is like a hot stove that no one realized was on.

About to catch fire any time. Like the chemistry is there but both were a hundred percent in denial.

"Tempting tempting tempting, tell me more about what'd you do to me honey? Tie me up and cover me in barbeque sauce. I like it weird." she cooed, blowing him a kiss as she walks through the swinging door. His eyes widen, and he makes an appalled sound.

"There's something seriously wrong with you kid." Mick points the spatchula at her, making a face as she leaves the kitchen laughing.

I shake my head and tie the apron around my waist, following her.

"You guys are odd. Just bang each other already." I comment as we begin to do the opening duties of pulling chairs down and opening the blinds. Georgia humphed and shrugs,

"If he actually moved his tight ass and did something, maybe I'd climb that. But he's slower than frozen molasses." she shakes her head, "and he thinks me being twenty-three and him being thirty-seven is too big an age difference. Sex is better with age, baby."

I just roll my eyes and unlock the doors. Georgia was turning on all the tv's with the gaggle of remotes and her eyes widen.

"Damn. Check it out, Graystone Academy student was attacked last night." Riley had gone to the highschool, Graystone Academy that was located in a town called Oak Burrow falls. It was about an hour's drive from Seattle. I was currently enrolled in online classes at Greystone U for a business marketing degree. The schools were owned by The Graystone family, some big old money rich family that donated their entire fortune to build the school in Oak Burrow falls then later the college on the outskirts of downtown Seattle. They were like Ivy league level campuses with hundreds of applicants a year.

"Damn, hopefully they catch whoever did it. That's scary." Georgia commented and flipped the news to the sports channel. There were supposed to be three games today. An OSU game, a Steelers and a Michigan game on, plus a Bruins game, so that meant crowds and tips.

"Oh, I almost forgot. How was that blind date the other night?" she asks. I roll my eyes. "Ugh, don't ask."

I work the floor and then a few hours in, jump behind the bar. There was a game on every tv and by four the bar was packed. Music was kept low and the sounds of the games played.

A group of tall men walked in and went to the far right side of the bar to one of the booths. I was grabbing drinks, collecting tips and taking orders. I had just grabbed a beer from the cooler and stood up. Right when I look at the person sitting in front of me, I do a double take. The same emerald green eyes from the other night stare back at me. instantly I recognize the hockey player from the penalty box.

"Oh, Hi!" I squeaked, unable to think of what else to say. He sat at the bar, wearing a black ski jacket with the name Boone stitched on the breast pocket. I slid the beer to the customer I was serving then wiped my hands on my apron and looked at the hockey player. His face is clean and not drenched in sweat, his beard is neatly trimmed and his hair is combed.

"What can I get you?" I asked. The corner of his mouth raised in a half smile.

"Just a water, please, Tabby." he asks, reading my nametag. I smiled and grabbed his drink, setting it down on the bar. "My name is actually Tabitha, it wouldn't fit on the nametag." I explained looking at the bar patrons close by to see if anyone was flagging me down.

"Do I know you from somewhere?" He asks. I smile, "I was at one of your games." I reply. His eyes widened and he sat up straighter.

"That's right! I knew you from somewhere but couldn't figure out where." he smiles. I return his smile wiping my hands on a bar cloth on my apron as I grab another beer.

"You threw beer on another guy and completely kicked his ass, if I remember correctly?" he cocks his head to the side.

"Yes, that drunk asshole should have kept his hands to himself." I say, glad the smell of beer washed out of my extensions.

"So judging by the name on your coat, your name is Boone? Unless you are wearing another man's coat. If so, I don't judge." I ask, nodding to his chest. He chuckles, "It's actually Oliver, but people also call me Boone." I raise my eyebrows at him, "Ah, so we both have incognito names," I nod, making him chuckle. Boone is momentarily distracted by a blonde viking looking man who comes over to talk to him. I look at Georgia who was behind the bar filling glasses for a tray. She waves her eyebrows at me and glances between me and Boone, mouthing, "He's' hot!' I nod, "I know." I wasn't gonna deny that fact. Oliver Boone was hot as fuck. She spun around when he took his jacket off, his slate gray under armor shirt clinging to his thick arms and broad chest. And holy moly he was a thicc boy. No wonder he was called the mountain, he was built like one.

'Oh my god!' I mouthed to Georgia who- because she was staring at both men- wasn't paying attention until the jug overflowed and she ended up dropping it. I chortle and help her clean up the spill before grabbing a second pitcher to fill with beer.

"I love thick men. The bigger, the better." Georgia mutters to me before taking the tray out to the floor.

"Did he offer you tickets to the next game like the gentleman he is?" the blonde asked me. He had his arm thrown over Boone's shoulders. I chuckle and shake my head.

"The last game I went to I ended up getting beer thrown on me. And I was kicked out for fighting." I explained, smiling.

"Well we can get you seats away from the assholes." his friend promises, flashing me a pearly white smile.

"Joch, let her do her job." Boone chided. The blonde, named Josh smiled at me before sticking his hand out, "I am Josh, spelled J-O-C-H." he introduced as I shake his hand. I give them both a confused look, "That's a very strange-"

"Spelling? Yea. I know. My parents are mean like that. I have a sister named Samantha spelled S-a-p-h-m-a-n-t-h-a. But we are not talking about my crazy, traumatic childhood. Oli, have you at least gotten this beautiful woman's number?

Have I taught you nothing? He is not this slow usually I promise." Joch asks, grinning with a Cheshire smile from Boone to me. Oh he was good. Best wingman award goes to the unfortunately named Joch. Boone gives him a look and exhales as he rubs his temples. A customer flags me over from down the bar and I excuse myself to go help them.

"I will be right back." I say holding my hand up, stepping away to help the customer.

Should I give him my number? I mean he is outrageously attractive. I grab the two coronas from the cooler and take the card to open the tab. Fuck it, I'll give him the number if he asks. He is hot.

CHAPTER 4

Boone

I take a sip of my water and watch as Tabitha cashes out a couple people before coming back over, "Sorry if I was being pushy, but my man Oliver here happens to be single and as his best friend, I will not let him miss this opportunity to get the number of a beautiful woman with amazing eyes." Joch says, grabbing my shoulders. She smiles, a dimple appearing on her cheek as she pours a beer from one of the tappers into a jug. Her smile is cute. And her eyes, one eye is full blue while the other is green with light brown through the entire bottom half. It was mesmerizing and I'm really glad making eye contact isn't rude because these eyes were definitely ones I wouldn't mind just staring at the whole night.

"It's called sectoral heterochromia, one eye is two colors, the other is one solid color." she explained.

"Beautiful. Isn't she super beautiful?" Joch asks, squeezing my shoulders, "Extremely." I reply honestly.

"Well I believe I have overstayed my welcome. Oliver, don't come back to the table without her number." Joch demands, giving a two finger salute before heading back to the table.

"He is very persistent, isn't he?" she says, handing the beer jug to one of the waitresses with blonde hair.

"Very. But he is a great captain. And my best friend." I sighed.

"So, if I can't convince you to come to a game, could I at least get your number, maybe?" I inquire, raising my voice a bit so she could hear me over the cheers from the groups of people watching the game.

"You don't waste any time do you?" She asked, cashing out a customer.

"Not when I put my mind to something." I replied. What was I doing? This was not usually how I would go about this. Usually I'd ask for a girl's number and if she said no, that was it. I never cared that much. But this girl...I didn't want to give up.

"Do you usually ask strangers for their number? I could be a serial killer for all you know." The cheeky smirk on her face has me laughing.

"I'm a risk taker." I shrug.

"That's a very big risk, you trusting someone not to be a killer *and* giving them your number?" she raises a brow suspiciously before putting her hands on the bar.

The smile on my face widens and I shake my head, "It's worth the risk if I get to talk to you again." Her smile drops when she looks behind me as a loud, obnoxious laughter bursts out from the frat guys table. Turning I see they were hassling the blonde waitress. She has a stoic look on her face mixed with anger. She's trying to get away from the table but they keep stepping in her way and laughing like it's some kind of game. Tabitha hisses a curse and walks around the bar, ducking under the side and goes toward the table. I don't like this. The boys at the table try to call the blonde back when Tabitha stops the one from blocking her again. They look at her like she's a new toy and it makes my skin itch.

From where I'm sitting, I can't hear the exchange but I'm on my feet the moment the blonde frat boy reaches for her. He grabs Tabitha by the arm and throws the pitcher of beer at her chest soaking her white shirt. Now I'm pissed.

"Fucker!" I bark, the bar stool loudly scrapes across the floor as I grab my jacket and storm through the crowd. The look on Tabitha's face is shock and anger. One of them, a tall lanky looking one with a literal fucking bowl cut, curves his arm around her to grab a handful of her ass, and pulls her toward him. I want to break his arm. Tabitha reacts by throwing her elbow back into his nose and strikes him in the throat with her palm making him squeal like a pig. Blonde boy grabs her shoulder and shoves her back hard.

"Whoa whoa hey!" I shout, catching Tabitha and moving her safely behind me and step between them so none of these assholes could touch her. I drape my jacket over her shoulders to cover her soaked shirt. "I think it's time for you assholes to leave." I growl. Drunk boy is chest to chest with me and I am a good foot and half taller than him so he has to tilt his head up to look at me. His eyes are droopy from the alcohol and his aftershave is nauseatingly strong.

"We're just having fun man. That's what she's here for! I can pay her." he hiccup-laughs. I frown at him. This asshole. I hate little bitch boys like this that acted like they owned the world. It was assholes like him that got away with murder because they had daddy's money. Tabitha lets out a sound of disgust.

"Bite me you cum wad!" She spits out.

"Fuck you, whore!" Bowl cut coughs, he takes a step toward her and Joch grabs his shoulder, stopping him, "Don't wanna do that." he warns.

"Take your asshole friends and get out." I growl at the blonde boy. I don't care that we're in public and anyone who recognizes me or Joch could whip out a cellphone and this would be all over the internet. If he wanted a fight, hell I did that for a living. What's one more off the ice? It'll be just like my rookie days when I was just an angry kid only this time I'm stronger.

"Pft, No way. We're celebrating our victory. You're looking at the next draft picks for the NHL." he sneers as his buddies whoop and cheer. Joch and I share a look, no fucking way these twats were gonna be drafted.

"Really?" Joch snorts. Blonde boy nods, his smirk growing as he straightens his wrinkled white polo sweater.

"Yea, I'm gonna play for the Skyhawks. And Duane here is going to the Bruins." So Bowl cuts name was Duane. Noted. Their low chances of being on the team are nonexistent now.

"I don't care if you're the next queen of England, all of you OUT!" a big built man wearing an apron yells. He has a crowbar in his hand. The blonde girl from before is behind him.

"Drunk and disorderly conduct and sexual harassment of a server doesn't seem like a good thing for draft pick does it?" Joch smirks at me.

"Lets see how Coach Cal and Coach Dallan feel?" I grit through my teeth. At the mention of the team coaches of their picks these boys go white.

"I will break all your knee caps if you don't get the fuck out of my bar." The guy with the crowbar roars. It appears the threats are enough and they end up being escorted out.

I turn back to Tabitha, "Are you ok?" I asked. she wipes her chin with the back of her hand, "I'm fine." she muttered, shaking her head and walking back towards the bar and into the back. Her face was red. The blonde waitress gave me a wave, "She's ok, I'll check on her." she said, following after her.

Joch slaps my back, "Hey come on man, we gotta get back to the table or head out." The patrons of the bar started to realize and recognize both of us and suddenly it started to get louder as people asked for pictures or autographs. Shit. If I stayed that meant cameras and eyes on me the entire time and then it would mean more attention on whoever I was with. I really want to keep talking to Tabitha but don't want it to end up on all the stupid internet news articles. Joch and I are taking a few photos with some of the patrons and I haven't seen her come back to the floor yet, a different woman is behind the bar at this point.

My phone starts to ring and my chest tightens when I see Marissa's name across the screen.

"I'll see you guys later." I barely say as I head outside and get into my truck.

CHAPTER 5

Tabitha

"Have you seen this man!" Riley calls out from the living room where she is cocooned in her blankets with her laptop on her lap.

I roll my eyes and walk into the living room with my bowl of cereal. I had gotten home last night and spent about forty minutes washing the smell of beer off me, again, luckily none of it got in my extensions but my shirt now has a yellowish stain on it and my bra cups were full of beer. It had been a college football night and there had been lots of drunk GU students in the bar. We had a new waitress too and she had spilt an entire tray of mixed drinks on me. Lovely.

When Riley got home from her job at the hospital a few hours ago, I told her everything that had happened the other night at the bar. She worked three twelves so this was the first I had seen her in five days. She immediately went to internet stalk him on all socials.

Currently I am changed into big, comfy, pink sweatpants and a black oversized shirt.

"Yes, I have and he is as gorgeous in person as in photos." I comment before eating a spoonful of cereal. Riley scrolls through photos of Boone on her computer. His instagram had professional photos mixed with ones he's taken himself of him at his house, jumping in the pool, I drool over the one mirror selfie of him in a full pale lavender suit he posted yesterday before his away game. The pants hug his thick waist and the pale shirt stretches over his broad shoulders and arms.

"Did he get your number?" she asks. I sigh, "No. Thanks to that idiot who doused me in beer, I wasn't able to." Maybe it was for the best? It had been a few days since the incident at the bar and he hasn't come back since. He was a professional hockey player, of course he was busy doing whatever they did other than playing hockey. He wouldn't still think about the random girl he met at a bar.

His jacket is currently slung over my chair in my room. When I finally emerged from the back he was gone and so was his blonde friend Joch. The front door opens and Perry prances into the house. I say prance because that's the only way to describe the walk she was doing. It was like a drunk reindeer in heels.

"Sorry I'm late! Traffic was a bitch." she pants, dropping her overnight bag on the recliner.

She plops down next to me and sinks down into the couch. Every week we have a lazy lounging day where we order food and watch movies and trash tv. It was seven am and all our blankets and pillows are in the living room.

"What did I miss?" she asks, grabbing a chocolate chip pancake from the bowl on the old wooden table. Riley had made a smorgasbord of breakfast foods like giant pancakes, and bacon. I made my muffins and they were on a plate on top of the oven cooling.

Riley turns her computer to show her, "Tabs got the attention of The Mountain! He came to her rescue at the bar after he flirted with her and remembered her from the hockey game." Perry lunges across me to her and grabs the computer.

"Are. You. Serious! Why didn't you tell me! He's hot!" she gushes. I roll my eyes, "Because I wanted an interesting story for our get together. A few drunk assholes got too handsy, the prick almost ripped out my nipple rings." I instinctively put a hand to my tit where my nipple is a little sore still, "Boone came in like a freaking big beast and was 'Get the fuck out.'" I start but Riley makes a noise that sounded like a gasp and gawk.

"This was after he asked if you wanted to go to a game! He also gave her his jacket." she gushes, kicking her feet.

Perry could have snapped her neck with how fast she turned it to look at her then to me.

"He asked you out?" she yells.

"Ow, Pear, please lower the voice." I wince, taking my dish to the sink. She trots after me, hanging on every word.

"He was going to but I got beer splashed onto me and when I came back after changing my shirt, he was gone. It was all chaos too." It was disappointing but Georgia had said he and Joch started to get a little swarmed with fans and he got a call and left right after.

"Hey, you should try to get in when they're practicing at the arena! I fucked a security guard that works there and he said its totally possible, he got me into one of the practices once. You can give him back the jacket and get his number." she suggested.

"Isn't that kinda stalkerish? Just showing up at his job?"

"Come on, he was practically drooling over you at the bar!" Riley gushed. Perrys smile widened.

"He was not, ok, he was maybe a little flirty but we talked for like two seconds and then I got drenched in beer and he gave me his jacket. If anything, he's probably looking for a lay." no need to get my hopes up for nothing. I dry my hands and lean back against the counter. Perry hopped up onto the spot next to me, "And so what if he is? You said so yourself last week you needed to get laid and I've fucked a couple hockey players in my life and they are always a fun fuck. So enjoy it and see what happens?" she advises. I sigh, last time I'd had sex it wasn't the best. Poor guy got whiskey dick half way through and I faked an orgasm to save him the embarrassment. We'd only gone on a couple dates before we slept together and after the worst sex ever, I never saw him again.

"Just take him the damn jacket and see where it goes." Riley insisted, "And dress in the cute jeans."

I can't believe I'm doing this, just waiting out here like a stalker. I had gotten to the practice rink a little bit ago and now I am just standing in front of the doors that had a big sign that read 'Closed for Private Practice'. It's cold today, my puffy jacket not able to stop the chill from sneaking under the fabric.

This is crazy. What am I thinking? I had gotten up and after a shower this morning, took Rileys advice and wore the cute jeans that made my ass look nice and a thin, dark olive green loose sweater over a black tank top.

"Hey! World's best bartender!" a voice calls from the parking lot behind me. It is Joch, he waves at me as he jogs toward the building, his honey blonde hair is in a low bun.I forgot how tall he was, I have to tilt my head up slightly.

"Oh hey, Josh with a C." I greeted. Joch had a huge bag over his shoulder, and wore a similar jacket to the one I had in my arms. He stands in front of me. "Are you waiting for Oli?" he guesses, giving me a flirty smirk when I straighten.

"Uh, sort of. I'm returning his jacket. I figured this would be the best place to check but I can't get into the building. Could you give this to him?" I ask, holding out the coat. Joch smiles and pulls out his key card from his pocket.

"Why don't you give it to him yourself? He should be on the ice practicing. Come on." he waves, swiping the keycard and opening the door, holding it open for me.

"Are you sure? I don't want to interrupt." I ask unsure. Joch's smile widens and he looks even more handsome, "Uh yes! He'll be happy to see you. He hasn't shut up about the bar since yesterday." he explained as we make our way down the hall. We pass hockey pictures and trophies of past teams. The team is scattered on the ice, some are shooting pucks, some are racing from one side to the other. I can't tell who is who since half of them don't have their jerseys on.

"Hey Oli! You have a visitor!" Joch shouts. I look from him to the ice and see Boone looking up at us waving.

"Have fun. I'm super late and need to lace up or coach will murder me." Joch groans, heading to the locker room door.

There are a couple spectators scattered around the seating area. All now looking up at me as I walk down the steps to the glass where Boone meets me halfway.

"Hey." I greet, smiling. He has sweat all over his face and neck, even his beard looks damp. He's one of the players not wearing his jersey, instead he is wearing a blue practice jersey.

"Hey! How are you?" he asks, returning the smile.

"I'm good. I, uh, wanted to give you your jacket back." I lift the jacket in my arms to show him.

He blinks and then looks at the jacket in my hands and I realized there was a layer of plexiglass between us, "Oh yea, I can leave it here or wherever." I stutter slightly. Boone chuckles.

"It's ok. I'm glad you came by today."

"You all are really good at skating, you make it look easy." I chuckle. "Have you ever skated before?" He asks. I shake my head, "Once or twice when I was a kid maybe but not really." Boone smirks and looks back as the coach blows his whistle. He has a look on his face that I read as mischievous.

"Hey, do you have anything planned for the rest of the day?" He asks.

"No. I just have a later shift for work tonight."

"What size shoe are you?" He calls, pushing from the wall and skating backwards.

"Seven, why?"

"Be right back. Meet me at the ice entrance." he yells, hopping through the small doorway off the ice. The way the rink is set up, there is a small door that opens to a walkway that leads directly to the athletes changing room so the players can get on and off the ice quickly. I do as he says and wait by the entrance to the ice rink. A few minutes later he comes back. He holds out a small pair of skates to me.

"Wait, am I allowed to do this? Won't you get in trouble?"

"Practice is over, so it should be ok.." he nods.

"Wait. Joch just got here though?" I questioned pointing to the hall he had gone down. Boone let out a laugh, "Yea, he's gonna be in the back rink tonight, he is on sugar plumb detail."

"What?" I laugh. I sit down on a bench and take my shoes off.

"It's the little kids skating time, he assists with the figure skating classes." He explaines. I couldn't help but awe at that. And chuckle, Picturing Joch in a pink tutu skating with a bunch of little kids. Boone kneels in front of me, he had taken all his pads off so he was in a black long sleeved under armor shirt and his black and blue hockey pants. He is a good foot and a half taller than me and his arms are thick like the rest of his build. His face was now dry, so he must have quickly washed it when he went to the back. My breath catches in my throat when his hand goes to my calf and he lifts my leg, putting the skate on and tying it. My pulse screams in my ears as I feel his hand lightly squeeze my ankle. Why was something so normal so hot? Boone, not even noticing, does the same thing with the other foot. Once the skate is tied he pats the side of the skate and looks up at me.

"Is this the part where you kill me and throw me into the zamboni?" I laugh. Boone covers his mouth as he lets out a snort..

"Nah, that's too messy. Plus, you've been seen with me by too many witnesses." he smirks, taking my hands and pulling me to my feet. He helps me onto the ice and I hold onto the wall. I knew how to do the little shuffle part, but I still clutched onto the side like the scared chicken I was. He glides over and holds his hand out to me. He smiles down at me, "Trust me?" He asks, making me chuckle. "Considering we've only met once before?"

"I promise, you won't fall-that much." I let out a snort at his cadence.

Slowly and shakily, I grab both his hands and let him pull me out onto the ice, Him skating backwards while pulling me along like a kid.

"Keep your feet straight." He instructs me.

"You make this look so easy, how do you do it?" I ask. It was amazing how this looks so effortless but was really fucking hard in reality.

"I've been playing hockey since I was seven so it's pretty much second nature at this point." He explains as we moved around the rink. Him pulling me along.

"So tell me about Tabitha, what should I know?" he asks as we make another round.

"Hmmm. well, I am twenty four, a bartender at TAPHOWZE. I currently live with my friend Riley in her house across town. And.... that's about it." I keep it vague and short. He shakes his head, "Nah, That can't be all. What's your favorite hobby? Do you have any siblings? Are you single?" he asks, tilting his head. I laugh at that.

"No, I am begrudgingly single. Not many guys want to date someone who depends on her looks for tips. And I seem to have only attracted the weird ones when I have been dating." I shrug. I don't miss the slight squeeze of his hand on mine when I verify I am single. "And I actually grew up in foster care so I don't know if I have any bio siblings." I add. He didn't need to know about the horrible woman that birthed me or the fact that she chose to do what she did over her own child. The abandonment issues were nonexistent in case you were wondering. I hated her for what she did.

"Well good on the single thing, and really sucks about the foster care thing. I'm sorry you had to go through that." He let go of my hand and I reach out for him, panicking a bit because we are in the center of the rink and I really don't want to fall on my ass.

"You're ok. You got it." he soothes. I catch my balance and push with the skate, able to keep myself upright without his help.

"See. You got it!" he praised. I look up at him through my eyelashes and feel my face blush.

"So tell me about you, Oliver Boone?" I ask. He skates backwards in front of me keeping an eye to make sure I don't fall.

"Well, I am a hockey player. I am almost thirty three. I grew up with a single mom, became a goon when I was in college. Basically I got into all the fights and then once I got to the NHL I joined the Skyhawks and now here I am." he explains.

"Bet your mom liked that you were getting into fights." I giggle, looking from my feet back up to him and he has a warm smile on his face.

"Probably not. She passed away right before I went to college." Aaaannnnd I feel like a complete ass now. Way to go Tabitha.

"Oh I am so sorry. What was she like?" I ask. I only vaguely remember what my mom was like before she chose drugs so I had no experience with a good mother.

"She was the best. She got sick when I was six and fought it off and on until my summer before college. You would never know she was sick by looking at her, she had this spirit about her that no one could dull. She went into remission when I was in middle school but then it came back in highschool." The vibrancy of how he spoke about his mom made my chest feel warm, but I can see the underlying sadness there in his emerald green eyes. It made me feel both happy and sad for him at once.

"Bet she was the mom yelling in the stands at every game?" I chuckle. Boones barking out a laugh has me surprised by the suddenness, "Oh yes. She was the mom that would cheer the loudest at practices, games. She almost got into it with a ref at one of my peewee games because a kid tripped me and it wasn't called. I mean, imagine a five foot two, hundred and ten pound woman yelling at a huge ref. She was amazing." he laughs. I had to laugh with him, his laugh was contagious.

Mid laugh I lost my balance, "Oh Shit!" my feet went out from under me and I ended up falling backwards onto my butt.

"Pffttt! I'm sorry! Are you ok?" Boone snickered, coming up next to me.

"My ass is freezing!" The shock of the cold had me squealing. When I fell, I had fallen onto a slush pile of wet ice so now I was soaking wet. Again. Boone bit his lip to not laugh as he helped me up.

"You always end up wet around me, don't you?" he chuckled, his voice low with a huskiness that made my belly heat. Did he know the effect he was having on me? There was no way he didn't know what he was doing.

"It seems to be the going theme with us, doesn't it?" I focus my gaze up into his eyes, feeling my face get redder from embarrassment. I wipe the ice off my butt.

"You ok? Anywhere else get.. wet, or hurt?" he asks, trying not to laugh but failing horribly.

"Maybe, but I'm too cold to tell right now. That's embarrassing." my face burns in embarrassment. Boone turns his head as he breaks into a fit of laughter, "I'm sorry, it's not funny. Pft." he keeps laughing and I give him a mocked offended look, "Ok not all of us can be professional skaters." I wince as the coldness on my ass has me starting to shiver, "My ass is freezing. I'm sending you the hospital bill." Boone helps me over to the door off the ice still snickering.

"I think you'll be ok. I'm no doctor though but everything seems fine. It looks the same as when you got here." He smirks.

"Ahh, that a confession that you checked out my ass?" I challenge His eyes widen and he scratches his beard, "I'm gonna plead the fifth on that one."

I nod, "Ok, that's not a denial." I scrunch my nose as I shake my head at him. He holds his hands up in surrender.

"I'm human. Feel free to check mine out too." he turns in a circle with his hands up letting me have the opportunity to check out his ass. I already did that when I came to the arena but up close it was still a nice impressive ass.

"Before you leave, is it possible I could finally get your number?" he asks once he faces me again, flashing me a smile. I nod. No fucking way was I leaving without this mans number.

"I'll make sure to save you under 'probably not a serial killer' since there is always a chance right?" he winks, and I bite my lip. *I bit my fucking lip.* What in the *Twilight* was I doing! This man has me matched for wit and sarcasm and it is kinda cute. Ok it was hot. Super hot.

"Of course. Can't be too careful."

"I'll walk you out front." he offers, handing me back my phone.

CHAPTER 6

Boone

God she is fucking cute. I watch as Tabitha walks to her car, of course my eyes are glued to her ass. I'm only human. She has a wet spot on the right cheek and back upper thigh of her pants from the wet ice and I can't help but chuckle a little. Once I'm changed and get in my truck, I realize with a laugh she had taken my jacket with her. I couldn't stop thinking about those beautiful eyes or her contagious laugh all night after the bar. How easy it was to talk to her and just how relaxed I felt around her. Whatever this was, I liked it. I like it alot.

My phone ringing has my good mood turning sour as I see the number. Fucking hell.

Gritting my teeth, I hit the bluetooth on the car, "What do you want Hank?" I spit through my teeth.

"Really? Is that how you greet your father?" he asks, making me roll my eyes. Hank was many things, but my father he was not. Biologically, yes he may be related to me but that's it. He lost the right to be my father the moment he stepped foot out the door leaving my mom to raise me alone while she was sick.

"I'm busy Hank, what is it?" I push, trying to keep the clipped tone out of my voice but not really caring if he was offended by it.

"Did you get the test done yet?" he sounds more irritable than normal.

"Yes, I got the tests done. I'll find out in a couple weeks what the results are and if they are going to move ahead with the biopsy." I explain robotically as I had done so much research and had gone over what the doctors had said. Hank makes a grunt of disapproval, "Couple weeks? Pft, Don't you have some kind of pull with that place? You donate enough to them. You'd think they'd be up and on this." skydaddy christ he whined like a posh bitch that wasn't used to hearing he had to wait. I fight the urge to hang up. Digging my fingers into the steering wheel.

"No. Hank. I don't have any *pull* with the hospital. That's not how it works." I growl. Hank tsked. "Money will get you anything boy. It's power." he would know, he had enough of it from his rich father inlaw.

"Bye Hank." I say, ending the call. I rest my forehead against the head rest. God I hate him. I inhaled deeply then exhaled just like I remembered to when I felt the burn of anger rushing through me. Tonight's game was gonna be a rough one and now I have this on my mind. It had been such a good day until now.

 My phone pings as I pull up to the gate of the arena a few hours later. It was Joch.

💬JOCH: Hey! How'd it go!

💬BOONE: Fine. Got her number.

💬JOCH: JUST FINE! Please tell me you made a move on her! She is hot!

💬BOONE: Look man I just got off the phone with Hank, Not really up for a discussion about Tabitha right now.

💬JOCH:.... Fuck man. What'd he want? You're already doing enough for that POS.

💬BOONE: To question me about the testing and making sure I did it and I'm not bs'n him. He actually thought because I donate to the hospital that I had some leeway with getting the results earlier. As if I controlled the testing results

My phone pinged with another new text and a smile immediately spread across my face.

💬TABITHA: Hey. it's Tabitha.....

💬BOONE: Hey

💬TABITHA: I realized when I got home ... I took your coat

💬 BOONE: Was this an accident? Or are you looking for just another reason to see me?

💬TABITHA: Total accident! I swear.

My phone pinged as Joch texted.

💬JOCH: ? you there?

I told Joch I'd call him later and immediately opened the text thread with Tabitha.

💬BOONE: Riiiiight. If you wanted to see me again all you had to do was say so, beautiful. It was fun. 10/10 would definitely wanna do that again.

💬TABITHA: Do I look like the type to be so desperate that she'd take your coat as a lame excuse to see you again??? And other than getting soaking wet, I would have to agree.

💬BOONE: There's nothing wrong with getting a little wet sometimes.
💬BOONE: Hell no. You seem like a go-getter. You see what you want and you get it.

💬TABITHA: Does that mean I can get you if I wanted? All to myself?

💬TABITHA: OMG! That was my roommate! PLEASE DO NOT ANSWER THAT!

💬TABITHA: I AM SO SORRY! She took my phone!

💬BOONE: Don't be. It's ok. But to be sure... how do I know this is really Tabitha?

💬TABITHA: [photo]

The attached photo was of Tabitha, she was at the bar; her shirt had BAR BITCH stretched across her chest. Her copper red hair was down and straightened. She looked down right sexy, the angle made her tits look amazing, but it was those eyes that just drew me in. The smokey eye makeup made those mismatched eyes pop.

💬TABITHA: It's getting pretty busy here, I gotta get back to work. Talk soon?

💬BOONE: Sure. I have a game tonight but text me later, I'll be up late. And Tabitha?

💬TABITHA: ? yea..

💬BOONE: To answer your roomates question, If you wanted me to yourself all you have to do is ask.

I was In the middle of getting into the in-ground hot tub when Tabitha calls. I'm happy to see her name across the screen, I used the photo she sent earlier to set it as her contact photo.

"Hey! Sorry, if it's late, I was just on my break and thought I'd say hi." she greets.

"How's work?" I ask, sitting on the edge with my legs dangling in the water.

"It's busy, as per usual. Just about to get off in a bit. What are you doing? How was the game?" she asks.

"Just sitting in the hot tub, It was a rough one." my shoulder was still stiff from the hit I had taken.

"Ohh that sounds like fun. I saw a bit of the game and it looked like it was rough. You ok?" ohh is that concern I hear?

"Yea, I'm good. Just a few bumps and bruises. How about you?" my neck cracks as I stretch, making me groan a bit.

She chuckles, "It's been a rough shift. Customers. The usual." my spine stiffens, "Have those assholes been back?" Joch had already reached out to the coaches and informed them of their new prospects' activities and it turns out this wasn't the first time they had been in trouble. If they had the stupidity to go back to the bar and bother Tabitha. The thought made me grind my teeth.

"No, just gets super busy and crowded around this time of year with all the games and sporting events. The long shifts suck but the money's good." I can hear the exhaustion in her voice.

"How much longer do you have in your shift?" I ask.

"About an hour. Why?"

"Wanna hangout?"

CHAPTER 7

Tabitha

I finished my shift and now am driving down the street into a cul-de-sac where my GPS tells me Boone lives. He had given me a passcode at the gate to give the security guard. I pass so many big houses on the drive to his house, I feel way out of place in the dented, scratched Corolla.

Boones house is a large gray- tannish brick two story house with a two car garage with one of those stone arches above the front doorway. It wasn't an oversized billionaire Kardashian mansion big like I thought, most of the houses were similar sizes. It was like a rich family type neighborhood. Parked in the driveway is a black RAM pickup truck. I only knew about this development because of the reports on the news of three break ins over the past few months. I notice a plumber's utility van a few houses down parked on the street as I walk up the driveway.

I send Boone a text letting him know I was here and a few minutes later I hear the sound of a door opening.

"Tabitha, hey." he greets, coming from around the side of the house. He is in just a pair of low swim shorts. Holy. Hell. His broad chest has a nice patch of dark hair on it that trails down the center of his torso to a little happy trail that disappears beneath his trunks.

"Sorry, I was in the back," he says, pointing his thumb over his shoulder towards a pathway around the side of the house. Momentarily I forget Why was I here again? Oh his jacket!

"Oh! Um here. This is yours. Figured since I was in the area I would drop it off." I stutter holding out the jacket to him. He takes it from me and smiles

"Well yea come on back. This is my home." he says motioning to the house. I nod, "Thanks for inviting me." I follow him around the side of the house, through a wooden gate into an amazing fenced in backyard. There is a covered patio to the right with a large sliding glass door. Straight ahead to the left is an in-ground hot tub that was designed to look like a natural hot spring with smooth decorative rocks all around the edge of it.

"Can I get you a drink?" he asks, glancing back at me. "Yingling ok?"
I scrunch my face agreeably nodding, "Always."

He hands me a bottle and we go to the sitting area between the pool and hot tub. He puts on a thin zip up hoodie and sits down across from me.

"Wow. this is amazing." I'm in awe, looking around at the lit up yard. The lights were dim so it wasn't too bright but casted a low glow giving the pool and hot tub a nice ambiance..

"Thanks, I just finished planting a couple of the trees in the back by the fence and was thinking of putting in a new fire pit in the middle back of the yard." he perks up, pointing to a few newer looking trees toward the fence line in the back.

"You planted them?" I raise a brow. He nods as he takes a pull from his bottle.

"I like taking care of the things around me. Adding some trees, plants, you name it. I've remodeled a couple houses with a buddy of mine for some families in the area we grew up in. It just feels good to help people." I'm caught off guard by this information, once again surprised by this unpredictable man. What else does he do?

"Color me impressed. You are full of surprises aren't you?" I smile, tipping my bottle to him before taking a sip. He rolls his shoulder and winces a little.

"You ok?" I grimace. I had seen the hit he'd taken on the ice while I was at the bar and it looked painful.

"Wounds of the lifestyle. Hockey can be a fickle dick sometimes." he groans a bit. A gust of wind blows through the yard and I shiver a little.

"This is really beautiful." I said, looking at the scene. He has a perfect view of the skyline in the distance.

"So how was work? Any problems tonight?" he asks.

I shake my head as I take another sip from my drink, "None more than usual, at least I didn't get a beer thrown on me for once." I smile. That hot tub looked so welcoming.

"I thought you smelled different," he points out.

"Yea, I switched from eu de beer to just some ed hardy spray from cvs." I shrug, making him laugh.

"I like it better than the beer smell."

"Same! I really like that I don't smell like I bathe in alcohol anymore."
Boone and I both break out in belly laughs. I shake my head.

"Hey, are you hungry?" he asks.

I tilt my head, raise my brows as I bring my bottle to my lips, "are you offering to cook for me?" I ask tilting the bottle back.

"I have some steaks I was going to make, tonight, I can fire the grill up." he offers.

"I could eat. I haven't eaten since my break." I nod. He stands and walks over to the grill.

"I'm about to make you the best steak you have ever eaten." he promises.

"That was the best steak I have eaten." I state as I lean back in my chair. I raise my second bottle up to him in a cheers, as he collects the plates and sets them in the kitchen before returning to the back yard.

"Ok I need to put my feet in this hot tub or I will regret it." I say toeing off my shoes and walk over to the edge, plopping down so my feet can dangle in the warm bubbly water. I almost moan at the feeling of the water. After being on my feet all day it was heavenly.

He laughs when I mutter 'fuck it.' and get into the hot tub fully clothed. Boones eyes widen, "Okay, If you were cold we could have just gone inside?" he laughs, pointing his thumb to the house. I shrug, "When will I ever get this chance again? It's a luxury I am gonna take advantage of." I sigh as the warm water and jets hit my legs and feet. I'm never leaving. He sits on the edge and puts his legs in the water.

"Anytime you want, just let me know and you can use it." He smiles while taking a drink from his beer.

I look at him and smile, "Ohhh careful on that, I could live in this hot tub. I mean it. I'll move right in." I chuckle, Boone shrugs, "Fine with me, rent is due on the first."

"So tell me more about Oliver Boone? How did you get the nickname 'The Mountain'? Was that a college thing?" I ask, leaning against the wall opposite of him. He raises a brow, the corner of his mouth cocking up into his signature smirk. My question had him snort, "Sort of. I uh, got the nickname because of my size in college and my bad temper too."

I cock my head to the side, "I can't really picture you with a bad temper but then again we're still strangers." I admit playing with the bottle in my hand. I know perfectly well that the nicest looking people could be the worst monsters.

"We still haven't ruled out if either of us is a serial killer yet, too." he pointed out tilting his bottle. I agreed.

"I had a bit of a temper after my mom passed. Anger at the world, at everyone. When I was on the ice I let all my anger out. Refused to let anyone get past me to the goalie. I was six three in college and two hundred thirty pounds, so me being the size I was and the beard, not to mention I wore a lot of flannel. I got the nickname Mountain man. Eventually it was shortened to Mountain."

"How much flannel?" I snort, holding my bottle to my lips.

He winces, "*So* much flannel." he squeezes his eyes closed. I giggle, picturing him in flannel with his beard. He would look like a lumberjack.

"Oh that's unfortunate. I think you'd look fine in flannel."

He nodded and held his arms out, " I thought so. But I wore it *all the time.* Now, I'm more stylish when it comes to clothing but oof." he takes a pull of his drink.

"What about you? Any equally embarrassing stories to share with the class? Tell me more about you." he asked.

"Well I grew up in foster care, bounced around a few homes. Nothing really stuck."

"So you ended up aging out of the system?" he asks..

"Not exactly," I play with one of the rings on my hands. "I actually ran away from my last foster home a few weeks before I turned eighteen. It wasn't a good placement and I knew they weren't going to adopt me. So rather than stick around and wait it out I just took control and made the choice to leave myself." *not entirely a lie.*

"Shit. I'm sorry you had to go through that." he says. I smile, "I'm here now though. I made it." I down the last of my drink.

He was quiet for a minute, staring out at the last sliver of light just beyond the treeline.

"I have a younger brother." He admits after a moment. "His name is Tate, he's ten. Most energetic, kindest kid I've met." He looks tormented as he speaks. My brows pull in as I listen to his next words,

"He has stage three leukemia." I suck in a breath. Oh shit.

"I only found out about him a few months ago, my *father* showed up after one of my practices asking for help because his son was sick." He spits out the word 'father' as if it is a bad taste as he lets out a humorless laugh. "The same cancer that killed my mom, was now killing his son. The irony." I just listened and let him talk. There was nothing I could say that would comfort him. I copied his movements and leaned against the edge next to him.

"I *should* forgive him. But I *can't*, he left my mom because she was sick. Left her to raise me alone and go through treatments. Now he wants my help? Tates just a kid. He doesn't deserve any of this so I got tested to see if I'm a match for a bone marrow transplant. I won't know the results for a few weeks but I can't help but think that he has something to gain from my help that's more than potentially saving Tate's life?" he wonders aloud. I push from the wall and float onto my back. His father sounded like an ass. As someone who grew up around people who hurt others like it was a sport, I could understand the conspiracy of someone suddenly coming back just to ask for help and feeling they had ulterior motives.

"Forgiveness is bullshit." I say.

CHAPTER 8

Boone

"You don't have to forgive him, you know." She says, drawing my attention. When I look at her, I am instantly captivated.

"Forgiveness is bullshit. Not everyone deserves to be forgiven. The idea of forgiveness is a complete piece of shit. People only say you should forgive others because they want to feel better about themselves. No one really cares if you actually *want* to forgive someone. They don't care how badly someone hurt you or how horrible they treated you, just that *you* forgive *them*. *'Because it's the right thing to do'* But the 'right thing' would have been them not doing the horrible shit in the first place." She's looking up at the sky as she speaks. I look over her silhouette, the way her shirt clings to her like a second skin, I am barely able to make out the faint outline of her nipples through the material. From the light illuminating the bottom of the tub, she looks so serene and something else I couldn't put my finger on.

"It's ok to never forgive someone." she finally looks at me with those beautiful mismatched eyes.

"Especially if they haven't *earned* it." she adds.

I shake my head, realization of the trauma dumping I had just done, my back straightens as I stand up, "I am so sorry for just piling this on you. It's not fair to you. I mean we barely know each other." I apologized, rubbing my forehead. *What was wrong with me!* I never talked this openly with anyone other than Joch or Casey. I barely know Tabitha but I just got word vomit around her.

"You're ok. Talking helps. Believe me, when I ran from my last foster home, all I did was talk to Riley and I hadn't even really met her until I got to her house." she explains. I cock an eyebrow. Tabitha sits up and pushes herself onto one of the built-in seats. Water drips from her hair, down her arms.

"It's ok, we're both trauma dumping. But we still haven't figured out if the other is a killer yet or not." We just looked at each other for a moment before we both burst out laughing. Tabitha lets out a melodic loud laugh that ends in a snort and it just makes us both laugh harder till we both almost had tears in our eyes. I feel like I was able to breathe finally and relax around her.

"It's a very interesting start of this little friendship we have here." she said. Line. Drawn. I nodded and felt content with that statement. Friends. I could be friends with her.

"It is. And I am looking forward to exploring this *friendship* with you." I give her a wink. I stand up and stretch my arms up over my head, "We should probably go inside, uhh… I can give you something to wear and you can throw your clothes in the dryer. Unless you would rather drive home in wet clothes? Ya know, keep the trend of you always leaving wet?" I offer. She smiles and nods.

"I'll take the first offer please. Riley would kill me if she had to drive to work in a wet seat tomorrow." she says standing up and following me toward the house.

"Jeez it's cold!" She shivers, crossing her arms in front of her chest. It is almost late

November and the weather has dropped to the low fifties so it is chilly and especially freezing at night.

Inside the patio door was the kitchen and to the far left was the hallway to the laundry room and garage. I show her to the laundry room and pull some clean pajama pants and a black shirt from the dryer. When I look at her, I try to keep my eyes from looking at her now see-through shirt and, *holy fuck,* I can faintly make out the outline of a pierced nipple. Immediately I'm looking at anything else other than the shirt as my cock stiffens a bit at this new knowledge.

'Do. Not. Picture your new friend naked.' I scream in my head.

"Here, throw those clothes into the dryer and I'll be back." I say closing the door behind me as I leave to go and change into dry clothes, hopefully keeping myself from getting a boner in front of the soaking wet girl downstairs. Friends. Remember. She's a friend. A very attractive, very single, friend with fucking pierced nipples and now my cock is hard. Dammit.

When I come down stairs now dressed in basketball shorts and a cutoff, Tabitha is just pulling her red hair into a bun, her eyes looking at the clock, and widening. "Oh shit. It's four am!" she gasps, looking at me. I blink at the clock, "Shit, no wonder my hands were all wrinkled, time flew by." I rub my neck, "Sorry for keeping you so long. I uh, don't really know what to do now, I usually get up around five."

"Breakfast?" she suggests, nodding to the pan on the oven.

"My clothes won't be dry for another forty-five minutes." she says, sitting at the island. I chuckle and go to the fridge to pull out eggs and cheese and some bacon.

I see Tabitha try to hide a yawn as I turn the heat on under the pan, cracking the eggs into the bowl and whisking them.

"I haven't made someone breakfast in a while so this is a first." I say, she smiles, "Oh well, I'm a lucky girl then. Hopefully It's gentle." she wiggles her shoulders. I chuckle and pour the eggs into the pan as the bacon sizzles.

"Coffee?" I offer. She nods, "I can help?" She stands up from the bar stool.

The sound of the front door unlocking has us both turning to the hallway that leads to the front door as Joch's voice calls down the hall.

"Honey, I'm home! Ready for our run? Oh." he pauses in the kitchen doorway. His eyes went from me to Tabitha. And he blinks.

Fuck. I forgot Joch and I were supposed to go on a run this morning.

"Wait, why are you here at four-thirty J?" I cock my eyebrow at him. His blonde hair is tied back into a ponytail and he has a pair of track pants and a hunter green hoodie on.

"You never get up on time, um, did I interrupt something?" he asks, pointing between us.

"Nope. Boone here was making me breakfast since he kept me up until now." Tabitha says. Joch claps his hands together and sat next to her,

"I'll take some, too." he asks. I give him a blank look.

"Doesn't Casey feed you?" I ask, moving the eggs around on the pan.

Joch laughs, "My sister? Cook? I'd get food poisoning if I ate her food." he leans closer to

Tabitha, "My sister lives with me, she does PR law stuff, super smart. But her cooking? Not so good." he mutters.

"Joch. stop bashing your sister's cooking, she's gotten better," I turn to Tabitha, "But yea, don't eat her food, it will make you sick." I nodded.

After we ate breakfast and Tabitha's clothes were dry she went to change. Joch had excused himself and went back home. Leaving us alone.

"I should probably head home. I have to work at five tonight. I am the closer." She says, folding the clothes I had lent her and set them on the table.

I went to say something but yawned.

"Probably a good idea. I'm sorry I kept you all night." I rub the back of my neck as I walk her to the door.

"Nah, it was fun. I'm still moving into that hot tub though." She smiles. I walk her to her car and opened the door for her.

"Let me know the move in date." I nodded. She backs out of the driveway and waved before she drove off.

Friends. Friends. Just friends…… Fuck. My cock did not want her to be just my friend but I can live with it. Just after I go rub one out to the image of her soaking wet in my kitchen with the see through shirt and piercings.

CHAPTER 9

Tabitha

I step out of the shower and wrap my towel around my body. I had gotten off work around midnight since I was so tired and dead on my feet, so Mick sent me home. After a fast shower, I felt ready for bed. I had so much fun talking to Boone last night it was so comfortable talking to him and being around him. As I walk to my room I stop when I hear the telltale squeak of the loose floorboard downstairs. This specific board that Riley named the Squeaker since it was super loud when it creaked. Riley was away for the week on a trip with her boyfriends and Perry was in the city. I tiptoe down the hall and look down the stairs. If I bent forward and looked to the right I would have a clear view of Riley's door so thats what I do. I see a shadow move in the kitchen and I bolt to my room as quietly as I could, grabbing my phone from my bed. And called 9-1-1.

"9-1-1 what is your emergency?" the operator asks.

"Someone broke into my house, I'm at 0515 Oakbrook." I whisper into the phone, I'm not able to say anything else because the phone makes a beep beep beep and the call drops. The call fucking DROPS?! Shit. The one spot in this house where cell service did not exist was the spot in front of my closet where I was standing. Shit this happened so many times.

I could hear the sound of the floorboard creak and I press my phone to my chest, locking my door and step back. Fuck fuck fuck. The gun box is in Rileys room too so I am fucked.

"Hello? Tabitha, you there?" a distant muffled voice calls. Boone's voice comes from my phone. When I had moved to lock the door I must have hit call on his contact.

"B-Boone! I think someone broke into the house, someone is downstairs." my voice sounds hoarse as I whisper. The rest of the house is quiet.

"Where are you?" he asks, the usual laughter in his voice is gone.

"I'm in my room upstairs." I whisper.

"Hang on, I'll be there in five minutes." he says, I can hear the sound of tires screech from in the background. "Stay on the phone with me, ok?" he says.

Memories flash in my mind of a lamp breaking, a door frame splintering as the panel is kicked in. My fucking heart is thundering in my chest and I feel like I'm gonna pass out. This felt all too familiar. My phone makes a low ping as the battery dies. You gotta be fucking kidding me.

"Shit. Shit fucking shit!" I silently curse, tossing the phone on the bed. Ok, I need to get out of the fucking house. I tighten the towel around me and tiptoe out of the room as silently as I can, avoiding the squeaky floorboards in the hall.. The house is dead quiet. Too quiet. Halfway down the steps, I glance at Rileys door and it is now wide open. My mouth opens and I quickly shut it to stop the cry. The front doors' multiple locks, the ones that I had all locked when I got home, were now all unlatched but one. "Fuck this." I leap down the step and go for the door pulling the security lock open and throwing open the door as I hear thunderous stomps from the kitchen coming towards me.

Hands grab onto my hair, pulling me back. The scream rips from my throat as I throw my body forward,taking both of us down. My head hits against the railing to the stairs.

No no no! I scream in my head. I'm able to get to my feet crying as I run from the house, down the stoop and to the road. My bare feet hit the cold street. I scream when headlights flash in my face blinding me as the sound of tires screech to a halt.

"Tabitha!" Boones voice shouts. The breath escapes my lungs as I run to him as he gets out of the truck. His fingers gently turn my jaw to the side where I feel the bruise forming on my temple.

"They're still inside." I gasp out as he reaches into his truck bed and pulls out a crowbar. Not one of the small ones, no. He has one of those heavy duty-yardstick long-three to four inches thick-crowbars.

"Get in the truck." he growls, its deep almost a snarl, making a beeline for the house. Taking long strides.

'Fuck that's hot.' my vagina says as I back up to the truck. Opening the passenger door and getting in. Boone goes into the house and after about five agonizingly slow minutes, he emerges as the police roll up.

"The house is trashed, whoever was in there is gone now." he says quickly putting the crowbar in the truck bed. He opens the back passenger door and pulls one of his duffle bags to him as the cops go to look through the house, one comes over to talk to me. He doesn't seem to care that I was in just a towel and nothing else. In fact he has a faint smile on his face when he realizes I am basically naked. He wets his lips as he looks me up and down.

"I need a statement miss." he sniffs.

"Here, all clean, I promise." Boone says, handing me a long sleeved sweater and black boxers. He seemed almost agitated as he glances at the cop that was trying to question me. He raises an eyebrow and cleared his throat before asking, "Maybe we give the lady a moment to dress, officer?" The officer blinks, seeing as Boone was bigger and taller than him he agrees then nods, "Yes, of course." before he steps away. Boone stands in front of the half open passenger door to block any onlookers. He uses a towel he had in his bag to give me a shroud of privacy and the action makes my stomach flip.

"Thank you." I whisper, pulling the sweater on and the boxers were like shorts on me but at least I wasn't naked now. Boone waited till I was fully dressed to look at me.

"Are you ok?" he asks, bundling the towel and leaning forward to toss it into the back seat. The closeness lets me get a whiff of his cologne, cedar and mint. His scent and the warm, protective energy he emanates has my nerves settling and makes me feel so at ease. He looks at my head where I'll likely have a bruise.

"Want the truth or the lie?" I chuckle, pulling my hair from the collar of the sweater. Boone moves a strand of damp hair out of my face, "The truth. Always." he asks. I take a breath and shake my head, "Probably not. I mean, someone was in that house. I *know* it." I stress as he takes my hand, beginning to roll the sleeves up so I didn't look like one of those tube things in front of a car dealership.

"I believe you. The back door was open when I checked." His verification should have helped me feel better but it just made me more uneasy. The neighborhood wasn't the most boujee one or the most dangerous one. It was older and sure the occasional break in happened but this didn't feel like the run of the mill break in. The intruder had been hiding, waiting for either me or Riley to come downstairs. Had it not been for the floorboard creaking, I shuddered at what could have happened. Boone gives my shoulder a firm squeeze. I welcomed it, placing my hand over his large one, leaning into his comfort.

"Thank you for coming." I say looking up at him. "Of course."

"Miss, we'll need to finish the statement." the officer interjects impatiently. Boone drops his hand and steps back letting me switch places with him to speak with the officer.

"So you said you came home and no one was there? The doors were all locked?" he asks. I nod, "Yea, I had a long shift and went up to shower. When I got out, I was in my room and heard the creak of the floorboard. They don't creak unless something heavy steps on them." I explain. The officer nods and jotted it down in the notebook he held. When he looks up, he glances at Boone and narrowed his eyes, "and you were on the phone when you heard this? Or were you also here?" he asked him.

"No, I accidentally called him after I called 9-1-1. I didn't want to stay in the house so I bolted for the door and whoever it was in the house came after me they grabbed my hair and I don't know we fell and that's how I hit my head. I guess they ran the other way when I opened the front door?" I shrug, feeling Boone tense next to me.

"So you were alone. No ex boyfriends, someone maybe hanging around the house that shouldn't be? No motive of any kind?" the officer dug.

"No? I work at a bar so occasionally you get a handsy customer. But I haven't had any issues lately. And even if I did, none of them would follow me home. Whoever broke in was here *before* I got home." I was confused as to where this was going.

"You are sure there isn't anything else? Nothing, not a crazy ex? It's not possible that maybe you fell and hit your head? You don't owe anyone money or-" Boone cuts him off, "She isn't a druggie and she doesn't have any exes hanging around." He growls protectively. Fuck he needed to stop doing things that made me want to do things friends don't do to each other. His entire body was tense and rigid and it is fucking hot.

"There was no sign of forced entry, and nothing looks to be missing, broken or left." the officer said, tapping his pen on the pad, "You're positive you saw someone in the house?" he asks sounding like he didn't believe me.

"I heard them, I could hear someone walking around downstairs. I felt them behind me. I was fucking grabbed." I press.

"Well no one is there now. They must have been scared off." the officer said, his eyes glancing down my body. I'm about to tell him to fuck a cactus but Boone is the one who speaks up.

"Ok so we can go now. Come on Tabs, you can stay at my place tonight." Boone cuts in stepping in front of me, ignoring the cop entirely.

"Let's grab you a change of clothes and I'll take you to my place." he says as he places an arm around me as we walk to the house. I don't even want to fight the offer because I am exhausted, it was almost one am. But he was such a cock wad.

Boone walks me back into the house, I had to just check Riley's room. I suck in a breath walking into the bedroom, black spray paint lined the walls above her bed.

I saw you

The paint was still wet as it dripped down the wall.

"No signs, my ass." Boone growls from behind me, turning to the door to grab the cop still standing out front.

"Go pack a bag." Boone calls to me.

Boone waits at the top of the stairs as I shove clothes into a bag. Once I am done, I make sure the front door is locked before He leads me to the truck, opening the passenger door for me like the gentleman he is. He takes me by surprise by putting his hands on my waist and he physically lifts me up into the trucks passenger seat. His hands are on my waist as I sit down and then he actually pulls the seatbelt out, securing me before he goes around to the driver seat. *Oh sweet baby lamb cakes.*

CHAPTER 10

Boone

Tabitha is quiet on the drive, no doubt she is exhausted considering it's almost two am by the time we get to my house. I show her the guest room and leave her to get settled for the night. She isn't hungry or thirsty and just wants to sleep. I understand. I myself am exhausted after the double practice and tomorrow morning I'd have one more practice before we had a game on Monday. I went to my room and changed into a pair of basketball shorts and climbed into bed.

It had been sheer luck that I was able to get to her as fast as I did. Seeing her in the road when I pulled up had me boiling mad. She had looked terrified and I was ready to fight whoever made her that scared. And worse is the faculty she was hurt too. That cop had infuriated me. He hadn't taken his scummy eyes off her legs or chest the entire time she was in that towel. It sparked an anger in me that I didn't recognize.

She is safe now. She is safe three doors down from me where I could get to her if she needed me. Anything she needed I would give. We are friends. Just friends…

I'm not asleep too long when a faint scream has me alert and lunging across the room. My heart thuds in my chest as I get to Tabitha's door.

"Tabitha? Hey you ok?" I knock, the door is locked and I don't want to kick it in unless I have to.

"Tabitha?" I ask again right as I hear her cry out. *Fuck the door.* My shoulder easily breaks it open and what I see has my heart aching. Tabitha is twisted in the sheets having what looks like a nightmare. Her face is pinched as she thrashes her body, she isn't breathing, she's holding her breath somehow. I need to wake her up.

"Tabitha. Hey. wake up. Wake up." I gently shake her shoulder. She jerks awake and pulls away from me taking a deep breath as her eyes look around the room taking in where she is.

"You're ok. It's ok. It's me. It's Boone." I reach out, rubbing circles on her back, "Hey. You're ok." I smooth my hand down her back. After taking a couple deep, shaky breaths she looks at me.

"I'm sorry. I'm sorry, I'm ok." Her voice is hoarse.

"It's ok, Don't apologize. Are you ok?" I ask. She runs a hand through her hair and nods, "I'm ok. Sorry I woke you. I'm fine now." that was a dismissal if I've ever heard one. I get up and go to the door.

"If you need me, I'm three down. *Anything* you need, come to me." I say. She nods.

"Thanks Boone." she says as I close the door.

When I walk down the stairs a few hours later, the sweet aroma of coffee has the house smelling heavenly. It is 9 am and I hadn't slept too much.

I walk into the kitchen and look to the left to where the living room is and see Tabitha sitting on the couch, glasses on, her hair in a messy bun on her head, looking like a sexy librarian. There's no way she slept after I left her room. The bags under her eyes tell me this.

"Hey, good morning." I greet. She looks up from the text book in her lap and smiles, "Hey.". Walking over with a hot mug of black coffee, I peek over her shoulder and bend forward, resting my free hand on the back of the couch, "Whatcha studying?" I ask. She had several lines highlighted.

"Oh, I have been doing some online classes for business and marketing." she explaines, turning slightly to look up at me and does a double take, her cheeks turning a slight shade of pink.

"Nice tattoo." she comments, setting the book aside and standing. I have a tattoo on my ribcage, *Vita in Motu, Veritas lux mea. Life is in motion and truth is my light.* Lifting my arm slightly to look at the ink I quickly realize I am shirtless and my black sweatpants are very low on my waist. I'm not used to having guests so I didn't even think when I came down this morning.

"Thanks. Do you have any?" I ask, following her to the kitchen where she poured herself coffee. I grab a shirt from the laundry basket on the table and pull it on.

"No." she answers after a moment. She stifles a yawn. She definitely hadn't slept. The police had said they were investigating the vandalism to the house but from how the dick wart acted I don't have much faith it'll be at the top of his list.

"Hope it isn't an issue,I was going to go to the grocery store, Is it ok if I use the truck?" she asks, sipping the black coffee and making a face as she tasted it. I smile at her, "No problem at all, I was going to the store today anyway, the fridge is pretty bare."

"I noticed, is it always that bare?" she asked, leaning on the counter. She was still wearing the same shirt I had given her last night and it went to her thighs. Her naked, slightly bronzed thighs.

"No. I was out of town for a game and I don't like to leave much in the fridge in case it goes bad." I sat on the stool across from her. "The bacon and eggs I made us the other night were the last bit of food in the house." I add, trying to adjust myself without being obvious.

She hums as she takes another sip, "Well, I will change then and we can go?" she says, setting the mug in the sink and rinsing it out before drying it with the dish towel. When she reaches up to put the mug away, the shirt rises up, giving me a slight view of the bottom of her ass in the sleep shorts she had changed into once we'd gotten home last night. Blood rushes to my cock and I want to hit myself because she was supposed to be my guest. Here I was practically eye-fucking her in my kitchen. Tabitha turns around and I put my drink to my lips, forgetting how hot it was and burn my lip. I stand behind the island, leaning over and rest my elbows on the table.

"I'll be ten minutes." she smiles, padding out of the kitchen.

I glance down at the tent in my pants, I am gonna be a little more than ten. Shit.

"I'm gonna jump in the shower fast so take your time." I called up the steps as I practically sprint to my room. *Just friends. Just fucking friends.* A friend that I was about to go think about as I masterbated in the shower like a fucking teenager. I needed to control my fucking dick.

After my fast shower I was in the kitchen making a list of what I needed from the store.

Tabitha came down in a heather gray hoodie that had the words *hangover hoodie* across the chest, and a pair of jeans that hugged her curves and made her ass look... nope! Nope. Not going there. She's just a friend. Just a friend. She smiled at me and, holy fuck, I can't deny she is hot as fuck but I was going to control myself. I wasn't about to ruin this friendship just because I was horny.

CHAPTER 11

Tabitha

Boone has on just a black Carhartt hoodie and dark wash wranglers. It was warming up a bit, but not too much for the time of year. I chose my hangover hoodie and pull my hair into a claw clip as I walk to the truck. I hadn't gotten any sleep this morning, every time I tried to sleep I was abused with nightmares. The sleep exhaustion would eventually get me but I knew that I would endure more nightmares like I usually did when I didn't get any sleep. Boone pulled on a black baseball cap and stretched, causing his hoodie to rise up and I could see the tuft of hair below his belly button.

I could lick a trail of kisses down below that torso. I shake the thoughts of me nipping kisses down Boones hips out of my mind. Skydaddy christ I needed to get laid or find my magic wand for some solo time in the huge guest bathroom.

"Ready?" I ask. He covered his mouth with his fist as he cleared his throat and nodded.

Did I say any of that outloud? I Prayed I didn't. I'd lay down in the driveway and let him run me over and end that misery if I did.

"Yep, ready to go m'lady." he says, opening the passenger door for me. Like last night, he helps me into the truck before he goes around to the driver side and climbs in. When he buckles up, he pushed his sleeves up to his elbows. His cologne was heavenly. Mint and something else I couldn't put my finger on. But it was so good. Even though there's a backup camera he does that thing where he puts one hand on the passenger headrest and looks back. Why the fuck is that hot?

"There's a grocery store about twenty minutes away that has some really good produce and is not as crowded on Sunday mornings." he explained as he turns out of the development.

"That must be good for you, being able to shop without getting mobbed by fans?" I ask, he lets out a chuckle, "Yea, it's a nice relief. I'm there so often that the novelty has worn off for the employees and the locals. Occasionally, I'll get the odd fan or two but it's not too crazy." Boone pulls into a small grocery store and parks the truck in a space.

"So what does "The Mountain" stock his fridge with?" I ask as he grabs a cart and we start down the first aisle.

"The normal fruits, veggies, carbs is the diet of the average hockey player." he said, placing a big bag of yellow potatoes in the cart. I giggle, "I wouldn't exactly place you in an average category." A look crosses Boones eyes and he cocks an eyebrow.

"Oh? So am I in a category of my own in your book, Tabitha?" he asks.

"Definitely above average." I wink, chuckling. I grab orange and yellow peppers and added them to the cart. We turn down the meat aisle and Boone grabbed five packets of bison and five of chicken breast.

"Ever have bison burgers?" he asks. I shake my head, "No, but I'll try anything once, within reason." the corner of Boones mouth raises in a sexy smirk. Shit, wait. What? *He's just a friend.* A friend that was letting me stay at his house for a few nights. A friend who was very hot and very attractive. And Fuck why had I stated I wanted to be just friends!

"Well it's the best meat you'll ever have, clean and easy on the stomach." he's looking at me all serious.

"That's what she said." I chuckle. What the fuck was I doing? *Am I really flirting with Oliver Boone!?* The guy who is letting me stay at his house-

"Did you just Michael Scott me?" he raises an eyebrow at me inquisitively.

"'Michael scott' you? That's not a thing." I shake my head, raising a brow right back.

"It most certainly is a thing." he assures me.

"No, it is not." I say back.

"Ok, then you just 'The Office'd' me." he defends, smiling. I cover my mouth as I laugh at the whole thing. He was such a flirt but I like it.

"You are insane." I shake my head, grabbing a few bottles of cloverlife hazelnut creamer.

"Please tell me you've seen The Office?" he gasps, making me roll my eyes playfully, "Yes, of course I have. John Krasinsky is a wet dream. Did you see him in 13 hours?" I swoon, fanning my face. Boone laughs.

"You would be a Jim fan."

"Oh let me guess, you're a Dwight fan?" I guess.

"The entire show is technically about Dwight becoming the manager. He's in every episode, always one of the main storylines."

This whole conversation was so entertaining and flowed so easily with him.

"Ok, but it's also about Jim and Pam falling in love too." I add as I reach up to grab a container of pretzels that are just out of reach even on my tiptoes. I feel someone behind me and got a whiff of mint and oak as Boone grabs the pretzels for me. His chest brushing against my back.

"Here you go." he says, handing them to me. My face warms at how close he is as my eyes look up into his eyes before he steps back.

JUST FRIENDS!

"Thank you." I mutter as he turns back to the cart unaware of the effect he had on me just now.

"Now, I also happen to love pringles so don't judge me when I grab like four flavors." he grins.

"Honey mustard is the best flavor." I call and he whips around giving me a thumbs up.

"Got it." he winks, vanishing around the corner only to return a few minutes later with two cans of honey mustard pringles and three of another flavor.

We push our full cart up to the checkout and I go to grab my stuff to separate it but Boone holds his hand out, "I got it, don't worry." he said.

"No, I can't let you buy my groceries." he shakes his head and brushes my hand away

"It's not a problem, Tabs." he smiles at me. I relent and he pays the swooning cashier.

When we get back to Boone's house, I help him put away the groceries and then he asks if I was hungry.

"I know we just got food but how does pizza sound?" he smirks.

"I could do a pizza."

This was all so crazy, I had just met Boone a week ago and now I was staying in his guest room. This friendship was very odd. But it felt... normal?

Like a little bubble of normalcy.

X X X X X

Boone had put on The Office and we were on the Christmas episode of season four when his phone lit up with Joch's photo and an absurd ringtone played.

"Hey Joch." he greets, after a moment his brow raised, "uh, no we were just eating and watching some tv, why? Wait what?" his eyes close and he lets out a groan.

"Yup. I get it. See ya." he ends the call and types on his phone. Hissing out a 'fuck' as he read the screen.

"What's wrong?" I ask from my spot on the couch. Boone's green eyes look at me, "I'm sorry," he starts, "Someone got a picture of us leaving the store." he holds out his phone to me, a news article displayed a slightly blurry photo of Boone and I, in the photo you could only see my back but Boone was clear. The title above it read, 'Has The Mountain been conquered?'

"Shit." I breathe. It was just of me from behind but still, I don't want my picture out there.

"Look, I should have been more careful. This is on me." He apologizes.

"Maybe I should go stay at Perrys?" I say, I should have figured that this friendship with Boone would come with this. He was a fucking NHL hockey player for fucks sake, of course he would have people taking his picture and following him. I chewed on my thumb nail, anxiety bubbling in my stomach.

"Paparazzi isn't allowed in the neighborhood, so you'll be fine here. I promise." Boone says.

"I don't really know why I'm surprised at this. You're a big time hockey player and I'm me." I say pulling my knees to my chest. Boones eyes soften.

"Look, I won't force you to stay. If you want to leave then I'll help you pack. But," He reaches out for my hand and gives it a squeeze, "I really like having you around."

"Maybe we can still hang out. But it might be best if I go."

My phone's sharp ringtone blaring had us both jumping. The goat screaming ringtone was Riley. The moment between Boone and I over.

"Hey Riles." I say brushing some hair behind my ear as I stand.

"Hey! What happened! Are you ok?" she asks, "Duke called Alex and said he saw the police report someone broke in, I finally got your voicemail and texts, stupid reception. Are you ok?" she gushes out.

"Yes I'm ok, um." I glance back at Boone and walk out onto the patio.

"Someone broke in before I got home. They vandalized your room." I explain everything to her, the spray paint. Everything.

"Fuck! Perry is at a big convention in New York then she goes to Australia, are you sure you are ok?" Riley asked. Riley was currently in Canada with her partners on a family trip and wouldn't be able to get home. Even if she could, there wasn't anything she could do. She was quiet for a moment before asking, "Did you take the gun?" I open my mouth to answer but stop because.... Oh shit. No I didn't. Under Rileys nightstand was a lockbox with a small ruger in it. A gift from her late step father when she was in highschool. I hadn't even thought to look once I saw the spray paint. Even if I did, I really don't think Boone would have been too keen on a gun in his house.

"I'll be on the first flight out in a couple days and I'll be home on Saturday. I can't get home any sooner." she winced.

"I'll be ok. I'm at Boones. But I may go stay at Perrys." Riley let out a squeal so shrill I pull the phone from my ear.

"What! So not only did he come to protect you at work and at the house but he let you stay with him!" she gasps, "Did you fuck him? Was it good?" I laugh and look back at the house, "No, I didn't. We're just friends." I say unfortunately.

"No way you actually believe that." Riley snorts.

I chew on my lip, no I don't. But that's what we were. Just friends.

This was hard, because I was having fun hanging around him but it would be better if I left.

Riley decides now is the perfect time to mention, "Perrys condo is under renovations. Her neighbors water line broke and flooded the three units so looks like you're staying chikadee." She giggles.

CHAPTER 12

TABITHA

Boone had to go to an early morning practice the next morning and I had to go to work. For the next couple of days, that was how our schedules went. Boone had a couple away games so I had the house to myself which wasn't too bad. He showed me how to set and arm the alarms and I was set.

Friday when I got back from work, Boone is in the backyard with a few of the other players from the team. The grill was going and a couple players were tossing a football back and forth. I recognized Joch's frame and blonde hair. He smiled when he saw me, standing from his seat. I opened the patio door and waved.

"World's best bartender!" he called, walking to me. I gave him a smile.

"Hey. Josh with a C." I say back. Boone was at the grill. He was dressed in a black long sleeved shirt with the sleeves rolled up showing off his forearms.

"Sorry 'bout this, it's a thing we do occasionally. Some of us hang out at each others' places. Team building and it is good for morale." Joch explained, throwing his arm around my shoulder.

"Makes sense." I agree. He smiled his beautiful smile at me.

"We have a camping trip in a few weeks too. As captain, I need to keep these boys hyped and energy up."

"Oh, for the love of god, give the girl a break, she just got home from work." a female's voice called. Joch rolled his eyes before acknowledging the woman.

"That. Is my sister, Casey." he pouted. Casey walked toward us, she was a few inches taller than me with chestnut brown hair that went to her shoulders, she had the body of a Dallas cowboy cheerleader. Her bronzed skin was flawless; she was dressed in a dark green hoodie and pair of jeans. Casey smiled at me, her brown eyes warm, "You must be the famous Tabitha." she stated, holding out her hand. I nod, giving her hand a shake.

"I wouldn't say famous, Joch seems to have the habit of exaggerating." I return her smile. Casey laughs. "You have no idea." she agreed. I look down at my uniform, "Are you going to join us? We have plenty of food." she asks, motioning to the table with the frozen steaks and meats.

"Yea, I'm just going to change first." I say. Halfway up the stairs, I couldn't stop the smile that spread on my face.

I change quickly into jeans and a white tshirt before rejoining the mini party down stairs.

Casey takes my hand the moment I am outside, "Come on, let me introduce you around." she says, pulling my hand.

"I thought I was going to be stuck surrounded by puck bunnies this year but you come along and save me from that hell." she chuckles.

"'Puck Bunnies?'" I question.

"The hockey groupies, the girls that soly fuck hockey players because they are hockey players. They aren't girlfriends, only one night stands or fuck buddies. But *god* are they annoying.

They also go for the married and taken players too. Fucking bitches." I don't miss the venom in her voice.

Casey introduces me to a few of the other hockey teammates. Each one greets me with warmth and smiles. After a little bit, Boone announces the food is ready and I make my way over to him, "Impromptu cookout?" I ask, giving him a smile. Boone returns the smile and hands me a Yingling, "It happens. This time turned out to be my house. Normally Joch has a big team cookout at his place every so often. He lives a couple houses down. Just wait till you see it, the team and their wives, girlfriend and kids all come. Joch loves hosting and his giant backyard shows." he points the metal spatula towards the fence of the house one over with a giant backyard.

"Sounds pretty cool." I say, taking a sip of my drink. Boone glances at me.

"He's having one the week after next. You should come." he says, plating the last of the burgers.

'Wives, girlfriends and kids go.' he had said. I am neither but he still included me. I guess there really isn't a label for someone who is staying with you because someone broke into her house and apparently had 'seen' them.

"Sure. I'd love to." I say.

CHAPTER 13

Boone

Watching Tabitha mingle with Casey and some of the team has my chest feeling warm. They welcomed her warmly and Casey took an immediate liking to her as anyone would. Casey sends me a smirk from where she sits next to Tabitha.

"Sooo this a thing with you two or what?" Joch draws out, pointing his pointer finger between me and Tabitha.

I give him a questioning look, "What do you mean? She's my friend. A new friend who is staying in my guest room. And fine, it is a little odd." I admit.

"Because she's fucking hot." my friend states. I sigh in response, "Yup."

Joch winces, "What did you get yourself into man?" he chuckles, shaking his head and clapping me on my back. I watch as Tabitha laughs at something Bohdie, our goalie, said. Throwing her head back and covering her mouth.

Casey had gotten up and now stood next to me. She lightly chuckles, grabbing a new bottle from the cooler next to the grill. I give her a look, "What?" I groan. I have known Casey for as long as I had known Joch. So when she gave me that catlike smile, I knew she was thinking something. She shakes her head, "Nothing. Nothing." she glances at Tanitha, "I like her. Keep her around." She says before rejoining the table.

CHAPTER 14

Tabitha

Two weeks after the break in, the cops called me to let me know they didn't find any fingerprints and there were no signs of forced entry.

"So what does that mean? What about the spray paint? Or the fact that I physically was attacked?" I ask. The cop on the other line didn't really have much to say.

"There's nothing that was left behind and we have no direction to go in. I'm sorry, ma'am. Unless you can think of anyone who could have done this, there is no trail to follow." he said. There was only one person who immediately came to mind but it was impossible, so I squash that thought.

"No. No one comes to mind." I say, gnawing on my pinky nail.

"Well If you think of anything, call us." he says before hanging up. So that is it then. The police were done with their investigation and I could go back to the house. No more staying at Boone's.

Georgia looked through the small window where we put order tickets at me, her brows furrowing, "You ok?" she asks.

I nod, "I need to head out early, gonna go get new locks for the house." I sigh, undoing my apron. "I got you covered with Mick." she winks, slapping my ass as I walk by her.

After a trip to Home Depot for new locks, I shoot a text to Boone to let him know the plan. He's at work so I don't expect a text back right away.

The house looks almost exactly as I left it. The full view glass storm door is shattered, glass covers the top step on the stoop.

"Shit." Did someone break in again? I can see the door to Riley's room is still open and the words still spray painted on the wall. It is so quiet as I walk through the house, double-checking everything to make sure I am alone. Once I do my walk through, I pull my hair up and go to work changing the locks and putting the new ones in. The house looks the same as it always does, it was my home for the past four years, my safety. I wasn't going to let some asshole burglar take away the feel of my safety. A headache starts to form when I see the broken glass on the kitchen floor too. The back storm door had been shattered as well and the glass was scattered on the floor. It takes a few extra minutes to sweep up but once that is done and the new locks are in the front door, I get to work getting the back locks switched out. The sound of a car beeping as it locks has me jump slightly. My grip on the screwdriver tightens.

"Tabs?" Boones' voice calls from the front. I put the screwdriver down and open the front door, super careful not to step in the glass I hadn't swept yet. I was surprised to see him. Practice must have ended early. Boone walks up the walkway with a worried look on his face. He points to the door as he approaches, "What happened?" he asks.

"I think someone tried to break in again." I sigh, looking at the damage. Not only was the door shattered, but there was a spiderweb crack in the front bay window I hadn't noticed before. *Fucking A man, what else did they break!* I swear if any of my shit is missing I will go apocalyptic. I didn't have much growing up and what little my mom couldn't pawn for money was few and far between.

Boone follows me into the house and while I go upstairs, he gets to work uninstalling the front storm door and back one for me.

"What time is Riley coming home?" he calls up the steps, I change out of my work clothes and into a pair of jeans and a snug black henley.

"She should be home tonight, so I can grab my stuff after the game and be out of your hair by tomorrow?" He dumps the last pieces of glass in the trash and looks at me as I walk into the kitchen.

"So I don't suppose you would wanna come watch the game tonight then? You would be sitting with Casey and you would be in one of the boxes?" he asks, leaning against the broom. I laugh and shake my head, "Are you gonna get sent to the penalty box again?" I take the broom and walk him to the truck. Boone smiles, "Probably, I try to be a good boy but sometimes the other boys don't play nice." he smirks. I roll my eyes, "So the other guys start it?"

"Of course. I'm a good boy, scouts honor." he promises holding up two fingers. I cross my arms over my chest and narrow my eyes at him, "A good boy who gets into at least two fights a game?" I nod. The corner of his beard raises into a half smile, "Ah so you did your research on me eh?" my cheeks heat a bit "Perry did. But I may have paid attention." I laugh.

Boone shakes his head, and puts his hands in his hoodie pockets, some of his dark hair sticks out from his backwards baseball cap and with his thick scruff, he just looks really fucking good. Like Too good. Ugh. Boone stares at me for a moment. Under his gaze my face heats and I shift on my feet, "What?" I ask, he looks like he wants to say something but closes his mouth, "Nothing, Casey will pick you up at five." he says giving me one of his sexy smiles before opening his door and getting into his truck.

"You can stay with me as long as you need by the way." he says, leaning his head out the window. His arm resting on the door. His sleeve is rolled up and *fuck me sideways please!* My vagina wants me to scream.

I put my hand on the truck door, leaning back a little.

"I don't wanna overstay, I feel bad being a burden." I admit. He rests his chin on his arm, "Nah, you'd never be a burden to me." he winks. Que the zap of heat straight to the vagina. Skydaddy Christ why did he have to be so fucking cute! He's looking up at me through his long lashes and it takes everything not to just kiss him.

'Avoid the eyes!' I tear my eyes from his, clearing my throat as I step back.

He waves as he pulls from the curb and as soon as he is gone, I cover my face letting out a groan, "Ohhh why does he have to be so hot!" I whine, "I'm in trouble."

CHAPTER 15

Tabitha

Five sharp Casey pulled up outside the house. She is dressed in a Skyhawks hoodie and black jeans. Her brown hair is pulled back into a slicked back ponytail.

"Hey! I brought you this since I figured Oliver wouldn't have given you any merch yet." she says, holding out a black Seattle Skyhawks hoodie and a baseball cap. The hoodie is a little big but comfortably big and the hat looked really cute.

"Thank you." Casey waves it off, "It's no problem. Joch has a closet of merch at the house, every hoodie, jacket, hat, anything with the team's logo on it, they get their pick of whatever they want." she explaines as I get into her suv.

"So," she starts, shooting me a sly smile, "What exactly is going on with you and Oliver?" she asks. Ok so right into it I guess.

"We're just friends. He is helping me out for a few days. I know you and I don't know each other but I promise I'm not like a gold digger or anything." I babble. Casey glances at me shaking her head, "Ok, we'll pretend that the 'just friend' statement is true for now. So the reason I ask, I love Oliver. He's like an annoying older brother and is probably one of the nicest, most genuine people I know. As one of his best friends, I am obligated to let you know if you hurt him, I will hurt you. In legal and physical ways." I stare at her, in both fear and understanding. But also confusion. The other night they seemed so close, like really close.

"You two haven't?" I trail off making her laugh, "Hell no! That would be like fucking my brother." That info actually makes me relax a bit for some reason. Casey pulls into a parking garage and shows the security her pass.

"I hope I didn't scare you off with what I said earlier?" Casey asks as we walk down the hallway to the elevator.

"Not at all. I get it, you and Boone are close and you're looking out for your friend." I understood, since Perry and Riley would do the exact same thing.

"Now, is there alcohol at these things?" I ask. Casey tosses her arm around my shoulder, "I knew I was going to like you." She smiles.

The family and friends box was what you would imagine it to look like. A big table with an ice bucket full of water, pop and beer. Three large bowls of mini chip bags, trail mix, candies and pretzels. Over along the far wall was a line of trays with mini sliders, hotdogs and deviled eggs. Straight ahead was a big window with four rows of seats in front of it. A few women stood around talking to each other. One of them, a tall woman with big blonde curls smiled and waved at Casey.

"Over there is Leanna, Mitchie and Rosea. They are wives. The blonde is the left defender, Hanson's wife. Aurora." Casey whispers, waving at her.

"The small brunette is Leanna. She is Tigs wife, he is the right winger, she is expecting her third baby." The brunette standing next to Aurora smiles at me, her stomach is slightly swollen and she laughs as she munches on a small bag of pretzels.

"Then that leaves us with the red head, that is Rosea, she is a fiance to another left winger. She's shy so don't take it personally if she doesn't approach you." I nod as we grab some candies and beer and take a seat in the first row.

Casey props her feet on the foot rail in front of her as she tosses some popcorn in her mouth.

"So what do you do for work?" She asks.

"I am a bartender, I work at TAPHOWZE a few blocks away from here." I reply looking down at the rink and watch as the players warm up.

"Ohh the boys go there after practice. That's the one with the cute blonde waitress right?" her eyes sparkle a little.

"The one with the tattoo on her temple? White blonde hair? That's Georgia." I say.

"Yea, the little one, always sassy and adorable." she nods.

"Yep, that is Georgia." I smile.

"Joch has been trying to get her to notice him for about six months, but I don't think he has a chance." she laughs. I jump a bit when she suddenly sits forward, "Oh! There is Oliver." she points to number fourteen, he skates around and I watched as he gets on his knees and does these stretches on the ice that looked like he was thrusting. I cock my head to the side. Oof, ok maybe I should watch hockey more often.

"Is hockey always so...."

"Erotic? Yea. The amount of thirst traps on tiktock are amazing. I mean watching men hump the ice for a warm up apparently makes women go feral." Aurora says, sitting on the other side of me.

"I'm Aurora." she introduces. I shake her hand almost being blinded by her giant ring on her finger. It's the size of a quarter.

"I'm tabitha." I say.

"Don't let anyone fool you, hockey players are some of the biggest sluts you will meet. I should know, mine was the biggest." she says.

"Until Hanson met you, then he put his slutty ways behind him. But we all know who the bigger slut is now." Casey chimes in.

"Sweetest boy ever but a big slut."

"Dashly." they both say in unison before giggling.

"Who is he?" I ask.

"He's a fresh recruit from college. He is on the injury list. Last year he and another player went through one of the plexiglass barricades and he got a huge glass piece in his hip, and fucked up his leg. He's still healing. Not a good chance of him playing till next year." Casey explains.

"Holy shit." I gasp. That sounded ouch.

"Yea, it was his second year too. But he'll be

back. He's a big boy.

CHAPTER 16

Boone

I skate around the rink waiting for the game to start. During my warm ups I glance up at the box where Casey and Tabitha are. I could see the flash of her copper red hair under a ball cap. Joch glided past me and bumps my shoulder, "Tabby-cat here?" he wiggles his brows.

"Yea, why?" I raise a brow, Joch smiles big, "Unless you started to sleep with Case and are all googly eyes, the only other person who'd be up there is Tabitha." he surmises, shrugging.

"I don't have googly eyes over her." I defend, Joch scoffs, "Sure man. Sure. I'm a fan of the slow-burn romcom so I'll let this play out.

Looking forward to the one bed trope chapter." he pushes off and goes to line up. *'One bed trope?'*

The hallways are always crazy after games so it was hard to find Casey and Tabitha, but I spot that copper hair and immediately a smile brakes out on my face. Her mismatched eyes meet mine and she smiles at me and, fuck, she looks adorable in that oversized hoodie. I walk over and give her a hug.

"Hey, glad you came. Did you have fun?" I greet her, stepping back.

Tabitha nods eagerly, "It was nice not getting covered in beer this time so that was a big plus, you only got into two fights." She puts her hands in the pockets of the hoodie.

"I was on my best behavior as promised." I say scrunching my nose at her as I smile.

"Because the other boys start it right?" she giggles. I swear this woman.Joch comes up behind me.

"We won, baby!" he cheers, messing up my hair.

"Let's head back home, I am starving!" Casey says as we start down the hall. She shot me a look and shook her head, not hiding the smile. I hear a quacking sound and Tabitha pulls her phone out of her back pocket.

"Hey Riley." she answers, the smile falls from her face, "What? Are you ok?" the panic rising in her voice, "I'll be right there!" she gasps while hanging up.

"What's wrong?" I ask. she runs her hands over her face, " Riley. She was attacked at the house."

"What do you need? What can I do?" I ask her, not sure what else I can do. Tabitha takes a few deep breaths, "Can you take me to the house?" she asks.

"Yes. Of course. Anything." I say and I meant it. Whatever she needs I'll do it.

"Hey, you guys go ahead. I'll catch up later." I call to Joch and Casey as we break away from the group.

The truck hadn't even come to a stop and Tabitha was jumping from the passenger seat. There were several cop cars and an ambulance parked out front of the bungalow, so I ended up having to park a few houses down. Tabitha ran past a police officer to a girl sitting on the stoop. She had dark brown hair pulled into a messed up ponytail that was a mess. She has a split lip and bloody nose. Definitely looks like she had been in a fight. Her eye makeup is smudged under her eyes.

"What happened!" Tabitha asked, holding Riley's face. She pushes her off and holds an ice pack to the back of her head.

"I came home and someone jumped me from behind. I didn't see their face. Ugh." she winces as Tabitha checks out her head.

"Alex and Dex are gonna be so pissed." She tries to laugh but it seemed painful. She opened one eye and saw me, her jaw dropped.

"Oh, hello." she says, blinking.

"Hi. I'm Oliver." I greet, giving her a wave. She looks at Tabitha, "Did I mess up a date? Oh my god, I am so sorry!" Tabitha shakes her head, "No, we were just at his game. Do you need to go to the hospital?" Riley waves her off her, "No don't be crazy, Dex is on his way and apparently he is not letting me out of his sight ever again." she explains.

"I just fixed the locks this morning, how did they get inside?" Tabitha asks. Riley shrugs, standing and turning to look at the house. I see her shirt has the name of a mechanic shop on the back with the name Dex on the sleeve that was torn.

"It's a big mess inside, the power was cut. Police say we should find another place to stay for a bit. Dex and Alex are on the way to get me."

I speak before thinking, "Tabitha can stay with me as long as she needs." Tabitha and Riley look at me, tabitha like I had two heads and Riley smiled approvingly.

"No, Boone, I can't ask that." Tabitha starts but I hold up my hand to stop her, "I'm offering. This is the second or third time in a week your house was broken into. You were attacked and this time someone else got hurt. I wouldn't be able to sleep at night knowing you are here alone. Who knows what could happen next time." It was true, there is no fucking way I was letting her stay here by herself. If she refused, I'd fucking camp out in her living room if I had to. Mom and I lived in a couple places that weren't the best as I was growing up. I knew there had been more than a few nights she had stayed up due to some sketchy people lingering around. She would act like she was just making sure the monsters under the bed or in the closet stayed away, but in reality, it was to make sure the monsters outside didn't come in. No fucking way was I letting her stay here without me.

"That is not a bad idea." Riley pipped in.

"I don't mind. Really. Some of your stuff is already in the guest room so it really is ok." I add. Tabitha licks her lips and looks at me, "Are you sure?"

"Yes. It's either you stay with me or I camp out on your couch. Your choice." I state. Riley laughs, "I like this guy."

"You can't do that, Boone." Tabitha counters, crossing her arms. *Ohh you feisty thing.* I think.

I mirror her and smile, "Watch me." I challenge. Her mouth drops open then she sighs, "Fine. Fine. I'll stay with you." she agrees, "But just for a few weeks." I step closer and smile down at her, "You are welcome to stay for as long as you need."

Tabitha clears her throat and looks at Riley.

"I am gonna get some stuff. Do you want me to grab you a bag?" Tabitha asks, Riley shakes her head and sits back down. She opened her mouth to say something and then hesitated.

"Um. the… *thing* is still in the box." I look at Tabitha and she nods then goes inside. Wondering what the fuck *the thing* is.

The moment she went inside, Riley looks at me. Her eyes were sizing me up and suddenly I feel like I am under a microscope. This was one of Tabithas best friends.

"I'm sorry we had to meet like this." I say, sitting next to her.

"Oliver. Let me just say, I know some *really* dangerous people. So if you hurt her, I *will* send them after you. Then Perry will rip you apart and dissolve you in bleach and hair dye." It was a promise, not a threat. I can only imagine what Perry was like but it made me happy to know that Tabitha has friends that were so protective over her that they would go to any length to defend her.

"I promise, I'm not gonna hurt her. She's a special one. I enjoy her company, our friendship is … *odd,* considering how we met, I will admit. But it's nice having her around, she's a good friend." my compliment seems to thaw the ice she had momentarily shown. I really do like Tabitha, as a friend and fuck, yea, she is smoking hot and I couln't deny that I hadn't occasionally let my mind wander to the thought of her in my bed, riding my cock, but we are FRIENDS! God, why was it so fucking hard to not have these thoughts?! It was easy with Casey. Hell, the small imagination of

Casey in my bed made me want to vomit and burn the sheets. But Tabitha….. My cock stiffened in my pants just thinking about her.

Riley narrows her eyes and observes me.

"Mh-hmm. Ok. I'll trust you. For now." I smile at her.

She sighs and shakes her head, "I have *no* idea how she does it. You're smoking hot and she's a babe and you two haven't banged yet?" she sighs. *Believe me I wonder the same thing too.*

"We're just friends." Tabitha hisses as she comes outside with a backpack.

A blue charger speeds down the road coming to a loud screeching stop right behind the ambulance. Riley stands.

"That would be Dexter. See ya chickadee." she says, kissing Tabitha on the cheek before walking to a tall tattooed man who covers his mouth with his hand when he sees her. Another guy gets out of the passenger seat, tugging at his blonde hair before gently taking her face in his hands. Tabitha had mentioned Riley was in some type of threesome relationship; those two must be her partners..

"Ready." Tabitha says. I stand and take the backpack from her, placing my hand on the small of her back as we walk to the truck.

Once we are in the driveway, I turn the car off and we just sit in silence for a moment. Tabitha leans forward and holds her face in her hands as she lets out a shuddering breath.

"Hey. Hey, it's ok. She is ok." I soothe, rubbing circles on her back.

Tabitha pushes back her hair, and looks at me. Her eyes are watery.

"I am so sorry, you played an amazing game and should be celebrating not dealing with my bullshit. I'm so sorry." She apologizes. I shake my head, "No, don't apologize. Come here." I pull her into my chest. She tenses for just a moment before she presses her head into my shoulder. The center console makes this sweet moment a little awkward.

"I don't know about you, but I could definitely use a drink." I say and feel her chuckle into my chest before pulling away. I stared at her, just looking at her eyes and her slightly tanned skin. Being this close I can see little freckles on her nose and cheeks, so faint almost invisible, but they make her even more adorable. Her eyes flash from mine down to my mouth. *'What are you thinking, you beautiful, beautiful woman?'* I wonder. Tabitha pulls back, some of her hair falling from her ponytail and instinctively I reach forward, brushing it behind her ear. As I do, I feel her lean into my touch. Her eyelids dip almost closing as she leans closer. My heart thuds in my chest because we are so close that if I just moved another inch I'd be kissing her. Tabitha sucks in a breath and leans back, shaking her head.

"I'm actually starving so, food?" she suggests. I nod and grab the bag from the back. I follow her in through the garage door, the urge to just push her against the wall, grab her amazing ass in my hands as I pick her up and kiss her speechless until we both were panting for air- rushes through my mind. Running my hand through that hair and yanking it back as I kiss down her neck while she ground against me. Then lay her on the kitchen table and tease her until she is writhing

beneath me and -NOPE! Stop. She is just a friend.

FRIEND!

"You ok?" Tabitha asks. She's at the island,

a bowl of cereal in her hand. I nod my head,

walking past a confused Tabitha. My cock straining

against my pants.

"Yeah, just a little amped still from the game.

I think I'm gonna go for a swim actually." I clear my

throat, taking my jacket off and head outside

unzipping my pants and rip off my shirt, kicking my

shoes off before I dive into the cold pool.

CHAPTER 16

Tabitha

Oh jesus take the mother fucking wheel. I spit out the mouthful of cereal into the bowl and cough. Boone pulls off his shirt and drops his pants before diving into the pool. Those thick legs and that hairy chest, that waist. My brows pull in, "Oh I'm in trouble." I wince as heat builds between my legs. He is sexy as fuck and I was definitely drooling. I take my bowl and dump its contents down the drain before drying it.

The guest room was pretty nice. Light gray walls with pale blue bedding and white pillows. A white oak dresser sits across from the bed with a tv mounted on the wall above it. The en suite bathroom is to the right of the dresser.

"Just clear your head." I say as I walk past the window only to let out a strangled groan when I see Boone swimming laps in the pool. His briefs are soaked to his skin and almost see through. He stops to catch his breath and I leap back from the window when his head turns to look up at me.

I need a cold shower. I can't think about Oliver Boone practically naked downstairs. Don't need to think about how hot he looks as he swims laps in the pool, his back muscles flexing. How his hand felt when he touched my face in the truck, or what his mouth might feel like on my skin, kissing down my chest, my stomach. How his breath would feel on my hot skin. I want to scream into the pillows.

My hand slips into the waistband of my jeans.

"Fuck!" I hiss, feeling how wet I am. I imagine it was Boone, that he was touching me, his calloused fingers circling my clit. What am I doing? Sure this was a completely normal thing, but to masterbate to the thought of my friend. My…phew.. Very attractive, very strong, built, New friend. I arch back against the pillows filling my head with images of Boone. Thoughts of his hot breath against my neck. Feeling his tongue circle around my nipples as I let out a cry. My fingers move faster. That wave of release just on the cusp when my phone lights up with a message startling me out of my concentration.

"Shit." I bark.

I had been added to a group chat that already had multiple texts in the thread.

"What the?"

💬<u>New Group Chat</u>💬

💬JoshWithAC: Hey! Camping trip is coming up! I need names of who is going!

💬Casey: Why was I added to this?

💬JoshWithAC: Had to add the world's best bartender to the group chat! Everyone say hi to TabbyCat!

💬Unknown number: Wohoo! Me and Len are in!

💬Unknown number: Kids will have a blast! Let Leanna know what we should bring?

💬Casey: Oliver you did invite Tabs to the camping trip right? Don't make the poor girl stay in that house alone! Tabitha you have to come! If he didn't invite you, consider this an invite!

💬JoshWithAC: YEASSSS! Oli I am disappointed in you for not already inviting her!

💬Boone: I hadn't actually gotten the chance to ask yet you vultures! Give me a break here!

My phone pinged with a new separate text from Boone.

💬Boone: Looks like Joch hard launched your addition to the friend group?

💬Tabitha: lol it appears so. They are not so happy you didn't mention the camping trip yet lol.

💬Boone: Would you like to go? It's a lot of fun. Most of the team goes with their wives and girlfriends. It's something we do right before it gets fully cold and before the season gets too chaotic.

💬Tabitha: When is it?

⊙Boone: It's in a couple weeks. We all bring campers and tents. It's really fun.

⊙Tabitha: I'm in! Hope it isn't too cold.

Thursday, I was enjoying the nice early morning cramming for a test when Boone came rushing down the steps into the kitchen, dressed in his workout attire, "I'm gonna be late! Crap." he muttered, grabbing his keys and jacket. He had come home super late last night, so I guess he overslept. Normally his practice was at eleven so I wasn't sure what he was late for.

"I'll see you after practice." he said breathily, I had filled his travel mug a while ago and turned to remind him to take it when he takes me by surprise by pressing his lips to my lips before he is out the garage door. I'm frozen in place because… he just kissed me. My mouth hangs open as I stare at the empty kitchen. My hands in the air front of me not sure what to do with them because WHAT THE FUCK!?

CHAPTER 17

Boone

The moment I'm in the truck the realization of what I just did, hit me.

"Fuck." I rasp, my mouth hangs open as I stare at the windshield. I had told Marissa I would stop by before practice and had woken up late. when I went into the kitchen and saw Tabitha there, hair in a messy bun, sweater hanging off her shoulder and her glasses on the tip of her nose as she focused on her textbooks. It was only supposed to be a 'See you later.' and she turned at the exact moment. I didn't realize how close I had been and it felt just like an oops kiss on top of her head but somehow I ended up kissing her on the lips. What had me more fucking freaking out was the fact that if I almost didn't want it to stop. Not only had I been stroking myself in the pool the other night-don't judge me- but now I was going to have her in the camper in closer proximity this weekend. I texted Marissa to let her know I wasn't able to meet her but would stop by soon.

By the time I got to the arena, most of the team was still getting warmed up. Joch gave me his trademark shit eating grin the moment I stepped onto the ice.

"Someone keep you in bed this morning Oli-Bear?" I flip him the finger, "Just Friends Joch." I grumble, elbowing him as he skates past. Joch spun and came up next to me.

"As team captain, it is my job to make sure every member of this team is morally and physically good to go. And in my professional opinion," he begins tapping his hand to his chest, "You are as the kids on tiktok say 'delulu', if you honestly fucking believe you and that beautiful woman, are 'just friends'..." he says making finger quotes on 'just friends'.

"Man, I am telling you. There is *nothing* going on with me and Tabby." I push. Even if I really want to. In so many positions.

"Really?" Joch drags out.

"I promise, nothing is going on."

Fucking liar.

Joch lets out a chortal through his nose, shaking his head, "Ok man. Then I guess you don't mind if I or Bohdie make a move on her then?" he grins at me as I narrow my eyes.

"She can make her own choices." my teeth clench tightly as I speak. Joch smirks, "Look, if you two are just friends, then good for you. But don't wait around till someone else tries to make a move for her then get all depresso when you miss your chance." he said, slapping my shoulder. "Especially if it's Bohdie."

"ALRIGHT! Let's practice, daddies!" Joch hollers to the team.

Joch is a pain in the ass, but also the best friend you could ask for. When I joined the team, he took one look at me and moved me around to different positions on the team, forcing me to learn to do more than be a goon. He saw the anger in me that was still there, and he also was the one who came to bat when the accident happened and is the main reason I was able to transfer teams so fast. He was the best person to be a captain since he threw everything he had into what he did, be it on the ice or off, keeping the team morale and making sure he was always there for everyone. He also ran a hard ship when it came to being serious about plays.

If he were to make a move on Tabitha.. *Wait a fucking second.*

Why did he specifically mention Bohdie? Thinking back to the cookout, Bohdie had been talking to Tabitha a lot but I hadn't thought anything of it.. Now? I wasn't sure what to think. But I didn't like it.

Some people have the shittiest timing in the world. Hank Greene-Louis was the one that somehow could tell when the worst time to call was. Currently I was naked, in the shower with a now softening cock, and not because I finished. Why was I rubbing one out in the shower? Again don't fucking judge me we've all done it. Tabitha. That's why. What I saw when I came back from practice this morning this is how the scenario went:

Tabitha was grabbing clean laundry from the drier to pack for the camping trip: blankets, sheets and some clothes. She was dressed in black leggings and a thin, dark gray pullover sweater, judging from the small bump of the piercing I still had no confirmation was real or not, she wasn't wearing a bra. Her copper hair was up in a clip and when she looked up at me through her eyelashes, still bent over, her body was fucking mouthwatering. The desire to just bend her over the washing machine, pull those leggings down and sink into her warm, hot. NOPE!

"You ok?" she had asked. I shook my head, clearing the image of what I wanted to do out of my mind, "What?" I asked.

Tabitha stood up, "You were kinda spacing out there. Do you think three blankets is enough?" she asked, holding up the laundry basket.

"Oh, um. Yeah that should be enough." I told her keeping my eyes off her face.

'About yesterday morning?" she trailed off. Oof the kiss. right.

"Gotta get ready." I said heading for the stairs. Ok I had been sort of avoiding her since the accidental kiss yesterday morning. Juvenile I know and I need to talk to her but I had no fucking clue what to say. 'Hey sorry for ambushing you but I really think you're hot and want you so bad I feel like a horny twenty year old.' fuck no!

"What time are we going to head out?" She called, a chip to her tone.

"A couple hours. The rental place is gonna drop off the camper in a bit so we should be ready

to go. I'm gonna take a shower real fast." I replied, sneaking one last glance at her ass before I jogged up the steps.

Now here I am letting my mind wander to the ideas of fucking my friend five different ways to Sunday when the phone rings. Que blue balls.

"What Hank?" I hiss. The sound he makes on the other end is something between a growl and a scoff. Or maybe he choked on his tongue. One could only hope.

"Show some more respect for your father, have the results come back yet?" he barks. My grip on the phone is tight enough that I could almost break it. This deadbeat cuck needs to stop testing me.

"No. It will be back soon." I almost snarl.

"It needs to be back faster!" he barks back.

"Did something happen to Tate?" the anger replaced by worry. Hank snorts, "You mean other than the cancer destroying his body and keeping his mother in this damned hospital? No. But the longer this damn test takes, the longer I have to come here." he complains. Unbelievable. He was complaining about *him* having to be at the hospital while his kid is dying. He didn't care that Tate was the one in the hospital, just that he had to consistently show up. How the fuck was he still Married to Tates mom?

"Otto has been asking." he snips. Ah so that's why! Otto was Tates grandfather and Hank's boss. He was still the same piece of shit deadbeat father as always.

"I'll let you know when the results are in." I snap hitting the end call button.

CHAPTER 18

Tabitha

Ok so yea. Ever since the kiss, we had maybe sort of both been avoiding each other. Him more than me. It had been almost two full days and things were a bit weird now at home. He would go for a swim as soon as he got home from practice and would swim laps for two hours. It was an accidental kiss! We should be able to move past it right? I mean It isn't like we had a drunk one night stand, I wouldn't mind being thrown onto the table and ravished don't get me wrong. It's been too long since I had any real sex other than my vibrator and I miss it. The feeling of another body. The connection.

Boone showered and hooked up the camper to the truck while I packed the last of the bags into the back seat.

Joch called the moment we left the driveway.

"Are you ready for an EPIC weekend?" he asks through the speakers.

I look at Boone and smile, "I guess," Boone smiles back and just like that, it feels like normal again. Hopefully it stays that way.

"We will be there a little later because *someone* decided to not pack the night before!" Joch says and then lets out a yelp as something hits him.

"Shut the fuck up, not all of us have time to get packed the week before." Casey snipped. I couldn't help but chuckle. Casey and Joch had a hilarious sibling comradery going on and it reminded me of how Perry and I were when I first moved into Riley's house. It was the three of us in a two bedroom for over two years, with Riley's longtime friend, Remy coming in and out as she repaired her relationship with her mother before she eventually moved into an apartment with her mom in Colorado. Perry eventually was able to move into her apartment in the city after her career as a makeup and hairstylist took off. Not gonna lie though, it got really heated sometimes with all that estrogen and different personalities in a small space.

"You two have fun, you'll probably be the only ones there for a little bit!" Joch yells as it sounds like something hits him again.

"Ok Joch we need to focus on driving. See you later." Boone laughs, hitting the end call button.

He shakes his head and mutters something under his breath.

"So how was practice?" I ask as I settle in my seat with a can of honey mustard pringles. Boone rolls his neck, "Not too bad. How about you?" He asks, reaching over and grabbing a chip from my hand to pop in his mouth.

"Same as always, super busy game days, guys trying to hit on me and the other waitstaff. I swear I get more numbers left on the table than tips some nights." It was true. Georgia and I took any numbers the guys left us and taped them to the pin board in the back kitchen and would give them out to the pushy customers that asked for our numbers.

"Risky for them to do that, giving their number to a stranger. I mean you could be a serial killer for all they know." I laugh as he recites exactly what I had said to him the day he came into the bar and asked for my number.

"Right! I mean I still can't believe I got your number. You still don't know if I'm a killer." I wink, popping a chip in my mouth and moaning at the delicious taste.

Boone returns the wink, "I'll take those odds, you haven't killed me yet."

"The weather is supposed to be nice this weekend, news says it'll get snowy before the Christmas season. I can't wait!" I stretch my arms up. It had gotten unusually warm as it got into December, warm enough that I was able to change into white shorts and a zip up hoodie. I pull my hair back in the claw clip and glance over at Boone, my face heating when I see his eyes looking at me for just a moment before turning back to the road.

We pull into the campsite around five, it was a nice woodsy area with a direct view of a beach and lake. The camping area was open and big enough for at least six camper vans.

"There's a cove with a natural hot spring and waterfall just down the path there." Boone pointed. He got to work anchoring the camper and getting it all set up.

"Want to explore?" I ask, looking around. The sun was still up so it was warm. Boone nods,

"Yea, just stay close. Don't need you getting lost." he says pulling out the grill and fire wood for the firepit. My smile drops.

"Don't you wanna go with me?" I ask, hoping he gets the hint.

"I gotta get this set up."

"Can I help?" I ask.

"Nah, I got it." And we are back to him ignoring me. Fuck this.

"Hey guys!" Bohdie calls as his truck pulls into the spot next to ours. I smile at him.

"Hey Bo." Bohdies hair is shorter and he had freshly shaved. I grab onto the grab bar next to his driver side door of his lifted truck and step onto the step up ledge..

"Hey, what happened to wanting to be all no shaving till new years?" I ask him. His brown eyes light up at my remembering his plan to grow out his hair and beard till january.

"I trimmed too much of it by mistake and just decided to shave it, plus it got too itchy. How are you? It's been a while." he leans his chin onto his arm that's resting on the door.

"I'm good. Hey, I'm actually about to go explore. Wanna come with?" I ask. The entire time we are talking I can feel Boones eyes on us. *Good. See, you're missing out.* Bohdie gives me an apologetic smile, "I need to get stuff set up but how about later?" he offers. I pout at him, "Fine. but you owe me." I wink and step away from his truck.

I put my hands in my pocket as I walk down the path, following the signs. Winter had come a little later than normal so there were still leaves on some trees even though it was early December. It was so serene. I snapped a few photos on my phone as I walked. Coming around the bend I found the cove, Boone was right. It is beautiful. Sand met clear water that went from shallow to deeper as it went closer to the waterfall, the cove was crescent shaped, rocks lined around the cut out and there was a small stream about twenty feet to the left that snaked off into the woods where the water from the waterfall emptied out into. It was beautiful. I kicked off my sandals and let my feet in the water. It was cold, but not too bad. I turn and continue back down the path but go left instead of right, the campsite I ended up at was not ours. There were a few tents around a fire and loud music blared from the beat up truck.

"Wrong way." I mutter turning around to go back.

"Hello there." a voice says. My skin prickles in alarm as I turn to see a guy emerging from one of the tents and walking to stand a few feet from me. He's probably mid to late twenties, with unbrushed blonde hair that made him look like a beach bum ken-doll. He wore a white wife beater with a teal Hawaiian shirt open over it, in his hand was a beer can. He swayed a little, probably having more than that one can.

"Now if this isn't the best thing I saw all day. Hi, I'm Chad." he smirks. Of course his name is Chad. Letting my face relax into the mask of resting bitch face I use when the greasy gross customer gets too close, I step back.

"Not interested." I deadpan as I calmly walk down the path. Chad follows me. He grabs my arm to stop me, "Whoa wait where are ya going baby? I know you from somewhere don't I?" his grip tightens to keep me from walking away. My heart pounds in my ears. "Nope, never saw you before." I reply, pulling my arm but his grip remains strong. He laughs, throwing his arm around me and tries leading me towards the tents and music.

"No thank you." I hiss. Chad clearly doesn't get what 'no' means as he doesn't let me go. I dig my nails into his wrist and drag them down his forearm leaving bloody claw marks. Chad lets out a yelp and jerks his hand back, cradling it to his chest. I take the chance and speed walk back down the path.

"Wait! Come back here you, *fucking bitch.*" he calls out the anger in his tone growing with every word. I come around the bend and run right in to Boones chest. Joch is a few feet behind him.

"Hey." he says, holding onto my shoulders. Boones eyes flash up and confusion is written all over his face when he hears what I hear, "Come back here." Chad calls as he comes into view. He sees Boone and lets out a laugh.

"Thanks for finding my girl, man." Chad calls, still holding his clawed hand. Boones brows shoot up his forehead.

"Excuse me?" he asks.

"Fuck off Chad. No means No." I bark. Boone holds up his hands, "Whoa, wait." he looks at me, "Did he try something with you? Did he hurt you?"

"Just forget it." I say grabbing his arm. Chad chose stupidity today, because when he gets closer he tries to make a grab for me, "Come on babe."

"Oliver! No!" Joch says but it's too late. Boone has Chad's arm in a death grip.

"Touch her and I'll break every bone in your arm." He hisses as Chad staggers back. I look at Boone, he is pissed. The anger radiates off him. Chad bolts down the way he came muttering obscenities.

"You ok Tabby-cat?" Joch asks not looking at me. His attention is on Boone.

"I had it handled." I say to Boone.

"Clearly." he gritted through his clenched teeth. *Jeez don't crack a molar.* My skin prickles with irritation.

"Are you actually mad at me right now? I said I had it handled." I gawk. What is his problem right now?

"You looked like you had it handled. You're welcome by the way. Maybe if it was Bohdie you would be more thankful that you were helped out." he snips back as he turns away from me, his back muscles tight as his fists clench at his sides.

"Ok fuck you." I hiss, getting in front of him, "Ever since the kiss you've been ignoring me and now you're mad at me? What's up with that by the way? What was that?" Boones eyes harden, "It was just a mistake. Ok. leave it at that. It won't happen again." He grounds out. My chest hurts. It feels like I've been slapped. He regrets the kiss.

"You are just a fucking magnet for trouble."

he tsks shaking his head and walking back towards

the campsite leaving me dumbfounded because

what the absolute fuck was that about? He was

mad at me? Me! For what?

Joch sighs as he rubs his neck, "Just give

him a little bit to cool off, are you ok?" He asks,

pinching the bridge of his nose.

"Yes. I am fine." I say, crossing my arms

over my chest.

Joch is dressed in blue and white swim

shorts and a blue shirt. His blonde hair was pulled

up into a small bun.

"Let's go join the others. The rest of the

team should be here by now." he says, holding his

arm out to loop it around my shoulders as we walk

down the path.

"Why is he mad at me?" I ask. I didn't understand since I did nothing wrong.

"He's not." Joch sighed, rubbing his neck with his free hand,

I looked at him to continue.

"He's protective just like we all are. And if you haven't noticed he is totally into you, Just let him cool off." he admits.

"He is not into me." I deny. Joch chuckles and shakes his head, "sure, sure." he says.

CHAPTER 19

Tabitha

When we get back to the campsite the other teammates that came are all scattered about, a few at the bonfire, some tossing a foam football back and forth on the beach. Boone is out on the beach playing with Hanson and Tig. He seemed to be fine, not all broody like he had just been before.

"Hey girl. You ok?" Casey asks, walking up next to me with a drink in her hand. She had on a pink hoodie and her brown hair was down, as per usual she looked stunningly beautiful. I nod, "Just Oliver being a moody baby." I roll my eyes, letting out a grumble. She glances from me to Boone, her lips pursed,

"Ohh boy, what did he do?" She asks.

"Blamed me for apparently being a trouble magnet. Not my fault." I say. She smiles, "Awee, you guys had your first argument. He'll get over it and will apologize once he cools off. Then he will come crawling back. Believe me." she assures me.

"Believe what?" Bohdie asks, walking up and sitting down next to me.

"That Oliver will get over his jealousy and stop being a putz." Casey smiles. Bohdie lets out a laugh, "Trouble in paradise?" he asks me. His brown eyes were like milk chocolate, so warm and friendly.

"No trouble on my end." I smirk. Bohdie nudges my shoulder and wrinkles his nose cutely, "Men are silly creatures, he'll come to his senses soon and realize how amazing you are." He says sincerely. I lean my head on his shoulder and smile at him, "You're sweet." I say taking a sip of my beer.

He looks at Joch and Tig fighting for the ball, his bottle midway to his lips muttering, "Shy creatures indeed."

The sun sets and everyone is getting food while waiting for it to get darker to light off the fireworks. Yea apparently this was another tradition that Joch had begun a few years back. I had cooled off a while ago but Boone still had kept his distance the past couple hours. I find him on a slightly out of sight Fishing dock, it's partially hidden from all the foliage. He was sitting on the end. Fine. I would go to him then. I walk down the dock to where he is.

"Mind if I sit down?" I ask, tapping his hip with my foot. He lets out a chuckle, "I don't bite." he replies.

"What if I ask you to?" I counter, sitting down. That got me a smirk. I pull my knees to my chest and pick at some of the old, weathered wood.

"I'm sorry about earlier." He says, dragging his eyes from the lake to look at me.

"I'm sorry I snapped at you, I may have overreacted." I apologized, looking at him. Boone gave me a soft smile before looking back at the water, "I was a little snappy with you too, I heard you tell him to fuck off and when he went to grab you. It set me off." he explains, "I won't apologize for defending you, but I am sorry for scaring you or making you uncomfortable." He added. I bumped him with my shoulder, "Thank you, and you didn't scare me, I was afraid you would get recognized and end up in trouble or hurt."

Boone leaned back resting on his hand, smiling as he shook his head before taking a swig from his beer bottle.

"I would have been ok, have a little faith in me, I'm a hockey player. Doing hard for a living is my daily thing." he says.

"You can't be hard all the time goof." I counter, taking a swig from my own bottle.

"Well, when you're around it's impossible not to be hard." he smirks as my face turns red at the innuendo. I lightly push at his arm, "Har Har!" I snort.

I mirror his position, leaning back with my hands behind me. Boone glanced down and gently placed his hand next to mine, our fingers overlapping each other playing lightly.

"Other than the unsavory character from earlier and my shitty attitude. Are you enjoying the trip?" He asks, looking out to the last bit of the sunset.

"Yea, it is really nice out here. I'm glad Casey and Joch told you to invite me." my face heats as his fingers continue to play with mine.

"Nah I would have invited you without them telling me to. They are just both very persistent." he chuckled and I couldn't have agreed more.

"One of their endearing qualities." I smile.

"I'm glad you came." Boone admits, I turn my head toward him and he sits forward, leaning closer to me so his shoulder is pressed against mine.

"Y-yeah. Me too." my voice comes out breathily. My heart hammers in my chest at the way he was looking at me. It was NOT how people who were just friends looked at eachother. Holy skydaddy he starts leaning closer.

Slowly Boone lowered his head towards me. He was so... so... So close. My body moves on its own, leaning against his and oh fuck he was gonna kiss me. And this time it would be on purpose.

My lips part and his eyes lower to them, just as he-

"Hey Oli! Tabby-cat come on. It's time for the fireworks." Joch calls, appearing around the patch of bushes at the end of the dock. I jerk back, face beet red quickly taking a pull from my drink.

Boone inhales deeply and breathes out, "Damn him."

"Yeah. On our way!" Boone calls. Boone looks down at me, fire in his eyes. I bite my lip, "I'm gonna. Just. yeah." I squeak out standing and almost sprint down the dock.

CHAPTER 20

Boone

Fucking Joch and his timing! Uggg! Tabitha practically ran from me after Joch interrupted our…. Whatever that was. Shit. What was that! She was there and it was definitely something. I almost kissed her and she practically sprinted faster than Usain Bolt to get away from me. Fuck.

"Oliver, come on!" Casey calls.

"I'm coming." I reply heading down the dock. The team was all gathered with partners around the tables. The ones with kids were all playing with sparklers or getting the s'mores ready to make.

Bohdie was by the fire talking to Tabitha and from his posture and how he was smiling at her, he was 100% flirting with her. She laughed as he handed her some sparklers but she refuses, shaking her head. Jochs' advice from the other day played in my head, *'Someone else will make a move,'* my pulse races because, was I watching one of my friends make a move on my girl who I probably had not just a friend's feelings for? She played with the end of one of her two loose french braids. Jealousy burns my veins.

Someone walks up to my side and a waft of cotton candy hits my nose making my stomach roll.

"Hey Oliver." the soft voice cooed. I want to puke when I hear her voice. Jannette Ilsa. She was a cheerleader for the Seattle SeaHawks football team, her light brown hair was curled to game day perfection as it framed around her face in beach waves.

"Jannette, nice to see you. What are you doing here?" I ask politely, she flips her hair over her shoulder as she smiles at me. She's wearing a light blue and white zip up hoodie and tiny shorts that showed off her long tan legs.

"So nice to see you again! I caught a ride with Cole, How have you been?" she asks, looking up at me through her thick fake lashes. I was gonna kill Cole when I found him. Jannette and I had briefly dated for a little bit a few years back and I broke it off. I wasn't going to be her accessory or trophy boyfriend, she only wanted the perks that came with being involved with me. She had also tried sleeping with half the team while dating me. Cole knew the rules of these trips, no puck bunnies or hookups or exes.

I looked up at Cole as he came up next to her, throwing an arm around her shoulders and kisses her temple, "I couldn't pass up the opportunity to bring my girl out with us all." he smiles. *'Oh this poor sap is so getting played by the manipulation queen.'* I think.

Cole is a huge player, having a new girlfriend/puck bunny every other month. Normally he isn't this clueless. Cole's attention is drawn by Joch and Tig as they start to throw a ball back and forth.

"So how have you been, Oli?" Jannette asks once he leaves.

"I've been good. Working hard with the team." I answer. I glance over to see Tabitha fully invested into whatever Bohdie is saying and nodding along. Her hand was on his arm as he spoke and it pissed me off.

"I have been busy too, practice and all the media stuff. It feels so nice to just relax with friends and get distractions from the chaos." her lower lip pulls in between her teeth. Oh so she is looking for a fuck. Shameless as ever.

"Maybe we could sneak off for a quick moment?" My eyebrows shoot up and out of habit I smile because I had almost forgotten how bold she could be.

"I don't really think that's a good Idea. what would Cole think?" Shaking my head and seeing the flash of confusion in her big brown eyes.

"Cole knows we aren't exclusive, he doesn't mind." she tries.

"Hey Oliver, we're gonna try to squeeze in a game of volleyball, you guys wanna play?" Bohdie calls, Tabitha has a look on her face I can't really read but she gives me a small smile as she looks from me to Jannetts hands around my arm. Bohdie has his hand on Tabitha's shoulder as he says something to her that has her smiling.

"I'm in!" Casey calls, throwing her arm around Tabitha's shoulder. Jannett squeals and jumps up and down, "We are so in!" she grabs my arm and pulls on it, "Come one Oli-pop! We can be on the same team!" she beams. "Uh, sure?" I look at Tabitha and see what looks like…no way…. Was that a flash of .. jealousy? Nah I have to be seeing things.

Casey has that look on her face, the look that someone got when they spot the person who cheated on her best friend and tried to fuck her brother. She makes a strange mnnnn sound in her throat before she spoke, "Jenny bell. Thought the rule was no puck bunnies and yet, here you are. Bad fake tits and all." she sneers. Jeannett sucks on her teeth and smiles, "They aren't fake." she states. I notice she doesn't deny the puck bunny status. Casey humphes, "Whatever helps you sleep at night." she says doing that thing where she scrunched her face and pursed her lips before walking over to Tabitha.

Yup, safe to say that Casey still held a grudge against 'Jenny-Bell.'

The net was set up on the beach, Bohdie, Casey, Tabitha and Joch were on one side. Me, Jannette, Tig and our left defenseman Ash, are on the other side.

"Alright let's get this going we have time for maybe two games before it gets dark!" Joch clapped his hands together. I set up in the back row, Jannette in front of me a few feet. I couldn't hear what she said, but she said something to

Tabitha when she walked past her. The ball is served and Jannette hits it over the net right into Tabitha's chest.

"Point!" Jannette gleefully cheered.

"How is that a point?" Casey asks, throwing her hands up.

Jannette shrugs her shoulder, "It's the rules," she says. Tabitha picks up the ball, shooting me a look.

"Right Oli-pop?" Jannette asks. Casey looks from her to me and raises a brow, I just shrug. She gives me a warning look and mouths, 'No.'

It was Joch's turn to serve so he called the serve and hit the ball. I pop it to Jannette who spikes it right at Tabitha, she drops low, bumping it with her fist up to Casey who spikes it between me and Tig. The ball hits the sand and Casey cheers.

"Woohoo! Point for us!" she laughs high-fiving Tabitha.

Bohdie lets out a whoop! and holds his hands up to Tabitha for a high- five, "Teamwork baby!" he laughs. The muscle in my jaw tics when I notice he closes his hands over hers, squeezing it for a moment longer than needed before letting go. Jannette smirks then pulls on a pouty face, "Bohdie, Tabitha get a room. We're trying to play a game here, not watch you two make puppy dog eyes at each other." she says loudly. Bohdie's cheeks go a light shade of pink and Tabitha's brows pull in, her gaze meets mine.

"Really?" she mouths at me.

Jannette retrieves the ball from under the net and when she stands, Tabitha's posture stiffens. Eyes locking on Jannette in a glare.

"Your serve Oli-pop." Jannette winks, blowing me a kiss.

"Jesus Jannette we get it, you wanna suck his dick. Could you try to not be such a pick me girl? You already scream desperate." Casey groans. Tabitha laughs, "It really is pathetic." she agrees, covering her mouth as she chuckles. I smile at the sound of her laugh. Jeanette's ears are red and she flips her hair over her shoulder. "Whatever." she huffs. *Jesus, could she act more like a teenager?*

I toss the ball up and serve it, Casey bumps it back over the net, Jannette jumps up and as she does she kicks sand into Tabitha's face making her jerk back right as she spikes the ball right into the side of Tabitha's face. It knocks her backward but she doesn't fall down, just bends forward, her left hand holding against her face as she rubs her eyes.

"Are you ok?" Casey asks as she bent over rubbing her cheek. Bohdie puts a hand on her back, "You good?" He asks. Tabitha nods and glares at Jeannette.

"What the hell was that Jeanette?" I hiss, grabbing her elbow. That was not cool at all.

"I play hard. Sorry." she smiles.

"Kicking sand at someone? Real childish." I huff. Tabitha grabs the ball and once Casey serves it, Jannette's foot kicks up sand again at Tabitha only this time, Tabitha grabs onto the ball and chucks it right into Jannettes face hitting her in the nose sending her down. All before I can say anything.

"My nose! Shit. I have a game the day after tomorrow!" Jannette cries.

"Oops, looks like I play hard too." Tabitha shrugs with a pout to her lips.

"That's my girl!" Bohdie laughs, patting her on the back.

'*His girl?*' .

Joch calls the game, "This is getting a little too violent for my liking. Let's end it here shall we?" he announces, snatching the ball from Jannette. I watch as Tabitha and Casey follow Bohdie back to the coolers. Like a bad rash Jannette is back on me. She's standing in front of me, napkin to her nose.

"Why did you bring trash like her around Oli? That's not like you." Her whiney voice is like nails on a chalkboard and I really have no clue what I ever saw in her to begin with.

"Excuse me? What did you call me?" Tabitha glares from across the camp fire. Jannette scrunches her face, "You're trash! He will never be into trash like you. Why are you even here?" she screeches. Hearing her call Tabitha trash set me on edge. Jannette was as shallow as they came, the cliche mean girl. I felt like an idiot for taking this long to see it.

"*Enough*, Jannette." the edge to my tone has her blinking in surprise. I wasn't going to listen to her shit anymore. Jannette gives me a sad puppy face. It looks ridiculous with her holding a tissue to her bloody nose.

"You seriously need a reality check. You're twenty seven not thirteen. The mean girl act is really sad at this point in your life don't you think?" Her mouth hangs open as I leave her by the net. Cole ends up trying to talk to her but she just sits in his truck yelling to go home.

"Hey, come on." I say to Tabitha, smiling at her and taking her hand. I have no fucking idea what I was doing. She smiles and gives me a curious look as I lead her down the path to the cove.

"What are we doing?" She asks. I pull my shirt off and kicked off my shoes. Grinning when I saw her face flush a shade of pink.

"Best place to watch the fireworks." I say beckoning her to follow me. She shrugs off her hoodie revealing a red bikini under the white tank top. I was happy to be waist deep in water

I must have been a little zoned out because suddenly a splash of water hits me in the face and she is a few feet in front of me.

"Oh. you little." I growl, lunging for her, she lets out a squeal and dodges my grab.

"No! Ah hah!" she laughs as I got her around the waist and pushed backwards, sending us both into the deeper water. My arms are still around her waist when we come up and she turns in my arms. Blood rushes to my cock because holy fuck, I now had confirmation that yes. Indeed. She had pierced nipples. The material of her bikini sticks to her skin letting the very clear outline of two small metal piercings. I audibly groan and rest my head on her shoulder, feeling goosebumps breakout on her skin.

"What?" she chuckles, her voice hitching when my lips press against her skin.

"You're killing me." I exhale.

"What do you mean?" she asks softly. My arms loosen, moving to hold her waist. I turn my head to look up at her. A loud crack above has her jumping and her head lifting up to look at the explosion of color in the sky. The fireworks had begun.

Tabitha let out a laugh, "Wow!" she gasps, smiling.

"This is amazing!" I don't pay any attention to the fireworks. My eyes were on her. Looking at her. Definitely not how I look at friends.

This was all too much. I stand up to full height. She looks up at me, a question in her eyes. This couldn't happen. It couldn't. And I had to tell her the truth. No matter how much this would hurt.

"We can't be friends." I admit. The look on her face has my chest feeling like I had been sucker punched in the heart.

"What do you mean?" she asks, trying to step away but I stop her by hooking my fingers into the belt loops of her shorts and pulling her back to me.

"I lied before. About the kiss. It wasn't a mistake."

"Then what was it?" She asks, the sharpness in her tone has me on edge a bit. She's confused, and I'm not making much sense.

"It wasn't a mistake." I say before pressing my lips to hers. The moment our lips touch, Tabitha pushes up onto her tiptoes, her fingertips digging into my shoulders as she hungrily kisses me back. Without breaking the kiss I bend my knees, grabbing her thighs and hoisting her up so her legs went around my waist, holding her up by the backs of her thighs as she presses herself to me.

"I don't think we can just be friends either now." she gasps as she rests her forehead against mine. I smile and pull her in for another kiss.

CHAPTER 21

Tabitha

Holy fuck fuck fuck fuck fuck fuck fuck fuck fuck fuck fuck fuck fuck fuck fuck fuck fuck fuck fuck fuck fuck fuck fuck fuck fuck fuck fuck fuck fuck fuck fuck fuck fuck fuck fuck fuck fuck fuck fuck fuck fuck fuck fuck fuck FUUUUCCCKKKKK!

Holy

Fuck

His lips, his tongue, his beard scratching my chin, his hands! HIM! It was better than I had imagined. He is hard everywhere.

Jannette had pissed me off earlier with her comments and then that stunt during the game. She had made it very clear that she wanted Boone and that I needed to keep out of her way. All her flirting with him had me feeling jealous yeah. She was all over him and he wasn't stopping her. But during the game, I knew; Bitch stood no chance.

Boone pulls away smiling a devilish grin and I guess what he is about to do but before I can escape- he launches us both backwards into the water.

"You are SO dead!" I laugh, splashing him. He laughs and ducks underwater Making me lose sight of him for a moment. Right before he comes up and grabs onto me, swinging me around.

Walking back to the campsite everything feels warm and fuzzy in my chest. Things with Jeannett way in the far recesses of my mind.

When we get back, Joch, Casey and the others were already in their campers and the fire is just a low glow.

"Want a s'more?" Boone asks, nodding to the left out bag of food.

"Hell yea, I love s'mores."

Boone holds the poker over the fire while I open the packet of chocolate. Just as the marshmallow was cooking, Boones' phone starts to ring. His brows pull in as immediate worry filled his eyes. He hands me the poker, "Here can you-" as soon as it was in my hands he turns away to take the call.

"Marissa, Hey." He breathes.

Marissa… who the fuck is Marissa?

CHAPTER 22

Boone

My heart launches onto my throat. If you've felt it before then you understand the feeling, the tightness in your throat as it constricts and trying to swallow feels like a foreign act. When I found out about Tate, I had immediately met up with his mother to explain everything about my birth father and I had told her I wanted to do what I could to help. Marissa, his mother, is from an affluent family, much to Hanks glee. He swindled his way into her fathers company and became the scummy CEO he always wanted to be; making the money his greedy dick wanted. The urge to warn her about Hank's fuckery, but I couldn't add more stress to her with Tate's diagnosis.

Seeing her name flashing on the screen had me feeling like the last time mom had been rushed to the hospital before she died.

"Marissa, what happened?" My voice is raspy and it feels like I swallowed chalk. It didn't help that I heard her sniffling and, fuck, she is crying.

"It's Tate. He had a seizure tonight." she sobbed. My knees feel weak. "Is..is he ok?" I ask as my eyes sting. Please no. Don't tell me he's gone. Not like this.

"He was walking around fine, trying to get some air outside and said he didn't feel too well; then he collapsed and began to have a seizure." she explained. The pain in her voice kills me because I *knew* that pain, the feeling of 'things were fine just a moment ago and now it's all upside down.

"Oliver, he… he was asking to see you. I know you have a lot going on right now," she trails off.

"I'll be there as soon as I can." I say. Through this whole thing I had honestly forgotten about Tabitha standing next to me. Marissa sniffles out a *thank you* and hangs up. I put my phone in my pocket, "I need to go. Tate." I trail off. Tabitha's eyes widen and she sucks in a breath, "Tate? Is he ok?"

"He had a seizure. I uh, I need to go. He was asking for me. I need to go see him." my lungs feel like they are in a vice. Tabitha nods, "I'll clean up here," she says as my phone rings again, this time it was the team PR manager, Devon.

"Hey Devon, look this isn't a good time right now." I start, making him laugh, "Ha! You're telling me! What is a puck bunny doing at a team and family only camping trip!" he hisses.

Oh this was not the time to fucking come at me like this. Devon was the jump down your throat and explode before getting the full story-type. Meaning he sucked at his job whenever it came to situations like now.

"You mean Jannette?" I ask getting into my truck.

"No! Not her. The redhead that not only was with you at the store but also injured another player's girlfriend? You know better! I can't believe you of all people would do this. I expect this from Bhoden not you." he barks.

"Is it my turn to talk?" I ask through my teeth.

When he didn't respond, I took a breath.

"Ok, good. First of all, her name is Tabitha, she is not a puck bunny she is my girlfriend, don't fucking listen to everything Jaenette says since she just wants a fuck and gets pissed when she is denied it. Now I need to deal with something, if you are done." I seethe hanging up. Tabitha opens the passenger door and climbs in.

"I told Casey and Joch, they are getting their stuff packed up. Something about Kaminskey needing Casey's help?" she explaines. I groan and bump my head onto the steering wheel.

"Shit. ok. I am really sorry about this." I say. Tabiths rubs my arm, "It's ok. Life is a continuous case of herpes that likes to flare up every so often with a bad yeast infection." A bark of laughter erupts from me, because... what?

CHAPTER 23

Tabitha

It turns out that the paparazzi were even worse than I thought. Kaminskey had gotten into a fist fight with one that barged his way into the NICU to get photos of his wife and son as they were being discharged. I felt so bad for them to have to go through that. To have a new baby and then some cuck shove a camera in your face. Casey was already taking care of everything and would have the cameraman arrested and Kam cleared. I decided to return one of the thirty missed calls from Perry. Oof, she had been in Australia for some big hair cosmetology convention and had been off her phone. I facetimed her and she immediately picked up.

"Girl! Where have you been!" she yells. She was in a hotel room. Her black hair is curled with rainbow extensions clipped in. I smile, "Hello to you too." I say as I lean back.

"I am so sorry I didn't call, I was so busy with the last two events I didn't have access to my phone because it was with my assistant. I already cursed her out for not even telling me about you and Riley's texts." she sighs, "I would have immediately came home had I known."

"And you would have ruined this big event that took you six years to get into. I'm ok. Riley is ok." I assure her. She lets out a laugh, "Oh I heard all about where you are and fine doesn't do it justice!" she gasps, "Are you at his house right now?" I turn the phone to show her the spacious living room.

"Yup. He just left." I say, laughing when I heard her squeal.

"Show me everything! Have you been in his room!" she cooed. I shake my head, "Pear, I'm not sleeping with him. Nothing like that has happened yet." I blush. Her eyes go wide, "Wait, something happened. I can tell. What happened? Did he try anything? Was it what you wanted? I can be on the first plane home." she fired off going from excited to protective to vengeful so fast.

"Sooo we may have... kissed. And made out." I bury my face in the oversized sleeve of Boones hoodie. Perry cheers, "Finally! I am so proud of you! How was it?" she asked. The smile was too big to hide. I looked at the phone and bit my lip, "It was," looking up I actually fucking giggled, "So hot." I sighed.

"It was like so much sexual tension had built up for so long and it was so good. He Is so amazing, I feel so comfortable around him." I explained. It was true. Boon just had this energy that he emanated that made me feel so at ease. Perry covered her mouth, "Oh I love this! Are you ready for the physical stuff thought?" She asked. I knew exactly what she meant. If I had sex with Boone that meant that he would see me naked. All of me. Including the scar.

"I will tell him eventually. We're taking it slow." I shrugged. Perry looked to her left, and nodded, "Be right there."

"I have to go. I will have my phone on me at all times so if you need anything call me." she urged.

"I will. Love you." I said.

"Love you." she winked before the call ended.

Since Boone was out for a few hours I decided to go for a run. It was around noon since we had gotten home around nine. With my pepper spray and taser strapped to my arm out of habit, I zipped up the hoodie and start my run.

The neighborhood was pretty swanky, big houses and rich families. Very not my life growing up that's for sure. I round one of those long shrub garden walls where it's just a line of shrubbery and a white work van catches my attention as I pass it. A guy with a short green mohawk was in the driver seat. I go around the cul de sac and head back home so I can shower and make food. Or at least that was the plan, Casey is pulling into her driveway when I get back home. She waves at me, "Hey. you wanna drink?" I look at my watch and laugh, "Pft, Isn't it a little early?" Casey shrugs, "It's still vacation. And you can tell me about your little thing with you and Oliver, because I know you two ain't just friends." she says, wiggling her fingers at me. I shake my head, "We're… figuring it out," I mutter, my hands on my hips as I swivel from one foot to the other, "Let me change and I'll come over?" I agree. Casey claps her hands, "Alright! I'll be back, with wine!" She calls walking up the driveway.

Joch and Caseys house is similar to Boone's, Casey's room was on the ground floor with her office while Jochs was upstairs.

We sit outside by an electric fireplace with a couple glasses.

"How is Kam?" I ask, taking my glass. Casey sighs, "He will be fine, I feel for his wife though, she was a mess. Fucking paparazzi scumbags." she shakes her head. Her brown hair is pulled up in a ponytail. She looks wary, tapping her nail on the rim of the glass before speaking.

"You should know, this life isn't for the weak. It can get super crazy and the paparazzi can be murderous with their invasiveness and they are shameless. The fans can get cruel." she explains before taking a sip from her glass. I know what she is doing. She was pretty much asking me if this was the life I could handle.

"I get that. I really do. I want to be a part of Boones life. If this is what it takes… I'll go with it." I say. I don't want to hide anymore. I don't want to constantly worry that I'll be found by my ex foster brother. I want to live my fucking life and be happy.

CHAPTER 24

Tabitha

I throw my head back and laugh, Casey covers her mouth as she laughs so hard she is wheezing.

"I thought I could hear banshee laughing." Boones voice calls. He walks into the backyard with Joch following behind him. Boone sits down next to me, "Hey, how's Tate?" I ask.

"He's ok. It was a reaction to meds." I look at my watch and saw the time was almost four. Wow. I had been hanging out with Casey for over five hours. That explains the waning buzz. We'd been talking about everything and anything. School college. Crappy dates.

Joch hands Boone a beer before walking over and sitting on the couch across from us.

"We having a little get together?" Tig calls from the fence line. Tig lived next door to Joch. He was with Bohdie. I waved at him and he smiled back giving me a little wave.

"Always!" Joch called. Soon enough, a few of the other players were sitting around the yard, hanging out and talking. The fire pit in the far left of the yard was going strong. Wow, they really did just randomly meet up at each other's houses acting like it was their own. Joch and Boone tossed a foam football around.

"So what's going on with you and Oliver?" Casey asks. I pull my eyes from Boone and Joch as they wrestle on the ground for the ball. Boone lets out a laugh as he jerks his arm up with the ball out of Jochs reach.

"No clue, why do you ask?" I smirk. She smiles, "I see the way you two look at each other, there is no way you two are 'just friends.'" I chew on my lip, the warm fuzzy feeling from the wine earlier wearing off, "I don't know." I say honestly. Boone looks over at me and winks. A zap of heat goes right to my crotch.

Casey lets out a sigh, "Slow burn romance."

Joch and Tig had set up a spot on the outdoor bar for the drinks and snacks. Casey had set up the margarita machine and I happily mixed the alcohols into the blender for the margs. I'm on my knees on the table as I pour the contents into the top of the mixer when I feel someone walk up.

"Careful." Boone says, coming up behind me. His hands hold onto my waist and like with the truck, he lifts me down from the table. I giggle and dust off the knees of the dress I had put on before coming to Casey's.

"Thank you." I smile at him. He reaches around me and grabs one of the solo cups with the frozen margarita in it.

"Wanna get out of here?" He says in my ear, I nod.

He takes my hand and we sneak out the side gate and jog across the yard, giggling like teenagers.

We sit along the pool ledge in Boones yard with our feet in the water. The weather is ok, not really that cold but there was a crispness as it got later in the evening that signaled snow was on the way just in time for Christmas. The sun was going down by now and the sounds of the get together from Jochs was starting to tone down too.

"You look nice in the dress." Boone says. I look down at the dress and then smile up at him, "Thank you." The dress was a simple knee length lavender dress with little flowers on it. Boone moves so he is standing in front of me, his hands resting on the sides of my knees.

"How drunk are you?" He asks.

"I'm not drunk at all. Just a slight buzz." I answer honestly.

"Why?" Boone smiles and his eyes drop to my lips.

"Because I want to make sure you're sober when I kiss you." He says before dipping his head and kissing me. *Fuuuckk.*

I tangle my hands through his short hair, pulling him closer to me. Moaning as I open my mouth to let him in. Boones hands grip my thighs and he lifts me up, pivoting so he was sitting and places me on his lap. His hands smooth up my legs under the hem of the dress, gripping my ass as I grind onto him. He's rock hard through his jeans. A small voice in my head says I should tell him. Tell him before it gets too far.

He makes me yelp when he suddenly stands, my legs go around his waist as his hands hold onto my ass so he doesn't drop me.

"Sorry, but I don't want to give the neighbors a show." He pants, pressing a kiss to the exposed skin of my throat, the feeling of his teeth grazing my skin has me shivering. He holds me tight, carrying me up through a secret side stairwell to his balcony. With one hand he pulls open the door and walks us inside.

Boones room is huge. A California king with a mahogany four post bedpost and canopy sits in the center against the wall. The matching dresser was across from the bed with a tv on the wall above it. He carries me over to the bed, kissing me as he sits back with me on top of him.

I have to tell him now. His hands go under my dress, one hand moves between my thighs where he's about to feel the skin and I pull back, "Wait!" I breathe. He halts all movements, "What, what is it?" he asks. I sit back, I have to tell him but I don't want to. It will be easier to do this now. He must take my silence as my second guessing the whole thing.

"Hey, we don't have to. It's ok." He says caressing my face. He's leaning back on one elbow, his hair is disheveled and his clothes are wrinkled. Ugh I just wanna grab him and kiss him.

"No. I want to. Really. I just need to warn you about something first." He tilts his head furrowing his brows. Closing my eyes I take a deep breath.

"There's a .. scar." I start, my eyes flash downward. His eyes go to my crotch as I pull the dress up to my hip. I open my legs more revealing the scar that starts at the very top of my inner right thigh close to the groin. The worst of it is covered by my underwear. Boones eyes widen and he pushes up into a full sitting position. Most of the scar is covered by my thong, but from what he sees, I know he can tell what the blotched words say.

The word 'Mine,' is burned across my groin and crotch in scribbled, slashing letters. It had settled to a light purplish brown color a few years ago instead of the pale skin color I had hoped for. Boone had a look of horror on his face as he takes in the mark.

"Who did this to you?" his voice cracks as he looks from the scar to me. The storm in his eyes building with rage.

I swallow the lump in my throat, "My ex foster brother was a sadistic prick who liked to torture me. The night I ran away it was because he gave me this." my voice doesn't break as I speak. I've only told the story to Perry and Riley, even with them I couldn't tell them the details of what happened in that house leading up to my escape.

Boone rolls us so I am on my back and he is kneeling between my legs. Carefully he lifts the dress up to my waist to reveal the scar.

"Can I?" he asks, looking up at me. Asking permission before touching me. Waiting until I say yes, he carefully hooks his fingers in the strings of my black thong and pulls it down my legs to reveal the full scar. The skin around the area is smooth so

I don't need to shave or wax much because the scar covers most of my crotch.

"Please tell me he is rotting in a cell or is dead." His voice is heavy as he tries to keep his anger in check. I look at the open patio door and scoff.

"I wish."

I suck in a sharp breath when I feel him gently place a kiss to the scar, my fingers grip the black bedspread as my back arches slightly.

"Does that hurt?" he asks, kissing my inner thigh. I shake my head, "No. It feels good." I mutter. *So fucking good.* He pressed kisses all up the scar. Over the words that my foster brother branded onto my body.

"Fuck. Oliver." I bite my fist as he presses a kiss directly above my clit. His beard hairs graze against the sensitive skin of my thighs. My hips buck up needing him to just fucking touch me! He's touched me everywhere but where I need him to.

Boone moves up my body pressing kisses against my soft stomach then my chest. Pulling the dress up higher as he does until he has me lift my arms so he can pull the dress off completely, leaving me in just my bra.

"You're so fucking beautiful." he murmurs as he kisses me. Claiming my mouth in a scorching kiss that makes my toes curl. My fingers pull at his shirt. He has too many clothes on. I want to see the body under the clothes, the one I had fantasized about most nights in my bed as I touched myself.

"You have too many clothes on." I growl as he presses his pelvis to mine, grinding against me. *Oh holy fuck he feels big!*

"Where are my manners?" he chuckles, sitting up on his knees and pulling his shirt over his head, tossing it to the floor, revealing his thick torso, hairy chest and tattoo. He moves off the bed as his hands go to his zipper and he undoes the button, pulling his jeans and boxers down freeing his cock. *And Oh. MY. Fuck.*

Holy skydaddy… he isn't just *big, he's thick.* Definitely a cock fitting of a man nicknamed 'The Mountain'. I was going to climb him like a fucking tree. His girth is just as I had thought. The heat that burns between my thighs in anticipation is making me crazy. His body made my mouth water. I've never wanted to taste a man as much as I wanted to taste him right now.

Boone strokes himself once, twice before climbing back onto the bed, hovering over me. His arms holding his weight so he doesn't crush me.

"See something you like?" His voice is thick and sends shivers through me. I want him. His tongue, his hands, his cock, his body. I want it all. He claims my mouth as my hands go to his cock, wrapping around his thick length and giving it a firm squeeze, running my thumb over his tip and feeling the precum already beading at the top. A groan escapes the back of his throat as he nips my ear, "You wicked thing." he murmurs, giving my ear another nip. When he sucks on the spot where my jaw and neck meet I can't help the whine that comes from me. He presses his hips down, grinding his cock against my cunt.

"Oliver!" I gasp. He grins against my neck.

"Fuck, you're so wet from just a little teasing." he growls, slipping his fingers down to rub my opening. I spread my legs wider and press my head into the mattress as he slips his two fingers into me, growling when he feels how drenched I am. He thrusts his thick fingers in and out of me as he moves down my body. I needed this fucking bra off.

"Scootch up and get comfortable," he instructs. Quickly I sit up, undo the clasp and throw the bra in a random direction as I slide further up the bed to the headboard. The moment my breasts were free, Boone closes his mouth around my left nipple, rolling the bud and the small barbell between his teeth. His fingers slide back inside me as he sucks on my nipple.

"I've thought about these so many times." he says, rolling his tongue over the piercing. They were sensitive. Making oh so sweet rolls of pleasure shoot down my spine straight to my core.

"Fuck!" I gasp, my legs spread more as he settles between them, smiling up at me, "I wonder how you taste, shall I find out?" My eyes almost roll back feeling his tongue lick up my slit and circle the top of my clit as he fucks me with his fingers. His beard tickles my thighs and I love it!

"Mmm. Just as I expected. You're fucking delicious." he growls diving his face into my pussy and sucking on my clit as he begins to give me the best head of my life.

"Oh god! Oh fuck!" I shout, grabbing the back of his head. Jesus skydaddy Christ his fucking tongue, his fingers. HIM.

"How are you so good at that!" I pant, in response he chuckles and lifts his head, licking his lips as he adds a third finger.

"Just naturally gifted. Much like you are with this fucking perfect body. *Fuck,* you taste so fucking good." Boone presses his tongue to my clit shaking his head as my orgasm is right there. So close. I'm about to shatter when he pulls his fingers out, placing a kiss to my scar before he climbs up my body, pressing the tip of his cock to my opening.

"If you want me to stop-" I cut him off, "Oliver Boone, If you stop I will literally kill you. Keep going, *Please!*" it was a borderline whine or beg and momentarily he is stunned but he smirks down at me, his brow cocked.

"My girl wants my cock that bad?" He asks. Slowly moving his cock against my clit. He is teasing me so deliciously bad that I grit my teeth. He takes my hands, pulling them up, pinning them above my head. The action, as much as I wish it didn't, triggers something and a faint memory flashes in my mind making my stomach roll. He sees this and lets go of my wrists.

"Hey," Boone soothes, cupping my face so I look at him. I look up into his green eyes, and his beautiful face.

"Stay with me, I'm here. You're safe. You're ok." His voice is so calm, his thumb strokes my cheek as my breathing hitches. He moves off me, sitting on his knees and pulls me into a sitting position.

"It's all you. You control everything here. Tell me what you want and I'll do it." he says, lifting one of my hands to his lips and placing gentle kisses to my fingertips. To my wrist, up my arm, then my shoulder. He kisses my collar bone then my neck. I close my eyes and tilt my head back as I get to my knees, tangling my hands into his hair and tugging his head up so I could kiss him.

Boone leans back, pulling me on top of him so my legs straddle his hips. His erection pressing against my belly. He hisses as I rub myself against his cock.

"It's all yours, baby. Claim it." he presses his lips to mine. I reach between us, lifting up and angling him to press the head of his cock against my entrance again. My hands grip his shoulders as I lower myself down onto him, his hips raising very slightly but he doesn't let himself move much more. Giving me full control over what happens. One of his hands held my hip, his fingers digging into my ass as I fully sheathed myself on him. Helping guide me.

"So fucking big." I pant as I rock back and forth on his cock, making him chuckle. Moving one hand to my breast and his other hand moves down from my ass cheek to grip my thigh.

"Don't move. A single. Muscle." I whisper in his ear. Knowing he would obey and it would drive him insane.

"As you wish m'lady. *Damn* You feel fucking fantastic." He moans as I start to ride him. He's using all his strength to keep his hips still. I could cry, both in pleasure and pain because this man is putting all the control over his body to me. Whatever I wanted to do he would let me and would give what I wanted to take.

Just for teasing sake I slow my movements and hold in the giggle when I feel his fingers dig into my thigh. He guides my hand back to grip his thigh, giving me better purchase with my movements. One hand holds his shoulder while the other grips his thigh above his knee.

CHAPTER 25

Boone

Holy. fucking. Christ. I could let her fuck me for days.

Sweat forms on my neck as Tabitha rides my cock. My hand bites into her ass so hard I worry it would bruise. She controlled everything here. I wouldn't do anything unless she wanted me to, including thrust into her amazing pussy. This was all about her. And I wasn't complaining at all, it was fucking fantastic. To watch her take control. Even if I wanted nothing more than to move with her, fuck her. Take her. All the things I want to do could wait.

Of all those things; nothing could compare to the sight of Tabitha, leaning back with her hands gripping my thighs as she rode me cowgirl style. Her breasts bouncing, head thrown back in pure bliss. I'm not religious at all but this was as close to heaven or Valhalla as I was probably ever going to get.

"Oliver." she pants. Fuck I love hearing my name on her lips. She lifts almost fully off of my cock before slamming back down. Letting gravity work as she rode me like the animal I was.

"Fuck, you feel so good fucking me." I groan, feeling her tighten. I smile up at her, rolling her nipples between my fingers. I can feel her walls tightening around my cock. She was close. I move my hand down so my thumb can rub her clit, slowly up and down in featherlight touches letting the juices coat my thumb before rubbing circles around the bud.

"That's it. Keep going. Grind that sweet pussy on my cock." I urged, my voice comes out breathy, "You're so *fucking* close, I can feel you almost there. Claim my cock. It's yours." Leaning further back so I can watch as she bounces up and down on my cock as I play with her clit. "Do you like this?" I ask, smiling when she nods. Her panting made her unable to form coherent words.

Tabitha leans forward. Resting her palms against my chest. Her eyes close as she starts to moan louder, her movements sporadic.

"So fucking hot, watching you use my cock to make yourself come. Fuck, baby keep going. Just like that. Oh fuck." I feel her tighten around my cock as I press my thumb to her clit, rubbing it in slow circles as her fingers dig into my chest as she moves faster. I was so so so tempted to just thrust my hips and help her get to her climax faster but this was all her. I hadn't realized how much I would enjoy watching her like this but here I was, ready to explode as her breaths came out short and hard letting her make me her fuck toy. I almost come the moment she lets out a blissful cry. Her pussy spasms on my cock, soaking me with her juices as she comes. It is a sight that I will burn into my memory. My girl getting off by using my cock. I lift my hips pumping into her slowly as she rides her climax out. The movement milking her orgasm as she cries out, "Keep doing that!"

I bite out a curse as I slowly thrust up into her. Feeling her tighten around my cock. It's perfection.

"Oh fuck. I'm." wetness coates my cock again and I smile as she cries out, orgasming a second time.

"Tell me what you want, Tabitha." I'm still hard and willing.

"Words. Baby. use your words." I beg when all she responds with is incoherent panting.

"I want you… to.. Fuck me." she gasps. I slow my thrusts. "How do you want me to fuck you?" I ask through gritted teeth. Her face is flushed red.

"From behind. Take me." she answers. I nod. Finally

I could weep.

"Then, on your knees, you fucking beautiful woman. And let me take care of you." my voice sounds husky and low, she sighs as she climbs off me, turning so I am able to see her amazing ass. I press a kiss to the back of her shoulder blade as I used my knees to spread her legs wider. My cock still slick with her juices as I position it at her entrance. Tabitha moans, pressing her ass back against my pelvis as I slide into her.

"That's it. My Good girl." my hand smooths down her spine and I feel her shiver. "Are you ready for me to move?" I ask, she nods. I grip her hips as I start to thrust. Tabitha grabbed one of the pillows and moaned into it. Letting out a string of curse words as I pump into her.

"Harder." She pants softly.

"What was that? I don't think I heard you clearly." I smirk, pulling out to the tip and stopping. "Words baby. Use them."

"I said, 'Fuck. Me. Harder.'" she grits. Yelping when my palm strikes her ass cheek.

"Yes ma'am. My cock is yours. Yours to do what you want with." my hips piston, thrusting harder as she pushes back to meet my thrusts. Tabitha pushes her face into the pillow and I reach around, pulling it from her.

"Don't muffle your moans baby. I want to hear you scream my name." I say, thrusting into her. Every fucking fantasy I had thought of over the past few weeks couldn't hold a candle to just how fucking amazing her body actually feels. She is vocal with her pleasure, her cries grow louder and louder and I am super happy I had the split decision to not take her by the pool where not only could we have been seen but most definitely would have been heard. I pull out of her, flipping her onto her back, she lets out a squeal as I re enter her. Her nails scratch down my back as she holds onto me.

Her legs wrap around my waist, "I can feel you gripping my cock, come for me baby. Let me feel you come on my cock again." I grunt, quickening my thrusts.

"Oliver!" she screams, arching her back as she comes. Her pussy squeezes my cock as I hit my limit and come so hard I see fucking stars.

A thin layer of sweat coats Tabitha's body, she groans as I pull out of her, my cum leaks out of her pussy. My eyes lock onto her mismatched ones as I smile at her, "Hi." she squeaks.

"Hi there." I reply, flopping down next to her, not breaking eye contact.

"So we're definitely not just friends anymore right?" she snickers. I bark out a laugh, "Baby, I don't think we ever were 'just friends', pretty sure we were just refusing to accept that we've wanted to fuck each others brains out since we met." I smile at her, pulling her in and press my lips to hers, my cock stiffening at the contact of her naked body..

"This fucking body. Christ, I can't get enough of you." I breathe kissing down her neck. She giggles and presses a hand to my chest.

"Ease up there cowboy." I kiss her on the nose and roll off the bed.

"I'll be right back." I say taking a few steps into my en suite bathroom. I run a washcloth under the sink and squeeze it out before walking back to the bed. Taking a moment to just admire the beautiful naked woman spread out before me like my own personal feast. I carefully wipe the cum off her pussy, placing a kiss over the scar. It enrages me to see it. That fucking psycho had hurt her, permanently marked her body. Instead of rotting he was walking around free somewhere.

I press kisses down the scar then one right over her clit. Tabitha sighs, her legs falling open. Her hips buck when my tongue prods her entrance.

"You are insatiable." she chuckles as I spread her lips and lick her slit from the bottom to top.

"I don't think I'm done with you yet." I muse, placing her legs over my shoulders before I start eating her pussy. She digs her heels into my back and a few moments later she comes all over my face and beard.

Yep I would definitely never get tired of this.

CHAPTER 26

Boone

After having probably the best sex of my life. I had the best sleep I've gotten in a while. Tabitha slept next to me, Her chest slowly rose and fell. Her copper red hair is a mess on the pillow. Her naked ass is pressed against my now hard dick.

"You're humping me." she mutters sleepily. I press my face into her shoulder blade wanting to just enjoy the moment longer of feeling her body against mine and inhaling the scent of her strawberry body lotion.

"I can't help it. I am fully addicted to your body, I want to keep you in this bed forever." I press a kiss to her shoulder blade and then her neck.

Tabitha twists around sliding her leg over my hip and getting on top of me, the sheet she had wrapped around her falls away from her body and I physically couldn't get any harder than I was right now. I wanted to be inside her again. Fuck I feel like a horny teenager. She presses a kiss to my chest and moves down my body quickly. It takes point two seconds to realize that she isn't getting out of bed.

"Oh fuck!" I bite into my fist as she takes my whole length into her hot mouth. My hand fists her hair as she bobs her head on my cock.

"Oh, Shit, Tabitha." If it wasn't for the shrill ringing of my phone going off in my jeans on the floor scaring the shit out of both of us, I would have probably coated her throat with cum. But no, I accidentally hit the back of her throat with my dick making her gag and almost choke, "Shit are you ok?" I ask as she waves me off while coughing so hard her eyes are red.

"I'm gonna fucking kill him." I growl, listening to Joch's ringtone going off. *Call me Baby* blares in my pants pocket.

Tabitha wipes her chin, giggling as I throw off the covers and see Joch texted me ten times. Oh shit. It was almost eight-forty five am and practice was at eight thirty. His photo popped up on the screen as the song began again.

"I know, I know I'm late. I just got up." I answer.

"Well good morning to you too." Joch greeted, "Where did you two sneak off to yesterday?" he asked.

"None of your business." I reply, pulling open my drawer and grabbing clean boxers and a shirt.

Joch chuckles, "Finally! Casey owes me twenty bucks."

"Fuck you." I say, pulling on my boxers and pants. Tabitha watches me from her spot on the bed, bundled in the blanket.

"Pretty sure Tj already did that. But hey, name the place big boy, I'll bring the lube." He purred.

"I'll see you at the arena." I said, as he calls out, "Give Tabs a kiss from me!"

"As much as I would love to stay in this bed all day, I have to go. I'm late." Tabitha pushes up onto her knees and crawls to the end of the bed and fuck me, I am hard again.

"See you later then?" She asks, running a hand up my chest before brushing her lips against mine.

"Fuuuck, Baby girl. I can't be late." I groan against her lips.

She gives my chest a slight push, "Then get going." she smiles. I fisted her hair and pull her to me, pressing a searing hot kiss to her lips, "I'll get you back for that later." I promise as I see the lust clouding her eyes.

She was gonna be the death of me.

"So you two still just friends?" Joch smiled at me after practice. I stand under the cold spray of the shower and roll my eyes, shaking my head.

"I'm not giving you a play by play of my sex life bro."

Joch drummed his hands on the cinderblock stall divider as he let out a 'Whoop!'

"Yes! Finally, Brother you two were moving so slow, thought you'd never get together. Proud of you!" He pulls back his blonde mane of hair, tying it into a bun before massaging beard oil into his blonde beard.

"What makes you think we had sex?" I challenge. He lets out a snort.

"The claw marks say it all. Is she coming to the game Thursday?" 'Claw marks'? I turned to the mirror and yep, sure enough my hell cat had left long scratches on my back. Hot.

"Probably. I have to ask her." I say, pulling on my boxers and jeans. My phone had several messages from fucking Hank and one from Tabitha that was a photo.

I couldn't stop the smile that spread across my face seeing it was a mirror selfie of her in a white t-shirt and a pair of ripped jeans. The photo was captioned, 'Got called in to work, looks like I'll see you later tonight. Xo.'

I send her a reply letting her know I'd have food waiting for her when she got off and right when I hit send my phone started ringing. Hank. Ignore.

I wasn't going to let him ruin my day. The results for the test would be back in three weeks. Then I would be able to donate my bone marrow to Tate and he would be ok.

We had back to back games this next week and I couldn't let Hank get in my head.

CHAPTER 27

Tabitha

Taphowze was super busy when I clocked in. The bar had Christmas lights put up around the tvs and the bar. Boone had texted me telling me to use the suv since the Corolla was acting up.

I pulled my hair into a clip as I jumped behind the bar.

"Hey Georgia." I call as she rushed from the kitchen carrying a tray of food. Her blonde hair was in a messy bun. And she was sans her normal makeup.

I sunk into the robotic act of taking orders, filling drinks, refilling drinks. Taking tips, cashing out. All muscle memory taking over. Before I know it, a few hours had passed. Finally, around six, the bar has cleared out enough for the closers to be good. Georgia wipes her forehead, "Thanks for coming in. It was crazy!" she's shoving her tips into her purse under the bar making room in her apron. Her fingers play with her pink lighter.

"No problem. I wasn't busy." I reply, drying a glass. Georgia narrows her eyes at me, and I raise a brow at her.

"What?" I ask.

"You got laid!" she squealed, covering her mouth as several patrons glanced over at us i shush her.

"How could you possibly know that?" Did I have a hickey? I didn't see anything earlier.

"You're not as… stiff as the other day. Good job girl. Landing yourself 'The Mountain.'" she winks.

"Ok. enough. I'll see you Sunday." I pull my coat on. When I step outside I'm greeted by a bright camera flash going off in my face.

"Fuck, what the hell?" I hiss. blinking away the spots that danced in my eyes.

A man with a balding head stands in front of me with a camera. He's wearing a red sweater and a black hat.

"Can I fucking help you?" Never be nice to creeps. Learned that lesson growing up. It's better to be rude than let them think they can be creepy with you.

"You're the girl who is in the photos with Oliver Boone. Are you his new girlfriend? Hookup? What's your name? You look young, is he really looking to settle down soon?" The man spewed off so many questions at once I couldn't even follow what he was asking but my guard went right up when he began asking about Boone. What photos was he talking about?

"No comment. Get the fuck away from me." I snarl, he stepped in my way, snapping more photos.

"Get the fuck away from me!" I yell, shoving him out of my way. He toppled backwards and I got into the truck, leaving as fast as I could.

By the time I got home, Boone was showered and drying his hair. The sight of him had my blood heating at the memory of last night. I set the keys down on the table and he gave me a smile.

"Hey, how was work?" He asked, followed by, "What's wrong?" when he saw my face.

"It was fine until some guy shoved a camera in my face and started asking me a bunch of questions about you. And photos of us?" Boones brows pulled in.

"What? When did this happen?" he comes to my side.

"It was as I was leaving work. He was a big, ratty looking guy, never saw him before. But he was talking about photos?"

Boone squeezes my shoulders, "I have no clue what's going on. But I can find out." He says grabbing his phone. Boone let out a string of curse words in both English and French. I didn't even know he spoke French.

"I found out what photos." he turns his phone to me. Its some news website with the title, *'The Mountain's secret girlfriend'* underneath is a photo of me and Boone at the team camping trip on the dock. Then another one of us sneaking away from everyone. I feel sick. More photos of me at the campsite talking to Bohdie. The article goes into talking about a "close source" to the team says that 'Tabitha is between two players at the moment, unable to choose from Oliver and Bhoden.'

"What!" I continue to read the article. According to this close personal friend, I have caused friction between the two friends. And as a new addition to the growing girlfriend lists the source doesn't think the relationship will last long as "they don't know each other too well." It's like a gut punch. That last part is true. I knew bits about Boone, like about his mom and some basic stuff. I knew about Tate. But that was really all I knew. Besides knowing how he felt inside me….Shit now I was getting wet just thinking about him being inside me. I knew about his taking ballet as a kid to help his balance.

"I know who did this. I'm gonna take care of it. I promise." Boone says.

"It's already out there. My photos. I didn't expect this would be happening this fast."

"This was all Jannette. She was jealous of you. She had to be the one to take the photos. She's vindictive enough." Boone explains.

"She was right about one thing. I *don't* know you too well. Everything happened so fast. I don't really know much about you."

Boone lets out a breath.

"Will you go somewhere with me?" He suddenly asked.

"Uh, sure. Where?"

He reaches over and picks up the keys, "Since this is getting more serious, then you *should* know more about me." he agrees.

I quickly figured out who he was talking about once we pulled into the parking garage of the Seattle Children's Hospital. Once we get to the fourth floor I follow Boone down the hall to a half closed door and knocks before opening it.

"Hey there kid." he greets.

"Oliver! Mom, it's Oliver!" a happy voice says from in the room.

I step into the room, it is decorated with drawings and pictures. It's very lived in, he'd been here for a long time. The little boy who I realize must be Tate, sat in the bed on his knees, he looked a little like Boone, the same smile and way his eyes lit up. He has slightly pale skin and dark bags under his eyes, in his arm was an IV that was connected to three bags hanging next to the bed. Boone high fived him and pulled up a chair next to the bed.

"Hey, I wanted to introduce you to someone." He said looking over to me and holding his hand out for me.

"Tate, this is Tabitha." he smiled. I walked over and Tate smiled up at me, he had on a Seattle Skyhawks fluffy robe over his hospital clothes. Tate smiled at me, "Are you his girlfriend?" He asked, "Tatum! Don't be rude." a woman who I hadn't even noticed walk in. She must have been Tates mom, Marissa.

She was dressed in light gray lounge pants and a matching oversized zip up sweater with a black shirt underneath it.

Her dark brown hair was pulled back into a bun. I'm a bit startled at how young she looks. She's almost Boones age and from what he told me about his father I wouldn't be surprised if Marissa was in her mid twenties.

"This is my friend Tabitha." Boone introduced.

She smiles at me and holds her hand out for me to shake, "I'm Marissa."

"Nice to meet you." I returned her warmth. Her eyes were so kind but there was a weariness to them. No doubt from spending months in the hospital watching her only child suffer from cancer. She looked as if she had lived years beyond what her actual age was.

"Oliver. Nice to see you as always." she nodded at Boone. Boone smiled back at her, "I just wanted to stop by and see my good luck charm before tomorrow's game." he said ruffling the hat that Tate had on his head.

"Tabby did you know Oliver is the best hockey player ever!" Tate asked me. His smile big and wide, he was so happy and energetic. You'd never know how sick he was.

I let out a giggle, "Really? I had no idea." I shot Boone a look of amazement, "You never told me you were the 'best player ever!' I wonder why you never said anything."

"It's because he is too hummer." Tate said scratching a new color on the picture he was drawing on the large tray across his bed.

"I think you mean 'Humble, sweetie." Marissa said, chuckling. Tate just shrugged, "Either way, the Skyhawks will win the Stanley this year! I'm gonna be at the game. Right mom?" Tate asked, looking at his mom. Marissa visibly tensed and nodded, "You betcha sweetie." If Tate noticed, he didn't show it. I felt the stab in my chest as I watched her, she moved around the room so easily, every inch probably burned into memory. Next to Tates bed was a smaller twin bed made up with a lilac blanket and a side table with an overnight bag sat on top of it. Of course she slept here too. Who wouldn't.

Tate talked Boones ear off and Boone was fully invested into everything Tate said. At one point Tate turned to me and started to ask me questions and Boone took the moment to step back and talk to Marissa.

CHAPTER 28

Boone

If my heart could squeeze any tighter it would at the sight of Tabitha with Tate. He was talking her ear off as he pulled out his Ipad to show her his favorite movie, D-3 the Mighty Ducks. Tabitha was so invested into the movie with him and when she said she had never seen the other movies, Tates eyes went wide and he shook his head, "Hold up! We can't start at movie three then! We gotta watch the whole enchilada." He started the first movie and was explaining to her Emilios character and why he was sent to teach the team.

"Where is Hank?" I asked Marissa. Her tired eyes close and she lets out a yoga sigh.

"He comes when he can." her lips stretch into a weary smile. My anger bubbles. Hank was choosing money over his kid again. Marissa was a legal partner in her fathers firm. When Tate first got sick she stepped away and took on less cases so she was able to be with her son. Like you know, a good parent.

"The doctor has a new chemo that has promising results in the trials that he thinks might help Tate." She says. That was something good. If it worked then he may not need a transplant.

Visiting hours were going to end soon and Tate was getting a little grouchy because he wanted to finish the movie with Tabitha. This was the hard part. Tabitha asked him if it was ok if she came back soon and they could have a movie marathon because she liked the Ducks. Tates face lit up like a

Christmas tree, he was so happy and it made leaving for the night easier.

Marissa walks us out to the hall to say goodbye, I have my arm around Tabitha's shoulders. It's then that I see the man in the suit at the end of the hall. I tense as he approaches. The last person I want to see right now.

"This is what you've been doing. Instead of *helping* your family. Parading around all over town with a trollop instead of being there for my son." he hisses. I remove my arm from around Tabitha's shoulders and stand in front of her.

"Hank!" Marissa looks at him appalled.

"Watch your fucking mouth, Hank." I growl. Hank's salty brown hair is slightly disheveled and I can smell the faint lingering scent of perfume. *He's cheating on his wife while his kid dies from cancer.*

I hated this man more than anything in the world, he disgusted me.

"No! You Ungrateful brat. I did everything to get you a good education while that woman spent every dime. And all I ask is that you help my son." I step into his space, getting right up in his face, "No. My *mother* made sure I had an education. She did *everything* and if you say. One. More. Word about my friend or my mother, I will punch your teeth in." my voice is low, threatening.

"The perfume smells nice by the way," I whisper.

Hank sputters and backs down like the pathetic worm he is.

"Enough, please!" Marissa whispers, stepping between us.

"He is asleep, say hi if you wish, but then go home." She says to Hank.

"So that was my birth father." I say to Tabitha as we get into the elevator.

I was going to immediately get to bed the moment I walk in the door, But when Tabitha takes off her hoodie and stretches out on the couch like a cat, I stop. I can see her nipple piercings poking through her tight white shirt. Even the black thin bralette couldn't hide anything. She stretches her arms up over her head, her back arching as she does. Her fucking body was magnificent.

Her gaze meets mine and her eyes darken.

"What?" she asks. I walk toward her slowly, taking in every inch of her from her fiery hair down to her white socks.

Her breathing hitches as I crawl over her. Running my hands up her ribcage and under her shirt to cup her breast.

"Getting to know you better."

"When did you get these?" I asked as my thumbs traced over the two small barbells, one through each nipple. Her eyes close and her head presses into the cushion as she inhales sharply at the touches.

"Th-three years ago. Perry got some piercings and I –Wanted to get them done." she shudders as I lean down, taking one of her nipples into my mouth, teasing the piercing with my tongue.

"I guess the theory about it making them more sensitive was right?" I chuckle, seeing her biting onto her lip as she lets out a soft moan. The entire time her hands are above her head, as I lap my tongue over the other nipple. My cock aches as it strains against my zipper. Tabitha's back arches into me and she presses her pelvis to mine grinding against me. Slipping one hand between our bodies I undo the top of her pants. She is soaked, my two fingers able to slip in easily. Fuck I need to be inside her. Tabitha moans as I move my fingers inside her, curling them so I could hit that spot that would drive her mad. My teeth sink onto her left nipple and she shrieks. Digging her nails into my scalp.

"Boone!" I smirk at this. My girl had super sensitive nipples and fuck her legs were starting to shake as I tease her nipple more.

"Fuck baby." I feel her climax, squeezing my fingers between her legs as she shakes.

"No god here, Baby girl, just me." I grin. She comes down from her orgasm, looking up at me with those beautiful blue and green eyes, "Don't stop. Harder please." the sight was erotic as fuck, slipping my fingers from her I manage to undo my pants, yanking hers down to her knees just enough so I could get inside her. She yelps as I flip her onto her stomach and enter her from behind.

"Oliver!" she cries out, squeezing my cock. Her face presses into the couch cushion and she lets out a loud moan as I start moving inside her. Groaning as the angle only left us with limited mobility due to her pants keeping her knees from opening more.

"Oh fuck, you feel so good." I pant, leaning against her back.

"I love the feeling of you inside me. *Fuck!* Oh my god Oliver!" her voice rose with every thrust. Across the living room was a mirror on the wall, an idea popped into my head. I wrap one arm under her chest and lifted her up so her back was flat against my chest.

"Look at yourself, baby girl. Look how fucking beautiful you are as you come on my cock." I whispered into her ear right before I closed my mouth over the spot on her neck. Locking my eyes on hers in the mirror. The sight was enough to make my balls tighten. Her shirt sits above her tits as the black bralette is pulled down around her elbows, her thighs spread just enough so my cock could slide in and out of her beautiful pussy.

Tabitha's head snapped back against my shoulder as she screams. Her orgasm rocking through her body right as mine hit me. And I was greatful I had put that fucking mirror up. Both of us collapse onto the couch. A layer of sweat coating both our bodies.

We stay as we were for a little bit letting our bodies come down and relax. Tabitha kicks off her pants before she stands, staggering slightly as she enters the downstairs bathroom. Coming back a few minutes later, standing in the doorway in just a thong and see through the shirt. Aaaannnnd my cock is hard again.

"Someone can't get enough can you?" she says.

"Only with you." I say.

She shoots me a devilish smirk that has me leaping from the couch, throwing her over my shoulder and carrying her up to my room.

CHAPTER 29

Tabitha

When Casey told me we were getting ready she was serious. She had her hair in heatless curls, a fresh spray tan and her lashes done. She dressed in blue skinny jeans, high riding boots and a Skyhawks Jersey with a white beanie. Casey was one of the full glam girls, I really can't wait to introduce her to Perry. They would get along well. I missed my friend. She was going to be home a few days after Christmas so I would see her soon.

When we arrived at the arena, I have on dark jeans, a long white sleeved turtle neck with a black and blue toque.

Paparazzi are everywhere outside the arena. Since the photos leaked by Jannette, they had already started to camp out front of the neighborhood gates.

"Once you and Oli go officially public, it'll be like Travis and Taylor with the media craze. But It'll pass after a while and not be as hectic." Casey says as we pull into the parking gate.

"I mean we haven't talked about it really now that you mentioned it. It's new to both of us so I don't really know." Mostly we have just been fucking like teenagers and not really doing dates yet. Casey blinks then lets out a breath, "I'm gonna throttle that boy." then she claps her hands, "Idea! I have the perfect jersey for you to wear over." she smiles. After a stop at the team shop, Casey leads me through the crowded back hall that the players would walk through to get to the ice, and she smiles at Bohdie.

"Hey good luck Goalie!" She calls. Bohdie smiles at her, his sandy blonde hair gelled back.

"Good luck." I wave as we moved through the crowd, he looks at my jersey and his face turns a shade of pink.

"Thank you." he calls.

"Shouldn't we be in the box? The game is about to start." I ask as she pulls me to the locker room area.

"Just have to wish my bro good luck." She has something up her sleeve. I can see the gleam in her eyes.

Joch and Boone are the first out of the locker room to head toward the ice, Boone caught sight of me and smiled. His eyes look at the jersey and he frowns. His eyes narrowed, "Where did you get that?" he asks. I look down at the jersey Casey had me wear. It was Bohdies. His number on the chest and back.

"I don't have anything else with the team name on it yet. It was a gift." I shrug. A muscle in Boones jaw ticks and he looks ahead, "He...Alright." he nods and continues down the hall. Irritation and confusion immediately burn up my spine because what was that about? Joch gave me a smile and followed after Boone.

"The fuck was that about? Is he mad at me?" I ask Casey. She was smiling as she threw an arm around my shoulders.

"Nah, He just needs to be clear of his intentions now." she grins and i get it now. This was her plan.

"Wait, that was why you had me wear Bohdies jersey?" I cock a brow.

"Trust me. Ok. Let's go to the box and watch the game." she laughs.

We get to the box right as the game starts and immediately I notice that Boone seems to be hitting extra hard tonight. You'd think someone pissed in his hockey skates. Halfway through the first quarter, someone from the team shop walks into the box and calls my name.

"I was asked to deliver this to you miss." he says, handing me a large black gift bag. I sit up from my seat and take the bag from his hand.

"Thank you."

When I open the bag I see a note on top of what looks like a shirt, jersey, and hoodie.

'Now you have the right number.'

Lifting the jersey out of the bag I see it has Boones name and number. His number is on all of them. Casey lets out a laugh, "Well, guess it's settled." She smiles. I look down at the ice, the fifteen minute halftime starts and my irritation grows. We never talked about us ever. Never had that conversation about me being his girlfriend or any of it. Hell I fucking was technically living with him and sleeping in his bed the past week. I could describe the feeling of his cock inside me and the way it felt in my mouth even the feeling of his cum as it dripped down my thighs in the shower. But god forbid we take a moment to have the "Hey we're official right?" Unless.... He wasn't sure about us being official. Boone and I had been fooling around for a few weeks now and we hadn't gone out in public on a date. My head feels like it's going to explode. What if he doesn't want to be official.... I'm good enough to fuck But not commit to?

"You ok?" Casey asks. She's looking at me concerned. I nod, "Yes. I'm OK. Just miffed." I say.

The game ends and I don't know the score because I leave early. I'm down in the hallway that leads to the locker room waiting.

"Hey Tabitha." someone says. I look up and smile at Bohdie. He's already showered and dressed before the team even is back.

"How did you get changed so fast?" I ask.

"Oh I wasn't in the second half, I jammed my shoulder in one of the fights. Coach said to ice it and see the doc." My eyes widen and I look at his left shoulder where an ice pack is bandage wrapped around his shoulder.

"Are you ok?"

"Yeah, I'll be fine. Just a little rest and ice is all it needs." He clears his throat and looks at me sheepishly, "So you want me to sign your jersey?" I nod and dig through my bag and grab a pink sharpie I have from work.

"Yeah! You're the best goalie ever!" Bohdies face turns red and I spin so he can sign the back of the jersey.

"Don't let the others hear you say that. But I appreciate it." he says. When I spin back around to face him my smile is big. It was impossible not to smile around Bohdie. He's adorable. He's like that golden retriever at the family party.

"I guess my favorite player has to be Boone since we're together now." I chuckle. Bohdie tilts his head and looks surprised. "Oh you two are together? I didn't know that. It's about time." He sputters.

"Boone didn't say anything about it?" I ask. Bohdie shakes his head, "hasn't said a thing to me." My smile doesn't falter when I see Boone standing behind Bohdie, in his full gear in the middle of the hallway staring at me and Bohdie. My smile does falter when I realize he's glaring and he's also storming over to us. Bohdie notices him and right as he says "Hey man." Boones hand goes around to cup the back of my neck as he lowers his mouth to mine. The whole thing screams *territorial male* and not gonna lie it's a little hot. He lets go of my neck and looks at Bohdie, "Stay in your lane Boden."

"My lane?" Bohdies face is pale as Boone gets into his face.

"You know *exactly* what I mean." he growls and walks off to the locker room.

"Well, that was intense. Wish I had someone like that." Bohdie cleared his throat. His face was beet red now. If I wasn't so riled up I'd tell him he'd find someone one day. But I was already charging into the locker room. Boone had never spoken to Bohdie like that before. And why would he be so rude to him?

Several players who were in the middle of undressing scrambled to cover their bits and pieces and Joch stood up from the bench he had been sitting on, just in his hockey pants and no shirt. His blonde mane of hair was a mess after the game. My eyes are locked on Oliver Boone.

"What was that about?" I cross my arms over my chest. Boone is shocked to see me but I can see the storm in his eyes still. His eyes narrow at Bohdies jersey I still had on.

"Take it off." he says. I gape at him.

"No. It was a gift." I say.

"He should know better than to give you one of his game jerseys." I raise a brow at him.

"Who?"

"Nothing. Look, we can talk after I get changed." oh fuck no he isn't blowing me off. No way am I just gonna walk out with my tail between my legs. Instead I raise a brow and smirk at him. He thinks Bohdie gave me this jersey.

"Now is a perfect time in my opinion."

"Tabs, maybe now isn't the best time." Joch chimes in, unease written all over his face as he looks from Boone to me.

"Oliver." my tone makes him wince.

He slams his locker and grabs my hand, pulling me through a set of doors to an empty adjoining locker room. I rip my hand from his and glare at him.

"What the fuck was that about with Bohdie huh?"

He shakes his head and goes to the showers ignoring my question. Pulling off his jersey and pants as he does, tossing them onto the center bench before he walks his bare ass into the open showers. Next to the showers is a large cubby of folded towels and some wrapped soap bars. He grabs a towel and soap as he passes it.

"Where are you going!"

"To shower, if you don't mind. I reek." He calls back, turning the shower on. The room fills with a light layer of steam.

"You owe Bohdie an apology." I state. Boone lets out a laugh, "Ha! After that stunt. Hell no." What was he talking about? What stunt did Bohdie pull? He was just talking to me and then Boone went all caveman.

"Ok, you need to explain to me now what am I missing Oliver?" I say. He lathers the soap into his hair and body, turning around to let me get a free show as he washes himself off. His muscles flexing as he rubs his shoulder and biceps. I wasn't going to let the fact that he was mouthwateringly sexy make me forget or ignore what happened.

"Bohdie has a thing for you. That is what you're missing." he says. Now it's my turn to let out a laugh. Because what!

"*That* is what has you all agro and like someone shoved a puck up your ass? You're *jealous*?" he was fucking jealous of Bohdie?

"Bohdie is one of the biggest fuck boys in the team. He may not seem like it but he has a higher body count than Joch and Tig put together. He does this. The whole innocent friend act then he makes his move." That was the most ridiculous thing I had ever heard.

"And you are jealous like a fucking child because why? Because I got some male attention? Another man looked at your new toy?"

Boones eyes shoot to mine, hurt and anger clouding them, "You are not a toy to me Tabitha." he glowered. I scoffed, "Really? Then why did you refer to me as your friend with Tate, or why didn't you correct Hank and Marissa? You said, 'she's just a friend.' So what am I? Your fuck toy? Your girlfriend? Does anyone on the team know we are together?" like a flash, Boone is in front of me, hand threaded through the back of my hair at the neck. His green eyes are blazing. Water dripping from his body.

"I don't tell 'fuck toys' personal shit about my life. I don't introduce 'fuck toys' to my little brother. I don't invite 'fuck toys' to live with me." he tightens his grip as he speaks and it sends a jolt of lust down my spine, "So no, Tabitha. You are not 'Just a fuck toy' you are the woman that I have fallen head over heels for and care for deeply." My knees felt weak.

He takes the bag from my hand and holds his jersey out to me. When I make no move to put it on he growls. Stepping closer to me he grabs the end of Bohdies jersey, ripping it down the center before pulling his jersey over my head in its place. The whole thing has me opening and closing my mouth like a fish. Because one that was hot. And two he did it so effortlessly.

"You sleep in my bed, you scream my name when you come, you wear my number, Baby girl." he spoke, His voice husky. He lifts my chin up to look at him. His green emerald eyes, stony-like as they bored into my own.

His thumb stroked my chin, "I don't share." he smirks, "Unless that is something you'd want, in which case we'd need to have a separate conversation." my face heats as he bends down so he is eye level with me.

"So what if I wanted to share with someone like Bohdie? I mean you never really officially claimed me." he's wound up from the game and the spark of jealousy in his eyes is actually kinda hot. I shouldn't push him but dammit I *want* him to be fired up.

He smiles at me, his eyes darkening as he backs me up against the lockers.

"Once I get you home I will claim you. Multiple times. In multiple ways." he promises.

"Now, you should go before I ravish you in the shower." He adds.

"I don't know. I kinda like seeing you riled up. Especially over the idea of me and Bohdie?" I smirk. Boone grinds his pelvis against me and I groan, tilting back my head giving him access to my neck. He bites onto my shoulder not too hard, but enough to leave a light mark.

"Don't joke with me on this Tabitha, I will take you right here, right now." He growled against my neck, setting me down and squeezing my ass.

"I'll be waiting outside." I roll my eyes and leave the locker room.

CHAPTER 30

Boone

I've never been the jealous type. Ever. But when I saw Tabitha turn up to the game wearing Bohdies number on her jersey, and then saw Bohdie with her afterward. The way he smiled at her..... something inside me sparked. I realize that maybe I should have been more clear about my intentions and feelings. As soon as we get home, that was exactly what I was going to do. I was going to make sure my girl knew how I felt.

The team had won and the adrenaline high was still strong. The moment I step out of the locker room I bristle at the sound of cameras clicking and Tabithas irritated voice saying, "Back off."

She stands at the entrance to the hallway that leads to the parking lot, a man is standing too close for comfort as he snaps photos of her. He's shoving the camera in her face and practically pushing her back with every step forward..

"Come on, which player are you fucking? Is it more than one? You showed up wearing Bohdens jersey but left the locker room with The Mountains, so two for one?" he asks, backing her up into a corner.

"Fuck off!" Tabitha growls at him.

"I'm not taking that answer. Come on! Are you a puck bunny or a wag?"

"Unless you want me to shove my skates up your ass. Move." I growl. The poor fuck looks like he is about to piss himself as I tower over him. I'm a good almost two feet taller than him.

"Let's go Boone." Tabitha says, grabbing my arm. We leave and get into the truck as paparazzi snap photos from the lot gates, Tabitha has her head low as she ducks into the passenger seat.

"Are you ok?" my hand rubs her knee, "Yea, I'm good. Can we go home?" She asks, slouching down in her seat. It hurts to see her uncomfortable. Even though the windows were heavily tinted, she looked worried.

The moment we pull into the development she seems to relax only slightly.

"Hey," I had to have this talk with her. She turns to look at me. I motioned for her to come to me and she giggled but climbed over the center console to sit on my lap, her legs straddling mine. Her hands resting on my shoulders.

"Are you ok?" I ask. She nods, "It was an asshole with a camera. I'll live." she forces a smile.

"Tabitha. I want to be with you. And I want you to be with me. I need to know that you are ok with being in my life with all the chaos that it comes with. It wouldn't be fair to not warn you of what comes with being with me." I explain as I cup her face in my large hands.

"The paparazzi, online comments. Can be brutal. And unfair. But if you decide to start this with me, you will not regret it." I had seen first hand how some of the guys had to go through it with their wives and girlfriends. The horrible things that could be said at them online was horrendous. The disgusting things that people would say or do. It took a thick skin to handle the bullshit people could say. If she did this with me, she would be subjected to the scrutiny of paparazzi and the public. If she chose not to then I would let her go- even if it killed me to. It wasn't fair to force her into misery she didn't want.

"It will take some getting used to, but I can handle it." she said, pecking my nose with a kiss.

"Really? Are you sure?" I ask.

"I lived through that hell house in my last foster home. Believe me. I got this."

"Sorry, but." She tugs on the jersey, "Can you help me, It's stuck. And I'm a little too warm." that glint of devilishness in her eyes.

"My boyfriend doesn't want me wearing a jersey that isn't his but the one he gave me is a little tight."

"Your boyfriend eh?" I chuckle lifting the ends of the jersey and her shirt up.

"Yea. His nickname is The Mountain. He plays hockey. And is extremely sexy." her hips roll against my pelvis and my cock hardens.

"What a lucky man. To have such a dedicated Girlfriend like you." I muse, pulling the jersey off so I could crumple it and toss it in the back seat. I'd buy her as many jerseys as she wanted. She has on a black lace bralette under the white long sleeved sweater.

I'm opening the door and tossing her over my shoulder and carrying her into the house.

CHAPTER 31

Tabitha

The news of two new break-ins has the entire neighborhood on edge. Kaminskey and his wife decided to move and Boone was going with a few other guys from the team to help them move. I was sitting at the table with my textbooks open and laptop in front of me. My hair in a messy bun with a claw clip on the top of my head. I had one more exam before the semester was over and I just wanted this to be done with.

"I'll be back in a bit. Have fun with Business insurance law." Boone smirked, pressing a kiss to my forehead.

"Ha-ha, business insurance law is totally amusing." I roll my eyes.

"Ohh sassy sassy." his eyes gleamed as he strode toward me, his hand cups my chin and he lifts my face to look up at him.

"Have I ever mentioned how absolutely sexy this look is? So many school fantasies." he mutters. His lips brushing against mine with every word.

"Careful or I'll have to give you a detention." I chuckle, playfully slapping his iron hard ass. His nose crinkles as he smiles down at me.

"I'll play with you later." he promised as his eyes appraise me.

"Text me what you want from the grocery store, as soon as I'm done here I'm gonna do a food run." I called.

"Anything for the lady of the house." he replies as he leaves through the front and I hear the sound of the key locking.

After another hour I give up and need a break. Both Boone and I are early birds so we had been up since five. It was ten when I decide to go to the grocery store, tossing the laundry into the drier before I leave, throwing one of Boones hoodies on as I do.

Shopping was different now that I was an official girlfriend of an NHL player. I would catch people looking at me and sometimes snapping photos on their phones. That and the unnerving feeling like I was being followed after that skeezy reporter cornered me outside of TAPHOWZE then managed to be at the arena too. I didn't say anything to Boone but...since the incident at the bar it feels as if a shadow is following me just out of sight. The feeling of being watched followed me at the store and the entire drive home.

Shaking it off the moment I step foot into the house and put away the groceries. Here I was home. Here I was safe.

Needless to say, since that night of mindblowing sex, I only slept in Boones- now our-room. Wow. Our room. Holy shit... wait.. Did this mean that this was also now my house?

I fold the clothes as I think more about my relationship with Boone. Everything happened so quickly but at the sametime it felt... Right. Normal. Being with him felt as normal as breathing. And it was fucking terrifying.

My swirling thoughts are interrupted the moment I walk into the bedroom.

I SEE YOU

The laundry basket falls to the carpet, my hands cover my mouth, taking in the sight before me. The red words dripping from the headboard onto the messy bedding. The photos had me wanting to cry. A couple dozen photos scattered across the bed. They were of me and Boone having sex. The first time we had sex, him kissing my scar, close up photos of my face as I came, Boone taking me from behind. I wanted to vomit but one realization shattered my panic and hysteria. The feeling of my heart jumping into my throat because;

1. Someone was in the house.

2. They might still be in the house.

3. My gun was locked away in the guest bedroom closet where I had stored it.

All these thoughts occurred in a microsecond and I don't think as I run down the steps to where the alarm pad was, pressing the silent alarm button before I'm outside and across the lawn, making a beeline to Joch and Caseys.

"Joch!" I yell, pounding my fists on the door.

I see Casey through the glass running across the foyer when she realizes it was me.

"Someones in the house." I gasp.

CHAPTER 32

Boone

"Easy now! Don't need to pull your back out before our away game." Joch grumbles as we set the couch down in the moving truck.

"Please, I'm not that old. I'm thirty three." I scoff, dusting my hands off onto my pants.

"And you're only what, a year younger than I am!" I pointed out. He was thirty two, normally guys retired by now but Joch was gonna play until he couldn't anymore. He had his eyes on becoming a coach when he retired.

He tilted his head at me, "Speaking of ages, how old is Tj?" he asked, picking up a cut in half watermelon and dipping a spoon into it. Where he got the watermelon I had no idea.

"Twenty four." I don't think I had asked when her birthday was, I would ask her when I got home. Home.
Our home. I liked the sound of that.
Joch watched me with a smirk on his face.

"What?" I ask.

"Just wondering when I should expect the wedding invitation." His mouth is full of watermelon.

"Give us a few months, why don't ya. We only just got together." I laugh. Joch narrows his eyes at me.

"And you are clearly in love with her." he points the spoon at me.
I gave him a smile, "Yea, I really am. I love her." I nod. Joch's phone starts to ring.

"Hey Case." After a moment Joch stands, his normally goofy grin gone.

"What happened?"

"Everything ok?" I ask. Joch's eyes shoot to me and I feel something sinking in my stomach.

"Yea he's with me. Ok. We're on our way."

"Your house got broken into."

Now I was on my feet, "What?" My phone! I needed to find my phone. I patted my pockets. *Where the fuck is it!* I yank the door to Jochs truck where I had last seen my phone. It was on the floor of the passenger side, the battery was dead. *Shit!*

"Hey, Kam! We'll be back." Joch called into the house.

Joch was not only the best friend you could ask for, but he was the most protective older brother when it came to Casey. He would move heaven and earth for her. Right now the look on his face was murderous as he broke every speeding law and almost drove through the gate to the development.

Four Police cruisers are outside the house when we pull up. Joch hadn't even stopped the car fully when I jump out. The front door is open and police are coming in and out. Tabitha. *Where are you beautiful girl?*

One of the officers tried to stop me from getting close to my house and I'm too panicked to give a fuck to be polite, "Thats my house!" I bark.

Where are you baby, where are you? not seeing her anywhere. What If she was inside…

"Oliver." Tabitha stands in Joch's driveway with Casey. Ok now I can breathe. The moment I'm within reach I scoop her up into my arms holding her tight.

"Are you ok? What happened?" I step back and hold her at arm's length looking over her body for any injuries.

"Someone was in the house. I don't know how, when I came home from grocery shopping, the doors were all locked. I went to put the laundry away and the bedroom...They left photos of us." she sniffled. Her fingers dug into my forearms.

"Photos? What photos?"

"Photos of *us* from your bedroom that first time." She stressed. Photos as in ones of us having sex. What the fuck! Rage shot through my body feeling her hands trembling. This fucker had somehow taken photos of our beautiful moment and used it as some twisted game. Tainting it.

The police officer approached, "Sir, we checked the house and no one is inside."

"Are you sure?" I ask.

"The only damage we can see is in the uh..
Bedroom." He clears his throat, glancing at Tabitha
quickly.

Tabitha covers her face and turns her head.
She looked ashamed. And I hate it. Someone had
came into my home and shattered her sense of
safety.

"Go to Casey's I'll grab us clothes and then
I'll get us a room tonight." I told her. She just
nodded and Casey put an arm around her.

"Joch." I nod towards them and he holds up
a thumbs up, "On it."

After speaking to the police I call Collin
Rothschile. He's the head of team security and

have him organize a cleaning company to clean the headboard and take care of a new camera security system too. While that happens, I get Tabitha and I a room at the Hyatt downtown. We have a game tomorrow night and I had all my stuff in the truck ready to leave. Something I really didn't want to do after today. Casey was staying behind for these next two games so Tabitha could stay at her and Jochs. But I still wasn't excited to leave her right now.

Tabitha sits on the bed with her arms around her knees. Her red hair in a loose bun. Whoever this sick fuck was that broke into the house had taken photos of us through what I figured out was the bedroom patio door. I was having a special film put over the doors to tint them so this would never happen again. It made me sick to think it happened in the first place.

I walk over, sitting on the end of the bed and pull her into my lap.

"Asking if you are ok is pretty dumb at this point right?" I smile, smoothing my hand up her leg.

"I've been better." she mutters.

"I am so sorry this happened." Something in her eyes told me something else was also bothering her, not just the break in.

"Tabitha, what is it?" I ask. She chews on her lip to the point I think she'll draw blood. She stands and pulls her robe tight around her, crossing her arms over her chest.

"The words on the headboard. Those were the same ones written on the wall at Riley's house." I shoot to my feet, "Are you sure?" Thinking back to that day I wasn't really sure I had paid much attention to the room, I had been more concerned about Tabitha.

"That's not all." She adds.

"Those words were what Marvin used to say to me."

"You think it somehow could be him?" She shakes her head, "After all these years? I highly doubt it. But it's not exactly a secret where I am anymore. Since that cunt leaked the photos. He would know exactly where to find me. This is like one of his sick games. If it is him I keep thinking what if he tries to..." I stood and grabbed onto her shoulders, "Baby, I won't let anything happen to you. I promise. He will never hurt you again." I'd kill him with my bare hands if he came near her.

"You don't know him like I do, he's *sadistic*. He-" she covers her mouth and looks away from me. I take her face in my hands,

"Talk to me Baby girl. Tell me. What did he do?" She takes a deep breath. My pulse races waiting on her answer and I prepare myself for whatever she tells me.

"He tortured me."

CHAPTER 33

Tabitha

"I lived with my last foster family for two years before I ran away. On paper the Gavins were a nice couple to be placed with, they were nice and welcoming. They had a son a couple years older than me. I was fifteen when I went to live with them." I began.

"I thought this was it, I was finally in a real home. But that didn't work out as I found out soon after getting settled in." I let out a humorless laugh.

"It started with the porn noises he would play through the wall when the parents were out, which was a lot since the dad was a doctor. They always went out on the weekends. Marvin would blast the porn through the walls all night keeping me up. He was into some sick shit.

"Then started the real bullying, he'd push me, tell me I was ugly. He hated if I had friends and made sure no one would want to hang around me at school. One night I woke up to him on top of me," Boone stiffened, his large body ridgid. "He was playing with himself while I slept."

"The sick fuck." Boone spat.

"I would be taking a shower and then when I would step out of the tub, he would be just standing there watching me, always trying to see me naked. I tried to tell the parents but they wouldn't listen. I knew I had to get away as soon as I could and I needed money so I started to work at restaurants or diners. I thought It would be a safe place from him for a bit. And it was. Until he would find out where I worked and would show up with his scummy friends and make a scene or find a way to make me get fired.

"I managed to last until I was seventeen, I got a job at Hooters and was on the track team. It was hard but I hid It from Marvin. Then one night after the parents had left for the weekend; He had found out I worked at Hooters, my paycheck was in my wallet and he took it after he beat the shit out of me. Once he went to take a shower I went to get my wallet. I needed it to cash my check. I should have left then and there. He caught me in his room and we got into a physical fight. He said 'If you're so willing to show off what's mine to others then maybe I should make it clear who you belong to.' he was on top of me. I fought him as hard as I could. I did get him in the face with his wood burning pen thing. That's where this scar on my hand is from," I show him the scar on my palm, " He held me down and he branded me. At one point I blacked out from the pain. When I came to he was gone. The house was quiet. Everything hurt. My leg was in so much pain. Grabbing what I could, I left the house and ran to the bus station." The memory of running to the station in the oversized sweatpants and changing in the small bathroom shoving the pillowcase into my pants against the burn. I blinked and suddenly was back in the house, watching everything from that night I met Perry at the station and she saw my leg.

Perry helped me into the house, my leg was hurting so fucking badly I couldn't walk. Riley ran into the bathroom to grab what she could to help my leg.

"It's going to get infected if we don't clean it." She yelled, coming from the bathroom with antiseptic and aloe and gauze.

"I'm so fucking sorry about this." she *gasped, opening the bottle. I nodded at her, "Just do it."*

Riley held onto me as Perry poured the antiseptic onto the burn. I screamed.

I squeeze my eyes closed and when I open them I was back in the hotel room with Boone.

"I had been in contact with Riley and called her from the station. Seventy two hours later I was in Seattle covered in bruises." I could see the question forming in his eyes.

"Did he….."

"No. He tried. One thing his piece of shit friend did was stop him. Guess he wasn't into me being out cold while he tried to fuck me." The storm of rage and pain I can see in Boones eyes at what he was hearing hurt my chest. I could feel the anger radiating off him.

"He'll never touch you again." He promises.

I don't realize he has tears in his eyes until he's standing in front of me. I have no idea how to react to this. He's crying for me. Boone takes my face in his hands, "I will do whatever it takes to keep you safe, baby. If this fucker is the one behind this, he will never come near you again."

This is the moment I fell in love with Oliver Boone.

CHAPTER 34

Boone

I stretch out my hips on the ice as we warm up for the game. It had been a total of six days since the house had been broken into and six days since I learned what Tabitha had gone through. Here I am in Minnesota playing the last away game before Christmas. While Tabitha was at work, I had replaced the headboard with a new one and moved the bed. The doors now had a polarizing tinted film over them so seeing from the outside in was impossible. The changes helped both of us be more at ease but she still closed the blinds tight before she had stripped off her clothes and proceeded to ride me like a horse. Not that I was complaining, I couldn't get enough of her. I just hated that she was always hesitant now before taking her clothes off in her own home.

Waking up next to her naked body pressed against me was pure bliss. Casey and Tabitha were off spending the day with Perry who had gotten back early from her trip.

Tonight we are playing against the Minnesota Bobcats. Tabitha had flown out this time with us and was in the stands with Casey. They had decided last minute to come.

As soon as that puck hit the ice it was game on. Number twenty two on the Bobcats seemed to have a hard-on for me. In hockey chirping was normal- you shit talk the other player and roast them to get them to be unfocused. This kid was gunning for me hard. I had been in this world most of my life and wasn't going to give him the satisfaction of reacting to any of his jabs. Even after we won and the game was done he just wouldn't stop running his mouth. I was able to ignore him, until he said something under his breath about the red head wearing my jersey.

"Bet she's a screamer." That one had me stopping and cocking my head to the side.

"The fuck did you just say?" My eyes narrow. A grin spreads across his face seeing he had hit a nerve. Only problem was this cuck had hit a live wire nerve that would explode if he applied even the *tiniest* pressure on. If he wasn't careful I would rock his shit.

"Just saying. Girl like that probably knows her way around a cock. Judging from those photos I've seen." he shrugged, "Maybe I can show her a few things and she can show me a few." my grip on my stick tightens as I ground my teeth. Oh how could I forget, A few of the photos that were left on the bed after the break in had leaked online. Thankfully it was only two of them, close ups of Tabitha's face as she finished and one of her from the back riding me.

"I won't bite. Much. I bet she's into that. Yea she looks like a pain slut."

"Lay off man." I warn through gritted teeth. This week had been hell for Tabitha because of those photos. She hadn't been at work as she had been getting harassed at the bar and Mick thought it best if she stayed home for a few days. Things were slowly getting back to normal since Joch took one for us and "accidentally" got locked out on his hotel balcony naked. Like I've said before, the best friend you could ever have.

"She looks like a pain slut. Maybe I should find out for myself."

My gloves and helmet are off, the crowd goes crazy as my fist connects with his face.

"If you go near her I'll break your fucking jaw." I growled as my fist connected with his jaw once more. I had no clue what Marvin looked like, but I pictured that this man was him. Each hit was harder than the last. I was angry. My girl is hurting and I can't fucking do anything!

Out of the corner of my eye I see Joch slam into another player that had been about to lunge onto me. It takes two refs to pull me off this guy.

"The fuck is wrong with your team Cubs!" Joch snaps at the Bobcats captain as we make our way towards the locker room. Jason Cubs was a dickwad.

"Too rough for your soft ass Collins?" he barks back.

"Not even close, baby boy. I love it hard. Just keep your wasted shots of sperm on a tighter leash." Joch spat.

"If your bitch can't take some chirping maybe he ought to retire early then."

"Jesus Cubs your mom really shoulda done us all a favor and swallowed you." Joch scoffs as he gets off the ice.

The hallway is pretty empty when I get out of the locker room dressed in the dark blue suit I wore to the arena. My gear slung over my back. I couldn't stop the smile forming when I see my girl snaking through the dispersing crowd to me. Her beautiful hair in a high ponytail, she has on a black Skyhawks jersey with my name on the back.

"Hey baby." I sigh, wrapping an arm around her, my hand resting right above her ass, as she pushes up onto her tiptoes to press a kiss to my lips.

"Are you ok?" her thumb rubbing the skin under the cut on my cheek.

"Yea, I'm ok. Just a punk kid that got under my skin." I glance up, and freeze. Standing at the end of the hall, head buzzed, smirking at me, is Viktor Zarko. As fast as I see him, he's gone. Not before he gave me a little wave first.

"Oliver? What's wrong?" Tabitha asks, trying to follow my look but isn't able to because of the height difference. She only came up to my chest in height. Suddenly it's like I wasn't in the arena, I'm in New York, standing in the street as police cruisers and ambulances surround me.

"Oliver, you ok man?" Joch grabs my shoulder, snapping me out of it.

"Let's get going." I nod, rubbing my hand up Tabitha's back.

"Hungry?" I ask, giving her a reassuring smile.

"Always." she laughs.

The faster I got out of this fucking city the better.

"Hey, what did you guys have planned for Christmas?" Joch asks randomly. Tabitha tilted her head, "Oh um, I really hadn't thought of it." she replied. Shit that's right it was December. Thanksgiving had gone by quietly, Tabitha and I had celebrated with Joch and Casey keeping it low key, but Christmas... This was the first Christmas I would spend with her.

"We'll let you know." I told him as we left the arena.

"Riley, Perry and I usually would all spend it together, watching movies and we would decorate the tree. I always love Christmas time. It's so cozy." Tabitha explained. I smile down at her, fuck she was adorable. I loved this woman so much.

"This year RIley is gonna be with the boys in Canada and Perry is going to be in New York." she adds.

"Well, then I say we do a Christmas decorating party. Oli, you and I do the outside lights? While the ladies yell at us about where to put them?" Joch nudges Casey.

"Or, you all freeze your asses off doing that while we go Christmas shopping?" Casey counters. Tabitha nods, "That sounds better." she laughs.

CHAPTER 35

Tabitha

"What is that heavenly smell?" Boone asks, walking into the kitchen. I smile at him, "Cinnamon blueberry muffins." I answered as I placed the fresh from the oven muffins on the cooling rack. Boone and I had decorated the living room with some Christmas decorations early this morning after our run. He had a huge eight foot artificial tree he had gotten years ago and we had decorated it with a bunch of ornaments that he had saved from his childhood.

Since my boyfriend would eat most anything I figured it would be a good idea to make muffins. And judging by the way he plucked one of the still hot muffins from the rack and shoved it in his mouth, I'd say it was a good choice. The kitchen had some garland and Christmas decorations placed around. The oven mitts were Christmas themed.

Laughter bubbled in my throat, "You're gonna burn your mouth!" I warn. He grabs me around the waist and pulls me to him, leaning down to kiss me.

"I can think of a way to help that." he purred, grabbing me by the back of my knees and lifting me up to place me on the end of the island that wasn't covered in baking. I sink into his touch as he kisses me, pulling me to the edge of the counter before he drops to his knees. Seeing over six foot tall Oliver Boone on his knees in front of me is like a fucking wet dream. His shirt morphes to his muscular shoulders and oh fuck. He places my legs over his shoulders as he moves my cotton shorts to the side and gives me a long, teasing lick. His beard tickles my thighs as he adjusts my legs.

My fingers dig into his hair, "Fuck!" I moan as he spreads my lips and presses kisses above my clit. He chuckles, standing up and threading his hands into my hair before he thrusts two fingers into me.

"Mmm!" I bite onto my lip as he curls his fingers inside me.

The smile spreads on his face as he watches me buck my hips against his hand.

"Good girl. Fuck my fingers." he whispers. My hips lift to match his thrusts. My breath comes out in short huffs as he quickens his pace, adding his thumb to rub my clit. My hands grip his shirt, pulling it up his back and he pulls his fingers away. I whine when he puts the fingers in his mouth and sucks on them.

"Don't worry, I'm not done with you yet." He growls picking me up. My legs wrap around his waist, his hands squeeze my ass as he carries me into the living room to lay me down onto the couch.

"Is this ok?" he asks hovering above me, I nod. I kick my shorts off as he kisses up my neck.

"Very."

Boone is hard against my stomach as I slip one hand down to stroke him through his pants. He groans when I squeeze his cock hard through the material, "Fuck baby." he bites into my shoulder. I free his cock from his pants. Boone hooks his hand under my right leg, lifting it as he pushes forward, sliding into me until his pelvis is pressed against mine.

"Oh fuck." I gasp, Pressing my hips up to take him deeper.

"You feel so fucking good." he breathes. Boone sucks on the side of my neck, his tongue licking circles on my skin making me break out in goosebumps.

"Do I feel good to you?" he asks. I nod, "Yes. So fucking good." I cry out when he slowed his thrusts.

"Oliver." It's a borderline beg because I am so close. I need to come. He repeats the same thing, building my climax up but right before the cusp he would slowly drag his cock out to almost the tip before he slowly pushes back in and pauses there.

"Oliver!" he chuckles at my frustration, kissing my chin and jaw.

"I fucking love when you say my name Baby girl. Seeing you all riled up." he pulls his cock almost out to the tip and stops.

I could cry at the tension building between my legs. It was so frustrating but the chills going up my spine had me wanting more.

"Please..."

His eye brows raise, "*Please* what?" the devilish grin spreads across his face.

"Please let me." He adds his finger to very *very* lightly circle my clit. Enough to make the edging almost cry worthy.

"You seem to have a little trouble with words, Baby girl. Maybe I should stop?" I'm gonna kill him if he stops. Seriously, I may commit murder. I can see the headline now: Girl kills boyfriend over orgasm denial.

"Please let me come." I beg. Boone places one hand above me to get a hold of the couch so he won't crush me with his weight.

His free hand grips my thigh as I hold onto him, kissing his neck and biting his collarbone, leaving little red kiss marks.

"Fuck, Tabitha." he gounds out as he pounds into me. His hips driving harder and deeper. Boone presses his forehead to mine, our skin is sweaty as he looks into my eyes, "I love you." he gasps out.

"I love you." he says again as he quickens his pace, "Oliver!" I cry. My eyes rolling back as I scream his name, "Oliver. I love you. *Fuck!*"

"Say that again. Say it again." He growls.

"I love you." The scream rips from my lips as wave after wave hits me as I come.

He lets out a roar as he comes right after me, his hips pinning mine down as I feel warmth coat my insides. Boone collapses onto the couch next to me, both of us spent and breathing hard. His words repeat in my head over and over.

He said he loved me. Holy shit. He said he loves me! And I said it back. I take his bearded face in my hand, turning it to face me.

"I love you." I look at him. He smiles at me, caressing my face as he looks at me with so much love.

"I love you, too."

Oliver Boone was in love with me. and I was totally in love with him. This man had cried for me, defended me, he had become my home.

"Is something burning?" Boone suddenly asks right as the scent of burning food fills the room.

"Shit!" I lunge off the couch and sprint into the kitchen butt naked to grab the now burnt muffins from the oven. Boones' laughter follows me.

CHAPTER 36

Tabitha

Busy days at work were my favorite. Time goes by so fast and the money is worth it especially during the holidays. Christmas is in four days and I couldn't be happier to spend the time with Boone.

"I don't know how you have so much energy, I just wanna climb into bed." Georgia whines. Her hair is down today, her makeup done in a smokey cat eye. She had on a pink Christmas sweater.

I gave her a smile, "I'm in a really good mood today." and I was, after I had tossed out the burnt muffins, Boone had carried me upstairs where he showed me just how much he loved me numerous times and numerous positions, a couple he was surprised I was flexible enough to do.

My body was pleasantly sore, but I didn't mind.

A man sat at the bar and waved me down, "Can I get a scotch neat please?" he asked. I nodded and grab the scotch pouring the glass and set it in front of him. He's about mid to late thirties, with a five o-clock shadow and a buzz cut.

"How are you this afternoon?" he asks, his voice a little gruff.

"Doing very well, it's always nice when it's busy." I smile at him. My hair is in a high ponytail, my bar bitch shirt hugs my chest under my black Skyhawks zip-up hoodie. It was only zipped up a quarter of the way. I was feeling on top of the world. The paparazzi had finally lessened up and I could actually get through a shift without anyone harassing me.

The customer pointed at the hoodie, "You a fan of the team?" I nod, "Considering her boyfriend is on the team she has to be." Georgia commented walking behind me. I'm gonna twist her nipple for that. I don't need who I am dating screamed from the rooftops more than it already is.

"Who's your boyfriend?" he asks. Uneasiness spreads in my stomach and I stop myself from saying Boones name.

"He is one of the coaching assistants." I reply. The man nods, setting his drink down. Something about him set off an alarm bell. His eyes…. They were too dark. Too.. something I can't put my finger on.

He stands, pulling out his wallet to set some bills on the bar before walking away, "Say hi to Oli for me."

he calls. I frown. He'd left me a hundred dollars for a tip.

"Say hi to Oli?" I mutter watching him go. That man knows Boone. He knows I am dating him. Georgia walks past and I shove the money into her apron.

"Here, scotch guy left a tip, you take it." I say quickly as I untie my apron. My stomach knotted as my alarm bells went off. Something about that man was off. Boone has a game tonight and I am driving with Casey so I had to get going.

It wasn't only me that had a strange day I realize. Something is off with Boone too. Judging by the way he is skating and being overly aggressive, I know something is wrong.

Casey's perfect brows were furrowed as she watched Boone during the game, "It might not be my business, but did you guys have a fight?" she leans over. I shake my head, "The absolute opposite. This morning was amazing. I have no clue what is wrong." I cringe when he body checks another player and a fight breaks out. Boones back hits the ice as the other player lands on top of him.

Both Casey and I jump to our feet as Joch and the refs pulls them apart, Boone spits blood out of his mouth. His hair is plastered to his forehead. He just sits in the penalty box with his head down until his time is over. After he gets back on the ice he once again gets into a fight with a player during the next play. This time he's knocked onto his back by the other team and it prompts Tig and Kaminskey to jump in. Boone takes a moment to get up and it scares the shit out of me. *Why isn't he getting up?* After a solid thirty seconds he moves and Tig helps Boone to his feet. He's ok it appears.

"He's ok." Casey says, rubbing her hand up my back. I can't wait for this game to be over.

They win by one goal. Casey and I wait where we usually do just down from the locker rooms. The team filters out one by one all dressed back in their suits they arrived in. Joch exits the locker room with a stoic look on his handsome face, "Something is up with him, I need your help." he says quietly to me.

I follow him into the now partially dark locker room where Boone is sitting against the locker on the floor. He had removed his pads and jersey, his skates were thrown haphazardly to the side. He sat in his under armor long sleeve with his elbows resting on his knees and his head in his hands. I patted Joch on the shoulder, "Let me talk to him."

"Hey hellcat. Nice fight moves out there. The other kids not play nice tonight?" I ask approaching him. He doesn't move. I take the seat on the bench in front of him and put my hand on his forearm.

"Go home with Case, babe." he says. The sound of his voice is off. It's strained, sore almost.

"Uh no, I'm going home with you. What's wrong?" I look at him. He keeps his head down and it's starting to worry me.

"Tabitha, please. Just go." He's trying to push me away, and I'm not gonna budge. Something is wrong, did he get hurt? A thousand scenarios are going through my head. None of them are good.

"Oliver, what is it? What's wrong?" When he finally looks up at me, I see his eyes are red, "I'm not a match." The crack of his voice catches me off guard. Tate. His test for the bone marrow transplant. I look at Joch, he closes his eyes and shakes his head.

"The test results came back. I'm not a match for Tate. I'm not a match and he's getting worse. I couldn't save my mom and I can't save Tate."

I lunge for him, wrapping my arms around his neck and holding him to me. His big arms go around my waist. His shoulders shake slightly and my heart breaks as his tears soak my shoulder.

"I'm sorry, I'm so sorry." was all I can say as I stroke his hair. Glancing back at Joch I give him a look, I didn't know what to do for him. He watched his mother die and now he is forced to watch his little brother die too. Joch kneels next to us and wraps an arm around Boones shoulders, resting his head against his friends.

"We'll figure this out man. I promise you. I'm gonna help you figure this out." Joch promises, his own voice steady even though I could see the tears forming in his bright hazel eyes.

Seeing both of these strong, powerful men breaking like this hurt. Boone had been my rock this entire time and now he needed me to be his. Joch continued to make promises to Boone that he would help him fix this anyway he could.

$$\times \quad \times \quad \times \quad \times \quad \times$$

Joch and I help Boone stand and Joch packs his gear while Boone showers.

"What can I do to help you?" I ask him as he wraps the towel around his waist. He has some bruises forming on his ribs from his fight. Boone holds the side of my face, his thumb rubbing my cheek, "Just be here, baby girl. That's all I need." He presses a kiss to my forehead.

"Are you sure?" I ask. Boone smiles at me.

"Yea, I'm sure. I love you, and I appreciate you." He's hurting right now and I can't fix this pain. I could only imagine what Marissa was going through.

"I love you too."

"I love you too man." Joch's voice called out from around the locker. Boone cracked a wide smile as did I because Joch was able to bring the mood up.

He held Boones gear bag, "I'll check on my results tonight, so will Tig and Kam. Bohdie's won't be back for a week at the most." he informed us. Boone tilted his head blinking in confusion.

"What? Results?"

Joch smiles, "I told you I would help you out anyway I could man, when you first got your test done I also got tested. I was at the hospital when you spoke to the nurse to schedule the testing, remember?" he explained, "When you finished the paperwork I told the nurse to schedule me too, then got Tig, Kam and Bohdie to get tested. All I mentioned was that Tate was a close family friend's kid who was sick. They didn't need to be told anything more."

My chest warmed as I looked at him. Joch Collins was probably the most amazing human being I had ever met after Boone. Boone storms over to his friend and throws his arms around his shoulder in a tight hug. Boone let out a shuddered sob, "Thank you." he breathed. Joch hugged him back.

"Ok. I appreciate the love bro, but you're naked and all the rubbing on me is gonna turn me on and Tj doesn't seem like the type to share her man." he laughs, patting Boone on the back.

"Seriously though, I'm gonna get a boner."

CHAPTER 37

Tabitha

Pictures popped up later that night online of Boone and I leaving the arena with Joch. The article titled *'The Mountain officially conquered! See photos of the redheaded beauty that has captured the heart of the NHL's heartthrob.'*

"It would appear that I have conquered you." Boone looks over my shoulder, his naked chest covered in sweat from his workout.

"Well, they aren't wrong." He wiggles his eyebrows at me, slapping my ass. I yelp and smack his arm. We're all in Joch's workout room at his house. There were three squat racks, a rack of dumbbells sit in front of the wall length mirror and two bench presses were set up in front of that.

They didn't have practice this morning so the two were in the basement working out. Boone kisses my temple before walking to the row of dumbbells.

"What if they ask about the photos?"

"I'll say no comment." he shrugs, picking up 2-75 pound dumbbells to start a set of curls. He's dressed in a cropped cutoff and black basketball shorts that are super low on his waist letting me see the V of his hips. I almost whine out of hornyness.

"Will that work?" I watch him, his muscles flexing as he lifts the weights. Those arms had been around me this morning when he had joined me in the shower and used his fingers to fuck me until I almost cried before he dropped to his knees and used his skilled tongue to finish me.

"Our relationship is no one's business." He huffs, setting the dumbbells down. Today I wore a black long sleeve shirt that was cropped, showing just a small sliver of skin and olive green and black plaid jeans.

Melissa had called this morning to let us know that Tate was starting a new treatment this afternoon and it looks promising. She spoke to Boone for a while and I don't know what they talked about but it seems to have helped him deal with the news of him not being a match. He was almost like normal, but I could see the worry in his eyes every time his phone rang.

"Are we still watching movies later?" I ask standing up.

Boone nodded, "Yea!" he comes up, circling his arms around my waist, "I'm gonna make your favorite food then once you're done eating I'm gonna ravish you my beautiful, delicious girlfriend." he promises peppering my face with hot kisses making me laugh.

"You're all sweaty!" I squeal, pushing him away. He has several away games coming up in the next weeks and it would be chaos. But Christmas day he was all mine. I watch him wipe the sweat from his forehead with the hem of his shirt. Normally I wasn't this bad, but lately one look at him was enough to ignite that heat between my legs. Our schedules would be hectic and we would have to go a few days without seeing each other, which I had been preparing for since it was getting close to the conference finals coming up in April. I had one semester left of school then would have my marketing and business degree. The days I wasn't busy working or doing school I was going to be hanging out with Casey or Perry. Since the paparazzi wasn't able to find out my name other than T.J, there wasn't much information on me.

They were starting to dig in again. Following me everywhere to the point Mick had security at the bar now. But they would only find dead ends. They wouldn't find *any* information on Tabitha Jones either. I didn't have any social media. And my real name wasn't Tabitha so they had no leads on me.

$$\times \quad \times \quad \times \quad \times \quad \times$$

On Christmas day we went Instagram official. While we were sitting in the living room watching the Christmas episodes of '*The Office*', Boone posted a black and white photo of our hands holding our coffee cups, and one from behind of me sitting in front of the tree on my knees with a present in my hands.

He captioned it *'Best Christmas morning spent with my heart. It's official I'm taken.'* posted with my permission. Within minutes it had thousands of likes, Boone had turned off the comments before posting and any of the photos he would post in the future he promised they would be turned off.

Boone handed me a gift and sat next to me on the couch, "One last one for you. Merry Christmas, beautiful." he smiles. He had already gotten me several things but I take the small box and tear the wrapping paper off and see a pandora box. Inside is an adorable necklace chain with a coffee cup, firefly and blue turtle charm on it. Along with a gold polished wave ring for my ring stacks.

"Awe, I love them!" I say, leaning over and kissing him, "Thank you."

This morning had started hot and heavy with him not only going down on me but using a new wand to tease the fuck out of me. And now that same heat reignited as his tongue explored my mouth while his hands wander up to my tits to play with my piercings.

"We have thirty minutes before were supposed to meet Joch and Casey." I pant as his fingers slip into my Christmas themed pajama pants.

"They can wait. Right now I want to fuck my girlfriend on the couch." he murmurs. Just as he starts to pull my pants down a thundering sound of someone knocking on the front door makes me jerk up which causes Boone to fall off onto the floor with a loud painful thud.

"Oh shit, are you ok?" I gasp as Jochs voice comes from the other side of the front door.

"Santa is here!"

"I'm going to kill him." Boone growls rubbing his head.

CHAPTER 38

Tabitha

New years had been fun as the entire team all got together and celebrated. Boone and I skipped out early and had gone back to our hotel where he teased me until ten seconds before midnight where he finally made me orgasm. We didn't get much sleep until the early hours of the morning.

It was officially halfway through January now. The guys only had some media interviews to do then they all had to hop on a plane to Denver for two games, it was going to be one of the last times the boys would be able to fully relax before they would be focused on getting to the playoffs and then the Stanley Cup. Boone pressed his body to mine as he kissed my neck.

"Just so you know, I have cameras everywhere. So if you wanna fuck, go home or do it in the bathroom." Joch barks from the squat rack.

"Seriously, watching you two rub against each other is like the beginning of a fucking porno." I stick my tongue out at him, "Jealous, Joch?" Joch flips me the bird, "I already offered a threesome and was turned down. So no." he countered shrugging.

"Not in this lifetime, bro." Boone deadpanned.

"What levels of depravity is he spewing this time?" Casey asked from the doorway.

"The usual. Are you ready? I'm starved." I asked untangling myself from Boone. Casey nodded. She was dressed in a cropped jean jacket with high waisted white ripped jeans.

"Have fun. Love you." I give him a quick peck.

"I love you too." he murmured against my mouth.

"And I love you as well." Joch mused.

Shopping with Casey was just what I needed. We hit up some stores downtown and finally stopped for food about two-ish meeting up with Perry.

"It's been too long!" Perry muses as she sets her bags down. She's dressed in a large oversized pink sweater and black jeans.

"I needed this." I sigh. Perry and Casey click right away. We're not even at the restaurant five minutes and Perry already has the bartender wrapped around her finger. We have three free first drinks in front of us. Both Casey and Perry choose wine, I choose titos lavender lemonade.

"So I gotta ask. As your bestie. How big is he?" I spit my drink out.

"Pear!" I cough,

"Ew!" Casey cringes.

Perry holds her hand up, "What? He's hot, and I'm curious." she shrugs.

"He gets the job done, that's all I'll say." I laugh. Perry shimmys her shoulders, "Ohh so he is big everywhere. Nice. I'm a little jealous."

Casey looks at the tv above the bar and snorts, "Oh speaking of. Look who it is." Boone is on the tv. From the look on his face, he's pissed. Casey sits forward, her hand under her chin as she focuses on the tv. Her brows furrow..

"Something is up." she mutters.

"Whatever it is he's pissed." I agree, "Is this normal for these things?" Perry asks. Boone looks irritated, like something was really pissing him off. Without the sound or captions we can't tell what is going on.

"Not usually. Sometimes the journalists can ask out of line questions to get a rise out of the players, but normally it isn't too bad. Oliver is known for keeping his cool. Whatever the questions are, it must be really pissing him off." she explained, her eyes locked on the t.v. as Boone stands and gives the reporter a curt nod and walks off as Tig takes his seat. I shoot him a quick text.

◯TABITHA: Hey you ok? Caught the end of the interview.

◯BOONE: All good.

His photo pops up as his ringtone plays.

"Hey." I answer.

"Hey, can you do me a favor? When you and Casey come up for the Denver game next week, I want you to stick to the hotel." he says.

"Uh, yea sure. Why though?" I ask, looking at Casey and Perry.

"Apparently the paparazzi are more into my personal life now than I thought. Asking more personal things. It's really fucked up. I don't want to put you through this shit." he explains.

"Do you still want me to come?" Casey tilts her head at my question.

"Yes, of course. I want to see you." I bite my lip to hide the huge smile on my face.

"Awee, Oliver Boone. Do you miss me?" I tease

"Maybe I do. Maybe I miss the feeling of you coming around my cock as I fuck you?"

"Damn, I *do* have you wrapped around my finger don't I?" I make the *wha-tcha* sound to mimic a whip.

Boone laughed, "Baby girl you can call it what you want. I just miss you." he said. The tone in his voice has my core clenching. I cleared my throat.

"I have to go now. But I'll talk to you later. I love you." he says, "I love you, too."
Casey gave me a look, "If you two get any more mushy I'm gonna vomit." she smirks.

"Right?" Perry agrees, taking the last sip of her wine.

"I need to get laid." she sighs looking at the bartender and flashing him her flirty smile.

CHAPTER 39

Boone

The smell of ice burns my nose as we set up in our spots. Tonight we are playing the Denver Avalanches. Their right defenseman is on me like a bee on a flower all night. The chirps and shit talking all night was comical and I can't lie a few of them were pretty good too. That was a part of the sport though, nothing was off limits with shit talking in hockey. The amount of times I heard shit about my mom, past girlfriends, other teammates, or now Tabitha, was too many to keep track. I wasn't going to give him the satisfaction of reacting to anything he said. Even if it was starting to get on my nerves. There was chirping then there was just being a pain in the fucking ass. This guy was the latter. The

Avalanches go to score but Bohdie blocks it, tossing the puck to Kam.

Kam passes me the puck and I take control of it, ready to pass it to Tig when a body rams into my side sending me into the wall. The puck flies out wide behind the goal and I'm right there with it, shooting it up to Tig as the Avalanche forward drives his stick into my ribs as we both hit the wall.

"Fuck!" I hiss not from the pain but from the immediate irritation this fucker caused. He lets out a laugh, shoving me one more time before turning away.

"That one is for Zarko." he smiles. My blood boils, "What the fuck did you just say?" I growl, tilting my head, how the fuck did this prick know Zarko? His smile widens.

"Paybacks a bitch Oli." he winks, skating past the goal, swiping his stick out so it sends a bunch of slush into Bohdies' face then taps his helmet with the top of his hockey stick. *Now I'm gonna hit this bitch. He fucked with my goalie.* My gloves and helmet hit the ice and I'm on him. The crowd goes wild, cheering and yelling. I drive my fist into his face, holding his jersey so he can't get away. It's a marriage of fists and punching. My adrenaline is keeping everything numb for now but once it wears off I know I'll be sore but I don't give a fuck..

"Stay the fuck away from my goalie." I say as a ref pulls me from the poor sap who was now crying on the ice. I spit out blood as I push my way to the bench. Mother fucker split my eyebrow I realize when I feel blood trickling down my face.

Tabitha is right there waiting when I leave the locker room. She pushes up onto her tiptoes to kiss me. She's wearing a pair of black leggings and the team jersey, her now faded coppery hair is in two loose braids under a light pink hat.

"Hey Baby girl." I sigh, scooping her into a hug and kissing her. The moment I do a hundred flashes go off as photographers snap photos.

"You ok?" She asks, rubbing her thumb over my taped up eyebrow.

"Yea, I'm ok. Just some prick trying to rile me up. It happens every season." I assure her. Looking up I immediately lock gazes with Viktor Zarko. His metallic gray eyes shine as he looks down at Tabitha, the smile on his face widening as he approaches us.

"Oliver." he smiles.

"Zarko." I don't hide the snappy tone from my voice. This fucker would never get any kindness or politeness from me.

"You're the guy from the bar." Tabitha says. I look down at her, pulling her closer to my side, "What?" I glare at Zarko. Why hadn't she said anything about him?

"I'm Viktor. I used to play on Oliver's first team out of college. Last I saw him was in New York in the back of a police car." My body goes rigid. He wouldn't.

"What are you doing here?" I ask. He adjusts the jacket and I feel sick. Captain is stitched over the breast pocket.

"Checking out the competition for my team." He has a new team! How?

"Fun. Boring game politics. I'm hungry and we need food. Let's go." Tabitha deadpans, treating him as if he were gum on the ground. She pulls on my arm and I follow her through the crowd.

"See you soon Oliver. See you angel eyes." Zarko calls. I don't miss the way her hand tightens on my arm.

I'm lost in thought the entire drive to the hotel. How could he be not only on a new team but also the fucking captian!

We're not even in the door to the room before Tabitha is pushing me onto the bed and telling me to explain. Ok, my turn to disclose some past trauma.

"When I graduated college, I was drafted to a team in New York. It was a year after my mom died so I was still a shit headed, aggressive asshole." I began, "I made friends with one of the other defenders, Viktor Zarko. In the mindset I was in, I thought he was the only one who understood me, and was the only one I could really trust." The anger I felt at that time in my life was so foreign to me that I didn't know how to process it. I was so caught off guard by it. "One night after a game we all went out to celebrate. Viktor and I were drunk, I found out later he was also on drugs. He suggested another bar and I just agreed. I wanted to dull the anger anyway I could.

"I knew he wasn't sober, but went anyway. As far as I knew he was the one who took me under his wing and was always looking out for me.

We hopped into his rental car and he drove off. A few blocks from the bar, Viktor ran a red light at an intersection. He t-boned another car, causing it to hit a patch of ice and spin into a pole. The driver was a nineteen year old single mother on her way to her night shift." for as long as I live, I'll never forget the look on her face when I ran to check on her. She was hunched over the steering wheel, her head turned to the side. Eyes open. She probably hadn't even had time to process what happened before she died. The photo of her baby was hanging on her mirror.

"She died on impact. When the cops showed up, Zarko tried to get me to say I was driving. But I couldn't, not after I saw the girl. He was pissed. He tried blaming me but Tyler, the other teammate in our car, had been snapchatting a girl and he had proof I wasn't driving. Zarko was arrested and subsequently kicked off the team.

After it got out why he was arrested, no other team would touch him."

"Let me guess, he didn't serve any jail time?" Tabitha guesses.

"He served six months. I traded teams and joined The Skyhawks, it was already something I had been in the process of doing but thanks to Joch it was expedited. I felt so much guilt over my choices that night."

Tabitha reaches out and cups my face, "It wasn't your fault you know that, right?"

"I know that now. It took me a little while to not think about it as my fault. But I know it wasn't mine. He's the one who killed her."

"How did he get on a new team after all this time?" she asks. I shake my head, "No clue, but I'm not gonna stress about it. He can't do anything to me." I say. I pull her into my chest and she snuggles up to me.

"Let's get some rest." I say.

CHAPTER 40

Tabitha

Casey was right. The following couple of weeks when Boone and I left the development, we were followed by paparazzi. The news of yet another break in had a majority of the news occupied as this time someone was home when it happened.

Basketball player Claude Higgins was at home working on putting up some shelving when he walked into his garage and was attacked by the intruder. Luckily he was ok but it once again had people demanding for the police to catch whoever this was.

Boone had media and training all day today. It was the busiest time leading up to who would play in the conference quarterfinals and it was coming up fast. So it was all games and media and practice. He had several away games going on and I had work so I wasn't able to go with him.

Currently I was wiping down the bar. Perry had refreshed my hair color, the dark red to copper ombre is now pulled up into a messy ponytail held by a claw clip. I nibble on some buttered toast when I have a chance to get some food in my stomach since I had the pleasure of waking up to my period this morning. Oh joy. So black loose overall jumpsuit with a long sleeved white shirt it was.

Luckily It was a slow afternoon, a group of people came into the bar, taking a seat at the table by the door. There were about five of them, four men and one woman. I put on my winning smile and approach the table.

"Hi, what can I get you?" The man closest to me is late twenties, has dirty blonde hair that's gelled back and a light five o'clock shadow. His soulless eyes gleamed. *No.* My smile drops when I see his one eyebrow. *No no no.* It feels like my lungs have been ripped from my chest and wrapped around my throat.

"I think we'll all just take some water for now please?" he says as I back up and stumble as I run into the back. *I can't fucking breathe!*

"Georgia, I need you to take that table by the door. No questions." I'm barely able to say. She nods, "Sure. you ok?" I hear her ask as I get around her, I barely make it into the bathroom in time to throw up in the toilet. *He was here. He was here!* Marvin. My ex foster brother was here!

When I peek through the kitchen door I do a double take. He was gone. The same five people are at the table but the man I was so positive of, where he sat, is a man with a dark green short mohawk.

"You ok kid?" Mick asks, eyeing me from the grill.

"Yea. I think so. I could have sworn that... nevermind." I shake my head.

"You look a little pale, you want me to make you something to eat?" He asked. I can't help but smile, The big softie.

"How about a turkey toasted club with extra bacon, no lettuce, no tomato?" he offers. Ohh Mick knew I loved his custom club sandwiches. Even though I had just vomited I'm suddenly hungry again.

"Thank you Mick." I sigh, earning a wink from him.

I went back to the bar and noticed a man wearing a basketball hat sitting a few spots down.

"Hello, what can I get you?" I smile trying to shake the anxiety.

"I'll take a ginger ale please, Tabitha." he said. I grab a glass from the shelf behind me and fill it with his requested drink. He takes his hat off and I straighten my posture. Viktor Zarko gives me a sideways smile.

"Here you go. Can I get you any food?" What is this, asshole day? All this stress isn't healthy.

"That was some game the other day huh?" he smirks.

Boone had a game the other day and they had lost. It was a rough one that had led to several fights, one landed Boone in the penalty box with Joch. Boone almost got ejected from the game at one point. I watched the entire thing on tv and-not gonna lie, it was pretty hot.

"Yea. It was." I hum.

"He always did have quite a temper. He once beat a man unconscious when he first started.

"Did he tell you that? Did he ever tell you about the night after our game in New York City? Such a tragic shame. That poor woman." Viktor asks, his hands folded in front of him.

I place my hands on the bar, narrowing my eyes at him, "Yea he did. He told me everything."

Viktor narrowed his eyes not fully buying it, "Oh, did he now? I'm sure he glossed over what he did, you never realy know who a person is-" I cut him off, "I know about the accident and the woman you killed by driving high and drunk. I know exactly who Oliver Boone is. And I know *exactly* who *you* are. Now get the fuck out of my bar." I demand.

Viktor blinks in surprise but recovers quickly.

"Such nice customer service, I can see why Oliver likes you. Your mouth is filthy." he tsks.

"I never said I was nice. Now, Get. The. Fuck. Out of my bar." my eyes bore into him with my best resting bitch face.

Viktor humphed and stands.

"Tell Oliver, I'll be in touch. Maybe I'll drop by and see him or maybe I'll ask this hairstylist I know to go out on a date. What was her name? Percy? Perry? Or maybe her name was Casey? She has such a nice personality." he shrugs.

"Leave her alone!" I snap, putting my hand into my apron to grab my phone.

Viktor chuckles, walking over to the opening of the bar top so he is towering over me. His cologne reeks like a department store.

"Oliver owes me, it would be so kind of him to throw a game. Let another deserving team into the playoffs. You're his girlfriend. Maybe you could convince him to throw the game next week?" I scoff, "Yea right. You really are insane."

Viktor glares at me, stepping closer, "Do what you're good at, suck his cock like the good slut you are and tell him to throw the game against Anaheim. Or else I may end up having some of my friends pay Perry a little visit. She still lives in the highrise alone right? It would be a shame if something happened to her. Balconies can be dangerous." anger burns my blood, he is threatening my friend.

"If you hurt her, I will kill you." I growl.

"Unlike you, I follow through with my promises." He stops and holds up a finger, "By the way, be careful driving in the snow this weekend. Corollas are known to not be good in the snow." my fingers dig into the bar top so hard I feel the wood under my nails.

"Good thing I don't drive a Corolla." I respond.

He smirks and puts his hat back on as he leaves. Mick calls that my food is done and I box it up making an excuse to leave.

The moment I am in the car I call Boone, getting his voicemail. Shit he is at media all day.

"Hey, I need you to call me. Right when you get this it's important." I say. My hands are shaking as I call Perry and Casey and tell them everything that happened. The moment I pull into the driveway Casey is at my door.

"Are you ok?" She asks. Perry is right behind her opening my door.

"Yea. Just freaked out. I really don't wanna be alone. Mind if I stay at yours?" I ask.

"Of course! You know you don't have to ask. You're family." she says.

"I'll chop his balls off." Perry says, throwing her arm around me and kissing my cheek.

Boone calls me around six freaking out. Twenty missed calls probably was overkill but it was an emergency.

"Hey are you ok?" he asks. I let out a laugh, "No, I am not ok. Viktor Zarko showed up to the bar and threatened me. He said if I didn't convince you to throw the next two games he would hurt Perry." I tell him everything that happened. Boone curses, "I'm so sorry baby. I never wanted you to be involved in any of this."

"It scared me, Oliver. He knew the car I drove. He threatened me." I play with my rings on my fingers.

"I'll take care of him. He won't bother you again." He says before hanging up. I glare at the phone. Immediately calling him back. Irritation lacing my voice when he answers.

"Forget something?"

"I love you." he chuckles.

"Oh, Do you? Mr. hang up after that ominous, 'I'll take care of it.'" I mock his voice, "What the hell does that mean anyway? You're a big bad hockey player on the ice not off it, you can't go around beating the shit out of guys. You'll go to jail and then it won't solve anything." I rant.

"Tabitha, stop!" he barks. I close my mouth.

"He threatened you. Scared you. He isn't going to get away with it. I'll see you tomorrow. I love you." he says before hanging up. I select the media file and text it to him.

⌕Tabitha: I took this before he left.

I send the video I had managed to record of Zarko threatening me.

Casey watched me from across the room on her spot on the couch. Her hair is thrown up in a messy bun on top of her head, she has on a light pink pajama set.

"Let me guess, he is going all protective Oliver on you?" she asks. I nod. "He is super protective when it comes to the people he loves. But he is also very clever about acting on it, don't worry he won't go nuts." she assures.

CHAPTER 41

Tabitha

The next morning I open the bar. I switched with Caroline since I was supposed to go with Casey to Vancuver to watch one of the conference games. If they won, the Skyhawks would play the Bruins in the next round. The news broke this morning on all Sports center news outlets playing the clip of Viktor Zarko trying to fix a national sporting event. Boone had gone to Ricard Donavan, the owner of the team, after our call and showed him the clip before anonymously tipping off the organization members. Some of the paparazzi had begun to buzz around the bar since people pointed out the location of the video. Best part,

Viktor was facing suspension from his team. When noon rolls around I head out to meet Casey.

We arrive at the hotel around three and I was supposed to meet Boone at the arena a few hours before the game to get food.

"You sure you don't want me to go with you?" Casey calls from the bathroom. I pull my boots on, "Yea, I'll see you at the arena." I say heading to the elevator. The parking lot is freshly plowed but it looks like it'll need to be redone since it was starting to snow again.

I'm digging in my bag for the keys to the truck when something hard rams into my side knocking me into the brick wall along the building.

Landing on my hands and knees as I hit the pavement. Pain explodes in my back when what I'm pretty sure is a foot stomps on my ribs. My attacker kicks me again in my side. It all happens so fast;

the next thing I know his hands are dragging me to my feet, holding me against the wall with a death grip on my shirt and coat. This man is a few inches taller than me, with broad arms. His hair is short and he's wearing a black leather jacket with a black ski cap. The moment everything somewhat stops spinning, I'm struggling to get him off me. Behind him I see Viktor Zarko leaning against my truck.

He's wearing a long black coat with a Cheshire smile across his stubby face.

"I warned you. I always keep my promises." he says.

"So you're the cliche bad guy with a henchman? Way to keep the stereotype," I groan as Mr, henchman punches me in the stomach.

Zarko holds up a leather glove clad finger as he steps toward me. His henchman jerks me forward, holding a knife to my throat. I want to vomit at the feeling of his body pressed against my back. The metal of the blade feels dull on my skin.

"All you had to do was one thing. One! And this could have been avoided. But no. Your little boyfriend had to go and ruin my life again."

""He didn't ruin anything!" I snap, "You ruined your life when you drove that car and killed that girl all those years ago. It was because of your own stupidity it wasn't his fault!" Viktors hand shoots out, clocking me in the face. The taste of blood explodes in my mouth. He grabs my jaw tightly in his hand, his fingers squeezing firmly.

"There's that filthy mouth again. Its time you shut the fuck up for once, angel eyes." *that nickname,* Only one person has ever called me that. I don't have any time to react because he leans back and punches me in the face. His henchman throws me to the ground, my head hits the asphalt and I start screaming as loud as I can.

Viktor grabs me by the hair but I'm thrashing too much. A kick to my back has me gasping as the air is knocked out of my lungs. I barely feel the next two kicks but It's right in the tits. Hands grab me by the throat and start to squeeze as a heavy weight sits on my chest. I don't know if it's Viktor or his henchman. I beat my hands against his, dragging my nails down his arms. Trying to claw and kick free but he's too heavy. My hands are pinned above my head as my vision starts to cloud. *No no no! Don't pass out!* I scream at myself. If I pass out I'm dead.

I think I hear the sound of a car horn and footsteps as a deep voice roars, "Get the fuck away from her!" The weight on my chest is removed and I can finally breathe. I roll onto my stomach and dry heave from how hard I'm coughing. Blood is running down my face from a cut on my forehead.

"Tabitha! Oh my god." I hear a voice I recognize as Caseys. She's kneeling in front of me, brushing my hair away from my face. She's barking into her phone to 9-1-1 I think? Everything is all spotty. I can't tell what's up and what's down. I try to push myself up but my head feels all fuzzy like I am on a tilt-a-whirl. All I can do is let out a groan as my arms wobble and I collapse to the ground as everything goes dark.

CHAPTER 42

Tabitha

I hate hospitals. So fucking much. My face hurts, my ribs and my tits hurt. I'm being wheeled through the hallway in the emergency room. I woke up in the ambulance and was able to keep awake even though I was so tired.

"Ma'am can you tell me your name?" the nurse asks me.

"Tabitha... James." I mutter, moving the oxygen mask back over my mouth and nose.

"Can you tell me where you feel pain?" I groan as the other nurse shifts the gurney as they push me into a trauma bay.

"Head, and chest."

A female police officer waits at the edge of the room.

"Miss, are you able to tell us what happened?" she asks. I can't answer over the sound of a loud voice shouting from down the hall.

"Where is she!"

"Oliver?" my voice cracks, muffled by the oxygen mask. The nurses are busy trying to assess my wounds and one of the interns goes to cut off my clothes and I freak out. Pushing them off. I'm tired of strangers touching me!

"Don't cut my shit! Fuck, I can take it off. Jesus fucking christ. Everyone just STOP TOUCHING ME!" I bark, lifting my shirt up and over my head so I was in just my bralette. The nurse to my left helps me ease the sweater over my head so it avoids my bloody hair. I wince.

"Ok, everyone OUT!" the nurse demands, she and one other nurse who was taking my vitals are the only ones in the room as the other three leave and the female officer closes the door behind them.

"Ok, Tabitha, we're going to sit you back so we can look at your ribs ok?" Nurse kick-ass says soothingly. They do an x-ray on my chest and I have no broken ribs, I would need to wear a sling for a few weeks because of my shoulder sprain. I have bruises all over my face and back.

"Ok this brow cut will need a couple stitches." she mentions.

"Can someone please get my boyfriend, he's the big hockey player bear man probably destroying the hallway to find me?" I ask.

The nurse finishes my vitals and goes to get Boone.

When Boone comes in, his hair is a mess, his beard has gravel in it and he has a bruise forming on his cheek bone.

"Hey." I squeak, reaching my good arm out to him. He closes his eyes and lets out a deep breath before putting his arms lightly around me.

"Oh my god, are you ok?"

"Are you ok?" we both asked at once.

Boone looks over all the injuries on my face. The nurse comes in with the thread to stitch me up.

The officer steps forward as the nurse begins stitching my eyebrow, "Miss. Are you able to give a statement?"

"Yes. I was attacked by Viktor Zarkov."

The room is a buzz for the next few hours. Turned out that both Oliver and Joch had to get their hands looked at because they had taken turns beating Zarko to a pulp. That figure I saw jump at the man helping Viktor, had been Joch tackling him to the ground right as Boone had gotten to Zarko. I got word that he had four police officers around his room two floors up from me. He would live. Unfortunately.

I was ok after getting fixed up and Casey helped me with getting discharged and we were getting settled into the hotel suite. Boone is a little irritated because I keep telling him to get his ass to the arena but he won't leave. The stubborn ass.

"Joch, take him with you. Oliver Boone I swear to the skydaddy that I don't even believe in if you don't go and win this game tonight or let Zarkos team be the ones to go to Boston. I will beat the ever living shit out of you with my one good arm." I growl at him. He had time to make it if he hurried and he knew that.

"Are you sure?" he asks. He wasn't going to leave unless I begged him too.

"Yes! I am with Casey and the security is outside the door. I will be safe. I am safe and I am ok. But I will not be happy If you stay here and miss the game tonight." I push.

"Are we going? I just need to know if I'm dragging him out the door or carrying him like a sexy fireman? Either way I'll do it. Just need to know now." Joch pipes up.

"But we need to go like now bro, coach is blowing up my phone needing to know if we're coming or not." He adds. Boone presses a kiss to my forehead.

"Call me if anything happens."

CHAPTER 43

Tabitha

It was official, The Skyhawks were heading to the Stanley cup! My shoulder is healed and I don't need the sling anymore. I had my finals and with Boone at training, doing media crap or practice it gave me a few days to myself to study and do homework. I also found the time to actually take down the Christmas decorations. I also had the strong urge to reorganize the closets. Boone has a huge closet that reminded me of a smaller version of Khloe Kardashian's. It's organized with all his suits hung in one section with the shoes neatly set in the built-in wall shoe rack with work boots, and regular shoes in the rows underneath. He has a safe in the top drawer of this island style dresser with all his watches inside. Half the closet was cleared out for me and it normally is not organized at all. But after about three hours, I have it organized by pants, sweaters, dresses, overalls.

My shoes are all lined up nicely. The cute storage containers had more winter sweaters in them and are now organized. The second drawer in the center island, below the watches, is a drawer for my underwear, bras, body suits and socks.

Casey and Perry were supposed to be stopping by after work for a drink, I go down to the kitchen to get started on making some to store in the freezer until they got here. The moment I taste the strawberry flavored tequila, bile rises in my throat and thankfully I'm already in front of the sink when my stomach rolls and everything in my stomach comes up.

"Ugh. gross." I grimace as my stomach rolls again and I throw up stomach acid for the next ten minutes. My stomach hurts and my back is coated in sweat. Once I finally am done throwing up I practically crawl up the steps into the master bathroom for a shower.

Thankfully the shower and brushing my teeth helped. As I change into sweats and a Heather gray t-shirt. I'm zipping up the hoodie when my stomach feels...off. I feel sore and a little stiff which is normal after just getting sick but my stomach itself feels not hard but tight? It's looking at my slightly plump boobs that have my eyes widening and me reaching for my phone. *Shit. Shit shit. THIS CAN'T BE WHAT I THINK IT IS.* Casey answers on the third ring.

I hear Perry burst through the front door mid sprint, "I'm here! I'm here, I'm here. Where are you!" she calls huffing as her footsteps thump up the steps.

"In the bathroom." Casey calls back. I'm sitting in the empty bathtub staring at the closed toilet seat lid.

Perry comes in and tries talking but holds up a hand because she has to catch her breath.

She had on her work clothes still, black leather pants and loose, flowy sheer black top. Her hair is curled into beach waves down her back.

"I...think...I got enough. Old lady behind the counter gave me the stink eye and serious attitude." she gulps, "Choice words were said. Needless to say I am officially trespassed from that CVS. But I got you the tests." She dry swallows, holding her chest trying to catch her breath as she drops the bag on the counter then proceeds to lay down on the floor of the bathroom.

"I don't think I'll get another result after four tests that say the same thing." I say pulling at my hair. I have taken four of the six tests Perry had brought me. Each one has the same result.

"Maybe we should all take one, just to be sure?" Casey suggests, "Girl, do not even put that energy on me. That would be like saying "come at me bro to karma." Perry shakes her head.

"Guys, I'm freaking the fuck out here." I say, my hands shaking as realization sets in just how fucked I am.

"Ok, let's not panic, I can get you in with my doctor today, We can get a confirmation." Casey soothes. She takes my hand and pulls me to my feet.

"Yeah, I mean false results happen like, thirty percent of the time." Perry agrees, "Hey, you're gonna be fine. we got you." her squeezing my hand gave me reassurance.

I'm ok. I'll be ok.

Two hours later; Casey, Perry and I wait in the Arby's drive through after the appointment. We get milkshakes and fries and burgers. Casey parks in the parking lot and we just stare.

"Holy. Shit." I break the quiet. Perry nods in agreement, taking a sip of her drink. She was in the back seat, but was leaning forward over the center console.

"Holy. Shit."

"Fuck." Casey breathes out.

I look at the positive blood test results in my hand. The doctor confirmed what the tests already told us.

I'm pregnant.

Apparently it isn't uncommon for some women to not know they were pregnant and show no signs. I was so confused since I was under the impression I had an implant in my arm, even had a little scar to prove it. Imagine my surprise when the doctor informed me that the scar tissue was there but there was in fact no implant in my arm. My ex foster parents were in the medical field and my foster mom had gotten me the implant after I had been with them for a few months. I remembered getting it. I remember since it was the same night I ran away. So that question lingered on what happened to the implant?

"So this entire time, you have just been raw doggin each other?" Perry asks, shoving a fry in her mouth.

"You know I never really stopped to think 'hey maybe we should put on a condom?' Fuck. We were so dumb." Never in my almost twenty four years had I ever thought I would not remember a freaking condom.

"How did the hospital not know you were pregnant?" Casey dipped a fry in her shake.

"I thought I was on my period, but apparently I was spotting and that can be normal- oh Fuck, how am I going to tell Boone?" It's less than two months before The Stanley cup! He was busy training and we had only just gotten into a good rhythm. I was about to graduate with my degree and start focusing on what to do with that. I can't be a mother! My own mother was a horrible mother, I don't have any idea what to do with a kid!

Casey could see the storm in my head and gave my shoulder a squeeze, "You need to tell Oliver. This is a big choice you both need to figure out. Whatever happens You know he will support you. He's head over heels in love with you." She's right. I know Boone would be supportive. But there was a small voice inside me that wondered that 'what if?' like what if this isn't what he wanted? What if this chased him off?

Boone comes home super early the next morning. He'd driven through the night after the game to get home early so we could spend the day together. He came into the bedroom, being quiet because he thought I was asleep. I listen to him go into the bathroom and turn the shower on. I hadn't slept all night, the anxiety was building a pit in my stomach. Climbing out of bed, my feet pad across the carpet and I knock on the door, "Hey babe." my voice rises an octave a bit as I pull my robe around myself before pushing open the door. Boone stands in the shower, letting me see a peak at that delicious naked body that I had missed the past week. I trail my eyes over every curve, every muscled soft crevice. He shut the water off and steps onto the bath mat.

"Hey baby." He smiles before wrapping the towel around his waist, I inch into the bathroom and set the test on the counter before moving back.

Boone slowed in his toweling off his hair and looked at the test before looking at me, his mouth hanging open.

I speak, trying to keep myself from having an anxiety attack, it comes out a little wobbly but I say it so he hears me.

"I'm pregnant."

Boom. Mic drop. Can't take it back now. The band aid is ripped off.

Boone places his hands on the counter, "Are you sure?" he asks, then squeezes his eyes shut, "Shit, wait duh, the test says positive so that means you are sure." He shakes his head.

"Yup. There's a very secretive bun in my oven. And it's very good at playing hide and seek.

At least for the past four and a half months if the one test was accurate." Boone looks at me, "Four! That means when Zarko..." anger flashes in his eyes. His fingers reach to caress my stomach.

"We're both ok. At least I think so." I say quickly, placing my hands over his as the tears burn my eyes and my lip trembles.

"I'm so sorry." my voice cracks. Boone shakes his head, "Why are you apologizing?" he cups my face, wiping a stray tear with his thumb.

"This is the worst timing. I didn't know I didn't still have my implant in my arm, I'm so sorry."

Boone smiles and tilts his head to rest his forehead on mine as he whispers, "Baby, this isn't your fault. It took both of us to make this happen. I'm not mad at you."

"What do you wanna do?" he asks.

"I'm scared." I admit. "I don't know how to take care of a baby, what if I fuck this kid up like my parents fucked me up?" Boone pulls me into his chest tightly.

"You have me, I'm not letting you go through this alone. I will be here for you every step. Whatever you choose." He kisses away each tear.

"Besides, no one really knows what they are doing when they have a kid. We'll learn. I'll read every what to expect book and watch all the how to parent videos. I'll teach the pee wee hockey. We'll do this together." my heart feels like it is going to explode. Even though I am terrified of this. I want it.

"So it's going to be a hockey player?" I chuckle.

"Hell yea. Little ninja baby will be the fastest player on the ice." He sniffles.

I nod as tears form in my eyes, "We're having a baby."

Boone let out a laugh, "Oh shit, we're having a baby."

He kisses me deeply. Oh fuck. This was happening. I was gonna have a baby.

Our kisses turn needy and urgent. I pull loose his towel and it falls to the floor. Boone grumbles, slowly backing us up to the bed.

"Are you sure you wanna do this?" He asks.

I nod.

CHAPTER 44

Boone

I was going to be a dad... Holy shit. Holy fucking shit! Obviously it was totally a stupid thing to not have used protection. Absolutely, but I don't regret it. Tabitha was chewing on her nail as we waited for the nurse to set up the ultrasound.

"What if something is wrong?" she asks me. I take her hand and squeeze it. She has been worrying about this visit for the past three days and I was too. I swear if Zarko did something to cause any issues with our baby, I would kill him.

"Hey," I brush her hair behind her ear, "No matter what it is we'll take care of it. We will adapt and figure it out. Ok? We got this." I assured her. I may have stayed up a few nights researching possible things that could happen to children if trauma happens before birth so I knew the possibilities but still was scared shitless.

"I understand you only recently found out about this pregnancy, and had trauma early on that you're concerned about?" the tech asked.

"Yes. There was some trauma. I didn't know and I'm... I just wanna make sure everything is ok."

She nodded, sucking in a breath as the tech moved the wand over Tabitha's stomach. After a few agonizing moments there was a sound like a wind tunnel *'whorp-whorp-whorp-whorp-whrop'* filled the room.

"There you are. There's your baby." The tech smiled, turning the screen to us.

Tabitha let out a shaky sob, "Is everything ok? It's ok right? Nothing is wrong with it?" she asked. The tech moved the wand around and smiled at her.

"Everything looks fine. Perfectly healthy baby." she said. Tabitha nodded and then looked at me, tears in her eyes as the biggest smile spread across her face.

"It's ok." she said. I nod as my own tears burn my eyes. I kiss her temple, "Congratulations baby." I whisper as she sobs..

Joch knew something was up the moment he got in the truck.

"Ok either you and TJ found a new position, in which case sharing is caring. Or something really good happened. You're walking like you got air under your feet." I pull out of the gate and shoot him a look.

"Ok, but this is literally a 'no one can know' kind of thing." I say. He crossed himself and took a bite out of his apple. I pulled up the photo of the sonogram on my phone and handed it to him. His mouth drops open.

"Tabithas pregnant."

"Holy shit, wait is this a good thing or is this a bad thing, I'm assuming by your mood it's a good thing?" he asks.

"It's a fucking amazing thing. I mean I'm kinda freaking out because holy shit I'm gonna be a dad but at the same time I'm like *I'm gonna be a dad.* You know?" holy shit I felt all jittery and my heart was hammering in my chest.

"How far along is she?" Joch asked.

I let out a low laugh, "That's the thing... She's already almost four and a half months."

"So," he squints his eyes as he did the math, "Christmas time? New years... but wait. That means when Zarko." my grip on the steering wheel tightened, "Yea we got checked out and everything is fine. The baby is ok thank god."

"Holy shit. Congrats man. you're gonna be a dad." Joch smiles and I notice him turning away and sniffling.

"Are you crying?" I cock a brow at him.

"No! Just got apple in my eye. It's salty." his voice cracks.

CHAPTER 45

Tabitha

"I swear if I have to smell a philly cheese one more time, I'm gonna vomit." I groaned, dumping my last table's dishes into the sink.

Charlotte smiled at me, "Just wait, When I was pregnant with Liam, just the thought of milk would make me projectile vomit." I groaned and rubbed a hand over my head, my hair twisted into two french braids. I had on a black zip up hoodie to hide the noticeable swell of my stomach.

"I don't know how I'm gonna do this." I sighed standing in front of the walk in to let the cold air hit me.

"How long are you going to keep it out of the news?" Georgia asked.

"As long as possible. There's already so much press around because of the finals coming up. I'm glad I got a few hours here." paparazzi had become so unbearable the past few weeks that Mick had told me to stay home since they were camping out around the bar. I let out a sigh and went to clear my last table before leaving for the day. A guy with a green mohawk stepped in my way and collided with me.

"Oh shit. Sorry." he apologized.

"I'm ok." I said brushing past him. I stopped and cocked my head giving the guy a second look.

He looked to be in his mid twenties, medium build dressed in a blue hoodie and jeans. His hair cut into a short green mohawk. That green hair. I had seen him before, on one of my first runs in the neighborhood, the day the Carmichaels house was broken into; he had been in a work truck outside one of the houses. And the day I thought I saw Marvin in the bar. I shook my head and went back behind the bar.

"I'm heading out." I said to Mick.

"Take care dear." he called.

Something didn't sit right with me after seeing that guy.

I had been doing a little shopping the past few weeks to get a few things for the baby. Most of them were online orders to prevent people from finding out about the pregnancy before we were ready to share it. Boone didn't want to announce anything at all and just keep everything within the friend group- an idea I agreed with one hundred percent. Casey had already paired up with Perry and gifted us twenty boxes of diapers and onesies.

Rosea and Leanna had brought over gifts of bottles and items I would actually need, one being a bottle warmer.

When I walked into the house I saw Bohdie, Joch and Boone all sitting in the living room confused over baby crib directions.

"I don't get this." Joch said trying to make heads or tails of it.

"I have a degree in engineering and I can't fucking figure this shit out." Bohdie shrugged. Joch scrunched up his face and looked at him, "Since when do you have an engineering degree?" Joch asked.

"What do you think I majored in at University?" He replied.

"Damn, youse a smart one ain't ya big guy." Joch winked. Boone cocked a brow, "Please don't fuck in my living room." he asked.

"Having fun?" I asked, leaning against the island.

Boone smiled as he came over and kissed me, "Hey." he said, giving my hip a squeeze.

"Just trying to put together a crib, beautiful." Joch called.

"I knew we should have asked Kam or Tig to help." Bohdie muttered.

"How was work?" Boone asked, grabbing a plate from the fridge and taking the saran wrap off it. He had started to make me turkey sandwiches every day to eat when I got home. I moaned as I took the first bite, "So good." he looked at me and I could see the heat in his eyes. He had been busy with the games and all the press over the past few weeks that we hadn't had any time for other things.

"Hey, uh guys I think we're gonna just do the crib another day." Boone called without even looking at them.

I stare at my reflection in the full body mirror, my breasts are a bit fuller and my stomach is getting slightly rounder every week. My hips were also a bit wider too. My body was changing.

Boone walked up behind me resting his large calloused hands on my naked hips "What is it?"

"Just looking at the changes." I commented.

Boone dipped his head and kissed my cheek. His hands move to hold my small bump, "If you would like my opinion? I think your body is beautiful." he murmured as he kissed my neck.

"Thank you." I grab the mauve robe from where it's hanging off the side of the mirror and wrap it around my body.

"I wanted to ask, did they find anything after the Carmichaels house was broken into?" Boone scratched his beard as he thought, "I don't think so why?" He picks out a pair of gray sweatpants from the clean laundry pile and pulls them up his thick legs.

"I remembered something from that day and I don't know if it is connected but I don't know." I cross my arms over my chest, "There was a van, a utility repair van outside the neighbors house that morning. I saw it on my run that morning and there was a guy with a short green mohawk. And I saw him at the bar." I explained. Boones brow furrowed, "You sure it was the same guy?"

I nodded, "I saw him a couple times, and now that I think about it, I saw that van around the neighborhood a few times." Boone grabbed a black tshirt and pulled it over his head.

"I'll call that detective that was here when our house was broken into." he said.

Boone was on the phone for a little bit and then the detective wanted to talk to me. I recounted everything I remembered and how I had seen this guy at the bar a couple times. By the end of the phone call he had enough to bring in the guy for questioning. He wanted me to ID him from the footage on the bar's security in the morning.

CHAPTER 46

Tabitha

Twelve days away from the biggest game of Boones career and he was cool as a cucumber. All week he had to dress up for media interviews meaning I got to oogle his ass in those snug fitted tailored pants while he got ready. His muscular, fit, body in those suits was so fucking hot.

"Baby girl, If you keep looking at me like that, I will bend you over this table." He smirked watching me in the mirror.

"Good luck. Baby Boone makes that impossible. But If you wanna bend me over your knee then have at it."

Boone groaned. "You are insatiable." he chuckled.

He was right, my hormones were raging whenever it came to him and I was already pregnant so what more could happen? I only had a few things to do today anyway. I had to meet up with the police detective and then grab my wallet from the bar. I was in such a rush yesterday I forgot it in my locker.

"I believe you were the one who went four rounds last night before finally being tired." I pointed out. Boone shook his head and stood in front of me, taking his tie and putting it around my neck to pull me in for a scorching kiss.

"If I didn't have media shit all day I would tie you up in our bed." he mused, his beard scratching my skin as he lightly sucked on my neck.

"Oh? Tell me more." I urge as his kisses move down to my collar bone. He climbs on top of me as his hand travels between my legs, his finger

dips inside me then circles my clit teasing me.

"Hey Oliver! You ready man?" Joch calls

from down stairs. *Go away!* I want to scream.

I groan as Boone pulls away, "Tell him you're

occupied." I laugh pulling him back. Boone laughs

as he leans back, "Be down in a moment." he

replies.

"I can be quick." I promised biting my lip.

Boones eyes lit up, "Let's see how quick." he winks.

The bar is bustling as usual when I walk in.

Georgia is behind the bar and smiles when she

sees me.

"I didn't know you worked today?" she asks

as I walk behind the bar, "I forgot my wallet," I say

looking around, "You need any help, It's pretty busy." I offer. I had already talked to the detective and Perry was supposed to come over later on to help me sort baby stuff.

"Nah, Char is in the back and we have Shawn and Luc taking care of the crowd." she explains, following me to the back area where a row of lockers are.

"How's Baby B?" she whispers. My hand goes to my stomach, "Pretty good, making me hungry for almost everything constantly." I smile as I rub my hand over my hidden bump.

"I remember that." she mutters. I cock my head, "What do you mean?" Georgia's eyes go wide as if she realizes she said that outloud.

"Nothing." she smiles before she hurries back to the front. Mick pokes his head out of the kitchen and sees me, "Hey, there was a guy in here earlier looking for you." he says.

"They leave a name?" I ask, putting my wallet into my bag.

"No, he was a little sketchy. Had a bit of scruff and bald head. I don't make it a habit of giving my employees schedules out and he didn't seem too pleased with that." he explained. I swallow the lump forming in my throat, "Thanks for looking out Boss. I'll see you." I wave and head out front.

Scruff... bald head. My pulse quickens, it couldn't be. There was no possible way it could be- someone steps in my line of sight at the entrance and I gasp. Viktor Zarko had just walked into TAPHOWZE. I pause at the swinging door, how the fuck is he here! I spin on my heels and peace out the back exit getting to the truck, locking the doors

before trying to call Boone.

"Oliver, It's me. I know you're busy but

please call me back. Viktor Zarko was at

TAPHOWZE." I have been calling him the entire

drive home but he wasn't answering. Joch and

Casey also aren't answering. I drop my purse on

the island and try Casey again. My eyes wander

around the kitchen and something catches my eye.

The butcher block where all the knives were

supposed to be. I say supposed to because it's

empty?

"What the.." the sound of keys jingling has

me spinning around and jerking back a few steps,

letting out a yell.

"Hey sis." Marvin smiles, leaning against the door frame of the laundry room.

CHAPTER 47

Boone

I look at my watch again, I have another three hours of interviews then I am free to go home. Most of the questions are asking me about how it felt to be retiring after all the years playing hockey, what I am going to do next? Asking me about my relationship, was a wedding in the future for me. I really just want to say, 'Yes I am retiring and my next thing I am going to do is enjoy being a father and marrying the love of my life.' but that would only open a can of worms I don't want opened. The team has been doing press all day and now I was getting a little irritated at some of the questions about Tabitha or as the media knew her as TJ. she had no social media so they weren't able to get any info on her really and that was something that always made them act more invasive than normal.

Joch gives me a thumbs up as he finished his interview.

"Are there any truths to the rumors going around that wedding bells are in your future? You took the internet by surprise by posting that Christmas picture of you and your girlfriend." the reporter, a woman named Darshna, asks. The top three buttons of her silk light blue blouse are undone. Her chocolate brown hair is in big curls that end right above her chest. I smile, "I really like to keep my personal life out of the public eye, more to respect the privacy of my partner." I notice her eye twitch at my response. She was the one who printed the story about one of our rookies' engagements right before he was going to ask and ruined it after he had been planning for months.

"The elusive TJ, reporters have had no luck getting a clear story about the lady who conquered The Mountain. A few of the recent photos show her wearing suspiciously baggy clothes and many are assuming that could mean a new addition to the Boone family is on the way? I guess congratulations are in order." a muscle in my jaw ticks at that comment. I steel my expression and adjust my posture. Darshna is a ruthless reporter and there is no way I will let her be the one to break this story.

"I think it's a shame that people make assumptions on someone's body simply because they wear what makes them comfortable. Isn't it a rule that you never assume a woman is pregnant just because she has gained a little weight? Your question is not only rude but offensive."

"So there's no truth to the rumors?"

"TJ values her privacy. And I do as well. Good on you for body shaming my partner." I stand.

"I think we're done here." I rip the mic off and drop it on my seat as I make my way out of the interview room and hear my name being called by one of the local reporters, normally I'd keep walking but his question has me stopping.

"Oliver, any comment on the release of Viktor Zarko?" he asks. I stop mid step, turning my head to look at him. He is a man in his forties with thinning brown hair, and a thick mustache. He's a local reporter named Harold, if I remember right.

"What did you just say?" I ask.

"Viktor Zarko was released last night on bail." he sputtered. Harold was old school with info and was always good for a true story. So I don't doubt what he has is correct.

I look at my media manager, Mitchel, "Where's my phone?" he patted his pockets and shook his head, "Office." I push past him and practically throw the door to the meeting room open where my jacket was draped over a chair and dig out my phone.

"Hey man, you ok?" Joch asks, a slice of lemon halfway to his mouth.

"No. Viktor was released last night." I grunt, cursing when I see I have seven missed calls from Tabitha. Along with an alert on the ring video feed in the garage. Tabitha's phone goes right to voicemail so I pull the feed to the garage up and feel my heart leap into my throat.

Tabitha was in the garage with a man who had a knife to her belly.

"Get the police to my house right now!" I roar at Mitchel. Joch is right behind me as I sprint down the hallway.

CHAPTER 48

Tabitha

I am looking at my living nightmare. Marvin stands across from me in the doorway to the laundry room. The island is the only thing between us. He's taller, still lanky, but filled out a bit more than the last time I had seen him. His hair is still the type of blonde that looks like wet sand. Above his left eye is the scar where his eyebrow should be. I had given him that scar the night he gave me mine. The memory was still fresh all these years ago.

"Get off me!" I screamed as Marvin sat on top of my legs. I was on my stomach and couldn't get him off me. I grabbed the first thing I could get

my hands on. He had been burning designs into wood for a school project earlier and the pen sat on its side, the hot tip cooling. In my struggle I managed to grab onto the pen, throwing my arm back, slashing it across his face, the hot curved part of the pen sliced across his brow taking the skin with it like a hot knife through butter. Marvin reared back holding his face.

"You bitch!" he roared, grabbing onto my hand that held the pen. He bent my wrist painfully, pressing the metal tip into the side of my palm burning the skin. The sight of my tears had him, to my disgust, hard. He smiled down at me. His free hand that was holding my neck tightened.

"It's time I show you who you belong to."

And Now he is standing in my fucking kitchen.

"It's been so long hasn't it." his eyes flash to my stomach and rage fills them. Instinctively I hold my arm around my belly protectively.

"You've been one busy whore, haven't you angel eyes." he accused, moving slowly to the side of the island. I mirror his movements, keeping as much space between us as I can. He sneers as he looks at the kitchen, "Nice digs. You hooked a rich one didn't you?"

"How did you find me?" I ask.

"It was easy after the news broke about you and loverboy. But I've known for a while where you were." he admits.

Marvin raises a brow, at my shocked face, "Oh I've known you were here for months. I could have got you that night at your old house, but I wanted you scared, and wanted that thrill of the hunt. So I let you *slip* through my grasp." he sucks on his teeth as he eye fucks me up and down.

"I *almost* had you too." Marvin glowered at me, scrunching his nose up and smiling.

"Being so close to you. All the things that I could have done to you went through my head and I would have enjoyed every moment of it."

I want to vomit. How did he manage to get into this house? The metallic gray work shirt with 'Plummer' on the pocket was the answer. The same brand that had been on the work van. It clicked.

"The break ins. It's been you this entire time hasn't it?" Ingenieus, disguising themselves as plumbers to break into houses in a rich neighborhood. No one would think twice about them. Fuck the police really *were* stupid if they let them get away with this that long.

"You'd be amazed at how easy hacking those doorbell cameras are. Shutting them off without anyone noticing or looping footage. It helps that the security here is fucking stupid." he laughs.

It's at this moment I see the large kitchen knife in his hand. That explains where the knives went. My phone is on the counter closer to him than me so calling for help is out of the plan. If I could get out the patio door maybe I could get to Caseys and hit her alarm. I may be five months pregnant but I am still fast. He must figure out my plan because he points the knife at me, "Don't be dumb, Natalie. She was and look at her." He points his knife to my right and I look over my shoulder.

My heart drops when I see Perry lying in the hallway on her side in a small puddle of blood.

"Perry!" I scream running to her. Her forehead is cut and she's unconscious, but she's breathing. Her keys are hooked to her belt loop and I try as best I can to grab the multi-keyed keyring quietly. Marvin comes up behind me and grabs me by the hair. I can't struggle because he holds the knife to my throat.

"Now that this ridiculous back and forth is over. Time to go." he muses before taking a long sniff of my hair. Bile rises in my throat and my spine stiffens when he lowers the knife to my stomach and applies slight pressure. Not enough to cut me but enough to get his point across. *No no no.*

"Oh? What's this, suddenly feeling cooperative?" He pulls me by the arm through the laundry room and into the garage.

"What no goons to help you with your bidding?" I spit.

"Zarko figured he'd let me have this little family reunion." And that answered my other question. There was no way Zarko could have known my real name and now I knew who had told him. This meant that Zarko was also involved in the break-ins.

"Imagine my surprise seeing my sister after seven years. Not only *whoring* herself out at the brothel, that I can forgive. But now you're unmarried and knocked up too!" he hisses. '*There he is.*' the corner of my mouth hitches into a dry smirk. The holier than thou, controlling, boy he always was is still in there. In his sick mind if he did it then it wasn't a "sin" but if I did it? Oh boy it's nothing but a sin and needing punishment. His control slowly unraveled before me. The thing about Marvin is once he loses control, he gets sloppy and his anger clouds his judgment. And I am about to make him to loose his fucking mind.

"Pissed you off that I was claimed by someone better than you? Someone who I went to *willingly and wanted*?" I sneer.

"You are *mine!* You should have stayed where you belong! I ripped out that birth control so you could be mine and now." his glare turns to my stomach, full of hatred. I step back again, "I was never yours, you sick fuck!" I hold up the pepper spray I'd grabbed from Perrys keys and unload it into his face. Marvin lets out a wail as the spray hits his eyes and I bolt into the house, him hot on my heels. Marvin grabs onto me right as Perry comes out of nowhere and lets out a yell as she hits him over the head with the wooden knife block. Marvin goes down like a brick.

Perry has a thin trail of blood down the side of her face, her black hair is a mess. But she's alive and ok.

"Perry!"

"Fuck, are you ok?" she gasps, pulling my gun out from her waistband.

"I grabbed it from the safe in the living room." Her voice is hoarse as she catches her breath. Thank fuck she remembered. Boone knew about the gun and I had only moved it to the bookcase the other day when he had gotten the new case that made it so the safe was like a fake stack of books.

"We gotta go. Gotta go." I say grabbing for my keys.

Like something out of a horror movie, Marvin is on his feet. He stabs Perry in the stomach, she screams, "Ah YOU DICK!" as he shoves her aside before he grabs me by the hair, yanking it hard, "Not so fast!" he growls. Blood coating his teeth.

"Get off her!" Perry yells jumping on his back. We fall back and crash through the glass patio door. I land hard on my side, pain radiates through my hip, my gun slides across the patio out of reach. Perry lands on top of Marvin. He flips her off his back and gets on top of me, I see the knife still in his hand right before he brings it down and stabs it into my thigh. The scream rips from my throat as I jerk back. *Shit! This fucker just stabbed me!* Oh now I am pissed. Perry is on him as she digs her nails into his face from behind and yanks his head back, he takes the knife with him. Blood seeps through my pants from the stab wound. *Oh I was gonna kill this one eyebrowed cunt.*

"Get off her!" Perry roars, pulling him back going for the knife. I wedge my foot between our bodies, kicking out from under him as we wrestle for the knife. Perry is once again on his back, putting her weight on his shoulder in some wrestling move as she twists the knife out of his hand, Marvins elbow snaps back, hitting her in the face, dazing her before he slams her head against the broken door frame knocking her out. The knife clatters across the glass covered patio, And I pray to a god I don't believe in that my best friend isn't dead.

The gun. Wheres the fucking gun!

I spot it just out of reach and scramble for it, slipping on the broken glass marbles and blood.

Mine or Perry's I don't know.

Just as my fingers graze the gun, Marvin is on me. His chest pressing to my back, as he wraps his forearm around my neck and pulls me tight against him, "I am gonna carve that fucking bastard child out of you." he hisses into my ear.

"I wonder how Oliver will feel, coming home to find you freshly fucked and cut open. Shall we find out?" Rage fills my body. This sick fuck wasn't going to hurt my baby. He hurt me and tortured me for years. No more. I am going to kill him. Letting out a roar, I pivot our bodies and then throw my weight back, using his force to my advantage sending us both into the shallow end of the freezing cold pool.

I'm on my feet fast. The water chills my bones. Its fucking COLD!

I lunge forward, grabbing the gun as Marvin comes at me but I'm already raising it, squeezing the trigger and shooting him in the shoulder. His body jerks back, pressing his hand to his bleeding shoulder letting out a string of curse words.

"You wont hurt my baby." I bark, keeping the gun aimed at him. I squeeze the trigger again but the gun makes that tell tale click sound of being jammed.

Mother fucking cock sucker!

Marvin grins and moves faster than I expect him to. He shoves me back against the concrete ledge, the hand holding the gun tight in his grip as he slams it against the siding. I have no choice but to let go of it, I have no clue where it goes because hands are around my throat as he begins to use his weight to dunk my head under water. Marvin lets me up for air only briefly. I thrash against him, trying to get free from his vice grip.

"You. Destroyed. Everything!" he screams in my face before shoving my head under water again. He pulls me up so I can see every new cut on his face, the scratches Perry gouged into his skin. The blood in his teeth. *I am so tired.* My arms feel so heavy. But I won't give up.

Fight! Tabitha. You need to fight bitch! A voice screams inside my head.

He holds me underwater, pressing me down so far my back touches the bottom of the pool.

Something hard presses against my back. If it wouldn't make me have a mouthful of water I would cry. My fingers find the tip of the knife. I'm pulled up and manage to suck in a breath of air, seeing Marvin smile before he presses his lips to mine in a disgusting, nauseating kiss.

Letting out a growl, I sink my teeth into his bottom lip and shove my thumb into his bleeding bullet wound. Marvin lets out a sound that was a cross between a pig and a rooster screeching. Pain erupts in my face as he hits me and pushes me back underwater. My fingers wrap around the handle of the knife. My feet are under me this time and I push up, using all my strength I bring that knife up and sink it to the hilt right into the spot between his collarbone and neck, letting out a wail as I do. Scrambling back until my shoulders hit the pool ledge. Marvin screams as he realizes how fucked up he is. My eyes go wide when he pulls the knife out and takes one step towards me. *What the ever loving fucking christ is this guy on! Why won't he die!*

He steps toward me again. Right as a gunshot shatters the silence and a bullet goes through his skull.

CHAPTER 49

Boone

I've never blacked out before. One moment I was in the truck, slamming it into park. The next moment I was in the backyard with Tabitha's gun in my hand shooting Marvin three times. My mom was born and raised in Texas so of course she owned a gun and taught me gun safety growing up and how to shoot. The moment I see him stop moving is when I go to my girl.

"Tabitha!" I yell. I set the gun down as I jump in the pool next to her.

"Are you ok? Look at me. Look at me baby." I hold her cut face in my hands. I have no idea if the baby is ok and I can't worry about it now because she is my top priority. Joch crouches down and grabs her under her arms, helping me hoist her out of the pool.

"Ow ow ow. Fucker got me in the leg. Oh, Joch," she grabs his arm and points behind him, "Perry! Go help Perry!" she urges. Joch moves around the glass and kneels down next to Perry.

She's groaning in pain, blood coming from her stomach.

"Oh fuck. That's a lot of blood." Joch curses.

"No shit. He got me in the stomach." Perry's voice shakes as she speaks. Joch takes his jacket off and presses it to her stomach.

Tabitha leans back on her hand and rubs her other hand over her belly, tears burning her eyes, "It was him. Marvin and Zarko were both behind the break-ins and he was in the house that night when I was attacked." she explained. She begins to shiver violently and thankfully the EMS chooses that moment to roll in as the cops clear the house and yard.

The EMS load Tabitha up in the ambulance, she's wrapped in so many warming blankets and has an IV started. She also has a death grip on my hand but I don't fucking care about the pain.

Casey's car screeches to a stop in her driveway and she sprints toward us, "Go with Perry! Someone needs to go with Perry!" Tabitha shouts.

Casey halts and I see her cover her mouth as she climbs into the ambulance that has Perry loaded up in.

"Is the baby ok?" Tabitha asks the emt in the back with us. The emt is a younger girl around Tabitha's age.

"We'll have a better idea once we get to the hospital, ok?" she smiles and steps up front as they set off the sirens and follow Perrys ambulance.

Tabitha looks at me and I press her hand to my mouth, "it's gonna be ok baby." I assure her and myself. She's ok. She has to be ok.

The first thing they do when we get to the ER is do an ultrasound. Tabitha refuses to let them do anything until she sees proof the baby is ok. I'm standing next to Tabitha, both of her hands hold mine tightly as she presses her forehead against them. It's a murderously slow few moments as the OB moves the doppler over her belly. We both erupt into sobs the moment we hear that wonderful quick wind tunnel *thru thur thru thur* sound of the heart beat and see the shape of the baby on the screen.

"There you are. Heartbeat is strong. Everything looks fine. We'll check again later and tomorrow to be safe. For now I'll have them monitor you two overnight for even the smallest change."

The doctor says as the nurses begin to take the wet clothes off Tabitha. One apologizes for having to cut her jeans off and Tabitha shakes her head, "Just get these things off me." she says.

I don't leave her side the entire time. Not even to change out of the wet clothes I'm wearing. It's only when Casey comes in with a change of clothes for both of us that I leave the room. She also begs me to check on Perry. Which I do.

She was in surgery to stitch up her stab wound and would make a full recovery. I take a minute in the hallway feeling my legs give out, Joch is right there to catch me.

"She's ok. She and the baby are ok." I force out as finally I feel the emotions hit me and Joch practically holds me up as I fall apart.

"I almost lost them both. That gunshot. I thought." I gasp out as Joch just hugs me tighter.

"I know man. I know." He soothes. Joch pulls away and holds my shoulders, "She's alive. She's alive- they both are. And they are well." he says. I nod wiping my nose and eyes. The fear I felt when I was running up the driveway and heard that first gunshot go off was something I never wanted to feel again. Losing the woman I love, along with our child would have destroyed me beyond repair.

I sniffle and put my hands on my hips, "I need to move out of that fucking house." I say and Joch snorts.

"You and every other person on the block."

he agrees. Joch hands me an apple and takes a

bite out of the other one.

"The entire fucking development needs an

fucking exorsism." he adds. News had already got

out about the entire thing at the house and Mitchel

was calling my phone nonstop. The reports have

videos of Perry being rushed into the ambulance

with Joch following and they also got the moment

Tabitha was brought to the ambulance. I

finally answer the phone on his tenth call.

"Number one. Is she ok, is everyone ok?"

he asks when I finally answer.

"Yeah, Mitch, everyone is alright." I sigh

sitting down.

"Ok, so it's all over the news about the

break in and the shooting. Tabitha being in the

hospital." he explains everything that is being

thrown around in the media. People are posting about prayers and wishing Tabitha a speedy recovery. Miraculously nothing about her being pregnant makes it to the press. At this point I wouldn't care if it had.

"They have a monitor on the baby just for precautions and want her to stay overnight. So I'll be missing the next game tomorrow." I tell him.

"Of course. Take the time you need." Mitch says. I'm very happy they fired my last PR manager. I look at Tabitha, she's sleeping finally. The nurses gave her something to help her sleep that was safe for the baby.

I can't leave the room. I'm too afraid of something happening to her. I barely sleep that night. Everytime the nurses come in to check on her I jump awake.

The nurse updates us on Perry the next morning. She's awake and moving around which is good. She'll be taking it easy the next few months.

She's apparently been flirting with the hospital security guard since she woke up. At one point Casey takes over and I'm forced to get some sleep under threat of being tranq'd by Tabitha.

Correction her exact words are, "Either you willingly get some sleep or I will have the nurses let Joch poke you in the ass cheek with a tranquilizer shot."

CHAPTER 50

Tabitha

A full eight days later and I am finally able to walk into the house. Casey had arranged for a full deep cleaning to be done on the entire downstairs, the pool was drained and covered, the patio door was replaced with a new one. She had it all done as fast as possible. The crime scene tape was gone. It was like nothing ever happened. But it did.

Both Perry and I would carry the scars for the rest of our lives. Perry had to have her spleen removed but she would live.

Zarko was arrested at the train station the same day as the attack. His green haired goon spilled the beans. He sold him out. Zarko and

Marvin had been working together for the past year and when I came into the picture Zarko saw it as a two birds one stone thing.

Boone was at the arena by force, my force. I had Bohdie and Joch practically kidnap him. The stanley cup was in four days and I am not going to let his career end with him just quietly leaving the sport he played most of his life. I wanted to watch my man get into one more fight on the ice before he didn't play anymore.

I have on a snug long sleeved black shirt that was cinched by the stomach showing off my bump, and a pair of dark gray leggings. Casey and I had gone to get our nails and hair done. The stylist did a great job of tidying up my long fringe curtain bangs.

"Hey. you ok?" Casey asked, walking in behind me. Perry shuffled in behind her wearing tennis shoes and a black jumpsuit with a large sweater over it.

"Yea. Just looking around." I say. My hand unconsciously rubbing over my growing baby bump, something I noticed was now a habit whenever I felt uneasy.

Casey gave my shoulder a squeeze. I will be staying with her for the next couple of days while the team is preparing for the big game. They all were in a hotel downtown. I was only here to grab some clothes. And my game day outfit.

"We have a few options, we can do the oversized hoodie and black pants. The jersey option. Or you can go full belly out and wear a tight shirt. It's really up to you." Casey calls, looking through the closet. Perry was laying on the bed since she isn't supposed to be moving around too much.

"I want Boones jersey, the dark wash jeans, and black sleeveless turtleneck," I said sitting on the bed. Casey set the choices in a garment bag.

"Hey, is Joch single?" Perry asks randomly as she scrolls through her phone. Casey and I gave her a look, she shrugs, "Ok, he's like a sexy viking god. It's me, what do you expect." she chuckles when I roll my eyes. *Took her long enough.*

"Ew. please don't ever describe my brother as a sexy viking god or I will throw up on you." Casey gags. Perry gives her a big smile, "No promises. Future sister in-law." She blows her a kiss and I laugh when Casey pretends she's going to puke.

CHAPTER 51

Boone

What a way to end an NHL career. I am flying down the Ice as we face the Bruins, the game is tied. Their left defenseman collided with me hard as their captain rammed into me from the other side.

Oh this fucker. I clench my jaw as my gloves come off and I hold my arms out.

"Wanna dance?" I ask. The Captain scoffs and pulls off his gloves and makes a 'come at me' gesture. I smirk. I never back down from a fight. I promised Tabitha I would go out with a bang. Might as well get sent to the penalty box while I'm at it.

Pain explodes in my jaw as he hits me with an uppercut, I smirk and hit him back harder, grabbing his jersey and we both go down onto the ice. At one point I start laughing as the Refs break up the fight. I have a bloody lip and the captain has a forming black eye. I think *aw fuck it,* and tackle him. The crowd goes ballistic. Now Joch and the other team's forward jumps in and the ref makes the call for me to go to the penalty box.

I look up at the glass and blow a kiss to my beautiful girl as I take my time out seat proudly, watching the guys I've played this sport with for the last fifteen years.

Joch passes the puck to Tig who hooks it around the Bruins goal, slapping it back to Kaminskey who blocks a hit from the Left wingman as he passes it back to Tig. I'm on my feet as Tig and the Bruins center fight for the puck. It flies out to their right forward and it's down to our goalie to stop it.

"Come on Bohdie. Come on." I growl watching as the forward slaps it to the goal and Bohdie stops it.

"Yes!" I whoop.

The timer beeps and I throw my helmet on practically penguin sliding on the ice as I skate out.

Bohdie passes me the puck and I take it back up the ice sending it to Joch and intercept one of the players, smashing him against the wall. Joch passes to Tig who sends it to Kam and he shoots the puck.

And it….

It goes in! The crowd explodes into cheers so loud it's deafening. The Seattle Skyhawks won The Stanley cup. Joch collides with me yelling and we both launch ourselves onto Kaminskey taking him down as we celebrate.

Joch skates over and accepts the giant cup from the man in the suit and we all set up for a picture. Joch holds the trophy out to me, "Last game, only appropriate that you hold it man." he says placing the cup in my lap. The entire team is practically laying on the ice as the camera man snaps the photo.

I spot my girl waiting by the ramp with Casey and Perry. She's dressed in dark jeans and my jersey. Only this one is a little more snug around the middle due to her belly deciding to grow, or as the pregnancy book states, 'pop'. I skate over and wrap her in a huge hug, Pressing my lips to hers as cameras go off. It's not just the kiss they are crazy for, it's the fact that I drop down to my knees on the ice and press a kiss to her belly that sets all the cameras off.

"Hard launching the pregnancy reveal." she laughs. Her mismatched eyes shine as I stand and press my lips to hers again.

"I love you." I say as I kiss her. Tabitha wraps her arms around my neck. I hear my name being called and turn to see Tate running toward me.

"Hey buddy!" I smile as he collides with me in a hug. Marissa is not far behind.

Tate was well enough to go home with the chemo working and he got the all clear to come to the game as long as he wore a mask and was careful with the crowds.

"Oliver that was amazing! You were like woosh and then they were aarrgg and then Whosh the goal!" Tates arms flailed as he bounced with excitement.

"I'm so happy to see you kid. You're my good luck charm of course I had to have you here." I say as Mariss mouths 'thank you.'

"He was bouncing all over the vip box the entire game, I thought he'd go through the ceiling." Tabitha chuckled, smiling at him. Tate was decked out in Seahawk sweatpants, a jersey and hat. Marissa looked a lot better too, her face was brighter and her eyes sparkled. She looked like she had begun to live again. Now that she didn't have to practically live at the hospital with her son and he could live at home now. The dark circles I'd gotten used to seeing under her eyes were long gone.

Casey and Perry and Tabitha all head off to meet up with the WAG's while the team does their last interviews. We make our way towards the locker room and it's lined with reporters. They shout my name and questions as I walk past.

"Oliver. Congratulations on the win. This is your last game on the ice. You're officially retiring from the NHL. What plans do you have next?" a reporter asks.

"I've been very fortunate to have played this amazing sport as long as I have. And I'm glad to be able to go out on such a high note. I really am looking forward to life after the NHL. Looking forward to being a father and being with the love of my life." I say honestly. I am Thirty four and have lived an amazing life so far. There was one more thing I planned on doing but Joch and Perry were gonna need to be involved, and it was going to be after the craziness of the win died down a bit. For the next few weeks the news was going to be talking about the win and the announcement of the pregnancy, I was not going to let them ruin this

huge surprise.

CHAPTER 52

Tabitha

For the next few weeks it was a beehive of chaos as the news and reporters were all covering the game, Boones retirement, and the baby announcement. I received my degree in the graduation ceremony. When they called my name, a chorus of cheers from Boone, Joch, Bohdie, Perry, Casey and Georgia had my face burning from laughing so hard. Who knew hockey players could scream so loud.

It was a relief when it finally tapered off and I could enjoy the last month of pregnancy pleasantly uncomfortable. Ninja baby as we had called it, since we didn't want to know if it was a boy or girl, was carrying low now and so every kick to my bladder had me having to pee. I stuck to lounge pants, leggings and cute jumpsuits. Today I chose a pair of dark gray scrunchie lounge pants from Target and a snug black shirt.

Boone and Joch had taken the role of peewee coaches and were coaching peewee hockey for kids ranging from four to six. I waddled into the hockey rink and immediately have to pee.

Oh the joys of pregnancy. Once I am finally able to make my way down to the first row of seats the practice is over. Joch lets out a loud whistle, "Damn, if you are the hottest pregnant lady I've ever seen." I roll my eyes and flip him the bird.

Boone smiles at me, skating over and giving me a peck, "Hey baby." he greets, he is dressed in jeans and a black thick long sleeved shirt. Fuck he looked good. What I wouldn't do to lick every inch of him and ugh, the worst part of this pregnancy was that in the ninth month sex became uncomfortable. I watch as Boone and Joch and Bohdie goof around playing keep away with a puck, when suddenly I feel something pop as the baby shifts position. My hand goes to my belly as I focus on the feeling trying to confirm if it's what I think it is.

"Babe." I say softly. Boone doesn't hear me as Joch has him in a headlock.

"Babe." I repeated a little louder, my eyes widening.

"Oliver!" I bark firmly. This time all three pairs of eyes look at me. To my hand holding my belly, then to the wetness spreading down my leg.

"My water broke."

For a comedically solid twenty seconds everyone is frozen. Then it's utter chaos.

Epilogue

Boone

"Alright team let's go." I call to the kids. The group of seventeen year olds all waddle out onto the ice. Following them is a very small figure in a too big shirt with the sleeves rolled almost all the way up, and a grown man's hockey helmet on. The chuckle grumbles in my chest as I skate over and crouch down so I'm eye level with the kid being assisted onto the ice by the team captain Shawn who is holding onto their two small hands before I meet them.

"You joining us today, bud?" I ask. The helmet nods and knocks forward, almost taking the kid off their feet. I smile and take the helmet off, letting the mop of dark blonde hair cover the little girl's eyes. She giggles and moves her hair from her face letting me see those adorable blue, brown mismatched eyes she had inherited from her mother.

"I did- I did my-my skates alls by myself." she says softly, playing with her fingers as she looks up at me.

"That you did, good job! You got the buckles tight enough?" I ask looking down at the blue skates to make sure they were tight enough. She nods her head. I scoop my daughter up in my arms and stand up, peppering her adorable freckled face with kisses as she lets out a scream of giggles. The sound could melt the cold heart of any living thing I swear.

"Alright, looks like we have a special guest joining us today boys." I announce carrying Nicole in one large arm as I glide around the rink. The team adored having Nicole join practice. It was hilarious when she was one and she would try to copy me but it would always just sound like she was yelling gibberish at them.

I spot a flash of copper out of the corner of my eye and smile. Standing in a pair of jeans and tight black TAPHOWZE Penalty Box Manager shirt, Tabitha watches us skate around the rink. Even from the other side of the ice I can feel the heat in her stare. Nicole squirms in my arms wanting to be down and I break the eye fucking stare off with my wife to let our daughter down onto the ice. Holding her tiny hands as she moved her feet fast wanting to zoom.

"Zoom! Daddy. Zoom!" she says. I hold onto her arms and start skating faster around the rink.

Not really that fast but enough that she lets out a loud gleeful scream. Nicole was the best of both Tabitha and I in all ways possible. The week we got her home and she kept us up until six am with colic, I realized that, yea this was the best thing I will ever have a part in creating. Not even winning the stanley cup could touch the excitement being a dad got me. That had been a whole other world compared to this.

After a few circles around the ice, I skate her over where Tabitha waits making sure to undo the skates so she doesn't kick and stab one of us.

Made that mistake once and have a scar on my arm from it.

"Hey baby." I greet dipping my head to kiss her. Tabitha nips my lip playfully before pulling back. The sex fiend. Her eyes look to Nicole and she holds her hands out.

"Ninja baby! Ready to go?" She asks Nicole and she practically jumps into Tabitha's arms.

Nicole plays with the rings on Tabitha's ring finger, her favorite is the engagement ring I had picked out the week she was born and then gave to Tabitha the day she came home from the hospital. The moment was interrupted by a particularly gassy blowout from our newborn daughter, but it was perfect by our standards. Tabitha had said yes. Obviously.

She had been terrified that she wouldn't be able to be a good mom, that she wouldn't be able to bond with her child. It was hard at first, she was afraid she would do something wrong or would not be able to be the mother Nicole deserved. I helped her as much as I could and we both went through therapy and had the support of the other parents on the team. Rosea helped her out a lot since she had gone through the same thing with her kids. Tabitha was a fantastic mom. Once Nicole learned to crawl, she had become Tabitha's shadow, a total mama's girl. Wherever Tabitha went, she followed. I was more than happy to discover that my little girl inherited my hockey gene. She may not know the rules but she loved to go to games and yell. Luckily she had plenty of uncles that loved to play hockey that could help teach her. The same uncles that will be more than happy to scare any boy or girl that comes around when she's old enough to date.

"Perry is going to take her tonight so we have the house to ourselves." Tabitha informs me. I cock my head, "Really now?" I ask, seeing that lust filled look in her eyes.

"So don't get too tired out here. I'll need you full of energy later." she winks. *Ohh just you wait.*

I had a few new ideas that would make my girl scream my name while she squeezed my cock. If we ended up with baby number two then so be it we honestly didn't care at this point. Tabitha mentioned she wouldn't mind if we had another.

I pull her in for a kiss and smile when we hear the sound of the teenagers behind me whistling and whooping. Tabitha pulls back and laughs.

"I'll see you at home." She adjusts her hold on Nicole and heads toward the exit.

"Alright! Back to work." I call turning back to the team and blowing my whistle.

END?

Acknowledgments

525

Dear younger me…… we did it.

I could not have done any of this without the help of my alphas, Kayla, Christine, and Anna. You are the reason this book is grammatically correct and I couldn't be more appreciative. I can not thank you enough for all of your help. You three helped me get to where I am. There are no other people in this world that I would trust to be my Alpha readers than you three. You show up and give me the most brutal, honest feedback and I am thankful for every comment from you. No matter how blunt or brutal.

Hope you all are ready for the next book…. It's going to be DARK.

Huge thank you to my cover designer Madison at Love lee creative designs. She is amazing and brought these covers out of my mind and onto paper! You made these covers perfect!

To my hubby. You are the force that drives me to be as great as I can be. You have supported me in whatever I choose to do, no matter what it is. There is no one in this world that compliments my life the way you do. You have seen me at my lowest point and loved me through every moment of it even when I couldn't love myself. You have helped me heal the most broken parts of my soul and I will forever love you.

A little about this series…. The Graystone series is a bunch of interconnected books that can almost be read in any order. I say almost because the only ones that need to be read in order will be three and four as those two are connected by the events that occur in book three. Up until finishing this book I had no ideas for the Skyhawks to have any other character books. But now..... I have a total of maybe three additional books in mind for the world of the Skyhawks. Specifically everyone's favorite booktok loving bestie Joch. but that will come in time !

Extras

Bad boy high school Football player with an attitude, meets his match with an injured volleyball player. They can't stand each other.

Things begin to change when she comes to his trailer in the middle of the night for help and he can't say no.

Shane and Summers' story begins in,

Until You

Coming soon.

www.ingramcontent.com/pod-product-compliance
Lightning Source LLC
Chambersburg PA
CBHW061851310726

48972CB00004B/969